The Dawn's Early Light

The Dawn's Early Light

A Mike Elliot Novel

Book I

Lee Duffy

Copyright © 2015 by Lee Duffy
Published by Lee Duffy

Rev. 8

ISBN: 978-0-9966053-1-1

All warfare is based on deception.

Sun Tzu
500 BC

1

Tunis, Tunisia, 0910 Hours, Day One

Mike Elliot wiped the sweat from his eyes with his sleeve and then raised his face to the sky. The sun was fiercely hot, but it soothed him. At thirty-five, he was fit and healthy again. He was mostly recovered from his wounds, at least the physical ones. The painful memories from his brutal past, however, still haunted him.

Six foot, trim, rugged, and muscular, he wore a simple, button-up sport shirt and tan slacks, attire appropriate for the North African climate. In faded green ink, he had a single, small tattoo in script on the inside of his left forearm—*De Oppresso Liber*.

Mike looked up at the big jet towering over him. The words *Air France* were painted across the plane's gleaming-white fuselage in bold, blue letters. Glossy red, white, and blue stripes decorated the vertical tail fin. The number 622 was stenciled across the base of the huge vertical stabilizer, itself silhouetted against the broad expanse of clear Mediterranean sky.

A line of evacuees, one hundred and fifty-six American embassy employees and their families, stretched across the hot tarmac, up the steps of a mobile stair truck, and into the Air France jet. Tunis was no longer safe for foreigners, and particularly for Americans.

With little warning, Tunisia had exploded into violence. An endless procession of bombings, riots, protests, and murders in recent weeks had tormented the country. As a result, the U.S. government was evacuating its non-essential embassy employees on this hastily chartered Air France jet.

Mike thought about his wife and trembled at the thought of the danger she was in here. Lynn was precious to him, but now she was leaving, along with the other family members of the U.S. embassy staff in Tunis.

He ran his hand through his short, sandy-colored hair. He was tired. Mike, a U.S. Army major assigned to the American embassy in Tunis, was in charge of coordinating the evacuation. He had worked through the previous night and had spent less than ten minutes with his wife in the past twenty-four hours.

Mike's past still haunted him sometimes. The emotional scars were always there just beneath the surface to remind him of the mistakes he had made. He could not let it happen again. All he wanted at this moment was for his wife to be away from this place, and to be safe. Guilt, remorse, and pain had consumed him after he was wounded, and Lynn had pulled him up from utter despair. If anything happened to her, he knew his own tortured soul would be forever damned.

Both a fuel truck and a catering truck drove up and stopped at the outer security perimeter in the distance. American and Tunisian security officers carefully inspected the vehicles and searched the drivers. An explosives detection canine swept the trucks. The agents even took a sample of aviation fuel from the fuel truck's bulk tank and tested it for contamination. Then a U.S. Marine hopped up onto the cab step of each truck, and the vehicles proceeded to the starboard side of the plane to load the catering carts and refuel the plane.

Mike spotted a young couple struggling with their bags and helped them get their luggage stacked on a cart. Two dozen other families stood in line waiting to board. Parents pulled or carried their kids and belongings. The kids dragged or cuddled teddy bears, dolls, or small blankets. The passengers were orderly and quick. They were anxious to be gone.

Lynn had already boarded, and Mike wanted a few moments to say goodbye. He walked past a group of federal agents clustered at the base of the forward stairs. They had finished their inspection and now waited to complete the boarding so the plane could depart.

Mike climbed the front steps past the still-boarding passengers and stepped into the plane. A young female flight attendant greeted the passengers as they came aboard. Mike could see another female flight attendant doing the same in the rear of the plane.

They were helping as much as possible to seat everyone, but there was still a lot of confusion and noise. Even with the extra space, the passengers struggled to find places for their many carry-on bags. Children complicated matters by chasing one another in the aisles. Kids battled with pillows over the tops of seatbacks.

The passengers aboard were already looking more relaxed. Those seated were smiling and chatting with their children, spouses, or neighbors. They knew they would soon be home and away from the madness of Tunisia.

All the security personnel, except for the two uniformed Marines who would accompany the plane to Frankfurt, had already disembarked. One Marine stood in the rear of the cabin calmly watching the pandemonium. The other stood in the cabin near the galley wall on the starboard side of the plane.

Mike stepped into the cockpit. The pilot, Captain Albert Granger, and his copilot, Jean-Pierre Didier, were in their seats when Mike entered. The flight engineer was out on the tarmac doing a preflight inspection of the plane. Mike chatted with the pilot and copilot in French for a moment, verified that they had filed a flight plan for Frankfurt, and then excused himself.

As he passed the plane's galley, he stepped through the drawn curtain and into a small alcove. Two Arab workers, wearing Air France uniforms, were stowing food carts full of meals, snacks, and drinks in the plane. The Marine who had accompanied the truck from the security checkpoint stood in the back of the elevated cargo section of the truck looking on.

One of the Arabs seemed startled when Mike walked in. The man glanced up nervously and then quickly resumed shoving a food cabinet into a slot in the galley wall. The man was huge, Mike noted, with massive, muscular shoulders. His bushy black beard and thick shaggy hair made his head look oversized, even for his large frame.

The smaller Arab was pulling bottles of wine from a cart and storing them in a galley shelf rack. In fluent Arabic, Mike asked the big one how it was going, but the man just looked away and hooked the container he was working on into its slot.

Mike stepped past the two men and stood next to the aircraft wall. He felt uneasy about the big one but couldn't quite put a finger on why. He glanced at the Marine who just shrugged in return. *The guy's just odd looking*, thought Mike, *and big.*

The big Arab, Abu Hassim, glanced at his confederate as he tugged on another serving cart. The smaller man, Abdul el-Aziz, nodded. The big man nodded in return and then turned toward the truck. He lumbered slowly, but deliberately, into the back of the raised truck bed toward the Marine. He pointed at the watch on his left wrist as he approached him. The Marine looked down at the watch curiously.

Mike felt that uneasiness return, and while keeping an eye on the worker behind him, he cautiously watched the other man as he walked into the truck toward the Marine. Abu Hassim reached the Marine and Mike saw immediately when the big man telegraphed a move—he was about to throw some kind of punch. Mike started forward when he caught a glimpse of movement behind him out of the corner of his right eye.

In the truck, the Marine never had time to look back up from the watch. The big Arab swung his elbow and slammed it into the Marine's throat. He was dead before he hit the floor.

The one behind Mike swung a wine bottle. Mike ducked and spun right, nailing his attacker on the right temple with a spinning back fist. The Arab crashed against the galley wall and slid down, blood running from the side of his head. Mike turned to face the big one.

The flight attendant welcoming the passengers not fifteen feet away was oblivious to the struggle going on behind her. The noise and tumult in the main cabin greatly over shadowed the fight going on just behind the galley curtain.

With uncanny speed for such a large man, the Arab quickly crossed the length of the truck and charged at Mike. Mike jumped forward and threw a left sidekick. He caught the man in the mid-section. The kick stunned Abu Hassim, but he still lunged for Mike, groping for a bear hug. Mike head-butted the big man hard enough to knock almost any person unconscious. It seemed to have no effect, other than the man shaking his head while he continued to clutch at Mike. He got his arms around Mike, who managed to keep his own arms outside of the bear hug. He repeatedly hammered his attacker in the ribs on both sides of his body. He threw knee kicks to the man's groin area, but the Arab's thick thigh muscles protected him.

Hassim gripped Mike tighter. He could feel the air rushing from his lungs. He spread his arms wide, and with open palms, slapped his hands together with a loud *thwack* on both of the man's ears simultaneously. Hassim was dazed, and shook his head even harder, but his grip only tightened. Mike could no longer breathe. He pulled his arms back and slapped the man's ears again. Abu Hassim seemed impervious.

Mike went for the Arab's eyes with his thumbs, but before he could complete the attack, Abdul struck from behind. He swung a bottle of wine and smashed it down on the back of Mike Elliot's head. He immediately saw a white-hot flash of light just behind his eyes as an electric pain radiated through his body. Time slowed. He felt intensely nauseous, and when Abu Hassim loosened his grip, Mike crumpled unconscious to the galley floor.

With a shaky hand, Abdul jerked a radio from his belt and called to Khalid Moussa outside on the ground with the fuel truck. Trembling and still bleeding, he said in Arabic, "Now."

Below, Khalid said something and motioned to the Marine watching them refueling. He pointed up at the catering truck, signaling with his hand to follow. The Marine looked at him quizzically, not understanding. He cupped a hand behind his ear trying to hear above the noise on the tarmac just what the Arab worker was trying to say.

The fuel man again motioned for the Marine to follow. The Arab started up a ladder on the side of the catering truck. The Marine looked around, unsure what to do. All of the U.S. agents were now on the other side of the plane by the stairs, watching the boarding, and not looking his way. He knew that three of his fellow Marines were up there with the caterers and passengers, so he shrugged and followed the Arab up the ladder. The second fuel man, Mohammed Halid, climbed the ladder behind them.

The Air France flight engineer stood near the fuel truck looking perplexed as the two Arabs and the Marine climbed the catering truck ladder and disappeared over the edge.

The first Arab reached the truck bed and turned to help the American come off the top step. As the Marine stepped onto the truck's platform, Abu Hassim, standing just inside the cargo section of the truck, threw his huge arm around his neck and cinched down with a chokehold. He dragged the struggling Marine into the truck as he crushed his windpipe. The young man went limp.

Mohammed and Khalid moved quickly into the truck. Khalid pulled a small suction cup from a side leg pocket and slapped it against the front inside wall of the truck, high in the upper right corner. He flipped a small lever attaching the cup to the wall. He slipped his finger into a loop attached to the cup and pulled, peeling back a thin layer of sheet metal.

Behind the wall was a concealed space. They began extracting weapons from the small compartment—compact Uzi submachine guns and semi-automatic pistols. Khalid tossed weapons to Abdul, Mohammed, and Abu. They each slung an Uzi over their shoulder and tucked a pistol into their belts.

Abdul carefully watched the curtain separating the galley from the entranceway. They remained undetected. He could hear the French flight attendant on the other side of the curtain as she greeted the passengers.

"Hello, welcome aboard, I'm Marie," she was saying to each one.

He also heard the scores of Americans who had already boarded as they giggled, laughed, and talked excitedly.

"They won't be laughing for long," he muttered in Arabic, wiping blood from the side of his face.

The men all crowded into the small galley. They closed and locked the starboard aircraft door where they had been loading the carts.

Abdul cautiously peeked through the curtain. He then turned to Abu and said, "There are two American soldiers in camouflage—one in the front and one in the rear." He raised his dark eyes in the direction of the aircraft's tail. "They appear to have only pistols. That is all I can see. There may be more guards. If so, we just have to deal with them." To all three men, he said, "We all saw many security men outside on the ground. They are relaxed and confident. Surprise will be ours. It is time."

"*Inshallah*," they all replied simultaneously.

Abdul picked up a box of paper cups from the counter and held it in front of Abu. "Take this," he instructed. "When I give you the signal, just as we planned, walk calmly to the rear of the plane. With your ID badge and uniform, they will not suspect anything. Take the American guard by surprise and get his pistol. Then, as quickly as possible, get the rear door closed. We will be close behind you."

Abdul turned to face the other men. "Mohammed, you will take the soldier in the front of the plane. Khalid, you must get the front passenger door closed where they are boarding. Use hostages to ensure that they do not try to open the doors from the outside. If they do try to enter the plane, we will kill as many Americans as possible before we die. I will go directly to the cockpit. We will take off immediately."

He paused for a moment to check his weapons, as did the other three men. Abdul snapped back the bolt on his Uzi and inspected it. The weapon's seven pounds felt solid and reassuring. He dropped the submachine gun to his side where it hung by its sling. He grabbed his pistol and dropped the magazine into the palm of his hand, then reinserted it. He pulled the slide back slightly and peered in to verify that a round was chambered.

Abdul let out a long breath. "Okay, we go. Shoot anyone who resists." Still wiping blood from his face, he nodded at Abu Hassim. The big man handed his Uzi to Mohammed, who slung the extra weapon behind his back. Abu then pulled his shirttail out to conceal his pistol. Again, he had to shake his head to try to clear his senses. His ears still rang fiercely from his altercation with the American.

Abdul looked at Abu Hassim, wondering if the man was injured. Hassim just nodded to the other men and stepped through the curtain. The remaining three men, their weapons held close against their chests, prepared themselves for combat. Just beyond the curtain, passengers talked loudly and children played noisily.

Abdul watched through a crack between the curtain and the wall as Abu made his way toward the rear of the plane. He moved steadily down the aisle clutching his box of paper cups. His intense, dark eyes remained locked on the young Marine standing at parade rest against the back wall of the plane.

The Marine noticed the man approaching before he was halfway down the aisle. The Arab seemed nervous. He was staring straight at him. Closer now, the Marine could see large beads of sweat on the man's forehead. The Arab's dark eyes began to dart back and forth from him to the open rear door.

The Marine was concerned, but not alarmed. He watched the approaching man, thinking that he was an airline employee. After all, he was wearing an Air France uniform. He had an ID badge. He had to pass through security to get on the plane. He knew that if he drew down on a Tunisian worker just because he appeared nervous about being around a bunch of Americans, it would be reported as an international incident. They might even transfer him out of embassy security.

Abu Hassim quickened his pace. He jostled a woman, and she almost fell. He approached within fifteen feet, still staring directly at the Marine. The young man knew now that something was wrong. He scrambled to draw his pistol. In the first attempt, he missed the quick-release snap securing the weapon in its holster. He tugged on the pistol grip a full two seconds, his eyes riveted on the hulk of a man bearing down on him. He looked down and hit the snap with his thumb.

In the next instant, several things happened at once.

Abu flung the box he was carrying at the man and lunged the last few feet, hitting him with his full weight. The Marine's head pounded hard against the rear bulkhead of the plane. Abu Hassim wrestled the Marine's pistol from its holster and viciously pummeled the young man with it, though the Marine was already dead from a broken neck.

Up in front, meanwhile, Abdul bounded forward and burst into the cockpit, waving his pistol as he yelled at the captain. "Take off!" he screamed in French.

Behind Abdul, in the galley, Khalid sprang toward the front passenger door. The doorway was crammed with families. He swung his submachine gun back and forth, clearing a path in front of him.

During all of this, Mohammed bolted from the galley behind Khalid to engage the second Marine near the front. The Marine had started to draw his pistol when he saw his buddy go down aft, but suddenly screams filled the air behind him. He spun around just as

Mohammed pushed the short barrel of an Uzi into his face. The Marine raised his arms. Mohammed lifted the man's handgun, stuffed it into his own belt, and then rammed the butt of his Uzi into the Marine's face. He toppled to the floor. Mohammed jerked his own pistol from his belt and fired one round into the unconscious man's head.

As Khalid reached the forward portside door, he roughly shoved Marie Dubois, the flight attendant, aside. She hit the bulkhead hard. A young woman at the top of the steps was just entering the plane. He jumped forward and kicked her, planting the hard sole of his boot squarely into her chest. Her arms flung out wide, and her bags scattered in all directions. She faced the sky as she fell backward over the families behind her on the steep steps. They toppled down the stairs, arms and legs flailing the air, piling on top of one another at the base of the steps. Those on the tarmac stared, incredulous, their mouths agape.

Khalid stood in the doorway and sprayed the air and tarmac with a zigzag burst of 9mm rounds at the scrambling people below. Bullets ricocheted off the tarmac and thudded into buses, buildings, people, and cars. Passengers scattered, dropping bundles of belongings, scooping up kids, screaming, diving. Two evacuees, a father and his five-year-old son, lay near death in rapidly spreading pools of blood, and many more were wounded.

Within mere feet of the gunfire, Marie squatted against the wall, eyes shut tightly, pressing her hands over her ears. To her, and the passengers, Mohammed's first shot and the noise of Khalid's machine gun fire in the cabin doorway felt like a rapid series of powerful explosions.

Mohammed left the dead Marine and headed aft. He scrambled over the passengers cowering in the aisles and seats. As he lurched toward the rear of the plane to help Abu Hassim, he bowled over anyone in his path, including several youngsters playing tag in the aisle.

On the rear steps, other passengers had also been boarding when the firing erupted from the front. They scrambled for their lives. Many dropped down on the steps or the floor covering their children. Abu and Mohammed struggled to close the door with a dozen passengers sprawled on the floor around their feet. The passengers screamed and covered their faces. They sat or huddled, frozen—their eyes wide at the sight and sound of these men and their terrifying weapons.

In the front, Abdul screamed a final order at the pilots and ran back to the passenger cabin. Khalid held his Uzi in his left hand and couldn't manage to close the forward door with his right hand alone. Abdul spotted the young flight attendant crouched in a corner. He grabbed Marie Dubois by the back of the hair, jerked her forward, and stuck his pistol into her ribs. He dragged her to the door, screaming at her repeatedly in French, "Close it!"

Marie could barely stand, but she reacted automatically. She did as Abdul ordered. Khalid backed into the plane, swinging his submachine gun back and forth, firing several short bursts as the flight attendant, flinching at every shot, clumsily pulled on the door; she swung it inwards and locked it into place. Abdul pushed her face against the small window.

In the aft section, Abu and Mohammed yelled, shoved, and kicked at passengers near the entryway. They shoved them into nearby seats or back out the door, yelling at them to shut up. The terrorists kicked and punched at anyone who did not move out of their way fast enough. The noise of screaming and crying women and children, and even men, was deafening.

Abu fired several pistol shots through the still open door to discourage any of the security men from trying to climb the steps over the tangle of passengers. Flight attendant Eva Martine had been greeting passengers entering the rear door when the chaos erupted. Now she stood frozen, eyes wide as if shell shocked, trying to comprehend.

Abu and Khalid finally succeeded in closing the rear door. Abu Hassim grabbed a hostage and jammed her face into one of the doorway portholes. Khalid shoved Eva's face against the other.

Abu remained aft watching both doors. Mohammed raced forward. As he ran, he brutally shoved and kicked any passengers in his way. One man, about forty, tried to tackle him. He shot him in the face, stepped over the body, and continued forward. No one else resisted.

He reached the forward section and flung aside the galley curtain, darting back to the starboard door. Mike Elliot still lay unconscious on the floor at his feet.

Mohammed peered through the cabin door window. He snatched a terrified female passenger from the front row of seats, dragged her into the galley, and pushed her up against the door's small window. He slammed her face against the glass hard enough to break her nose. She whimpered. Her breath came in ragged gasps. Blood streamed from her nose and smeared the tiny window. Mohammed fought to catch his own elusive breath as he held his pistol to her head.

Less than sixty seconds had passed since Abu first stepped out of the galley—the terrorists had managed to overpower the remaining two Marines and lock all four aircraft doors.

The U.S. federal agents began picking themselves up from the tarmac. The chief officer, Johnson, barked a few sharp commands to get the remaining passengers to safety. Tunisian police sirens wailed in the distance.

Johnson bounded up the front steps, jumping and climbing over passengers huddled there. Several of his men followed. He cupped his hands and peered in through the porthole in the closed door, the Glock 17 in his right hand clanging against the window. He could see the young flight attendant's face pressed against the tiny window. Abdul put his pistol against Marie's temple. She closed her eyes and sobbed.

Johnson could do nothing. He stepped back and stood there for several seconds at the top of the stairs, his pistol now hanging uselessly by his side. He cursed to himself. Through the window, next to the flight attendant, he could see Abdul staring back defiantly. Johnson was desperate to free the hostages, but he knew that if he tried to open the aircraft door it would cause a bloodbath. Abdul pulled back and shoved the woman's face back against the window.

From all four aircraft doors, American agents could see only the face of a frightened female passenger pressed against each small porthole window. Blood and tears streaked the windows in crazy quilt-work patterns.

Abdul yelled in French at flight attendant Marie Dubois, "Do not move!" He signaled to Mohammed, who was on the opposite door, to watch her.

Abdul then dashed back to the cockpit. "Why aren't we taking off?" the terrorist screamed, jamming his pistol into the back of Captain Granger's neck. The captain hesitated, and Abdul drew back his pistol and slapped the pilot in the head with it. Granger fell forward, covering his head; a trickle of blood ran down his neck and onto his white shirt. Then Abdul pressed the gun to Granger's head.

"Now!" screamed Abdul. The captain and copilot started flipping switches. The engines began turning. Captain Granger reached up and set his transponder to *7-5-0-0*—hijacked.

The copilot, Jean-Pierre Didier, yelled, "We're still blocked by the stairs and the food truck. And we're not fueled," he protested. "The truck is still out there with the hose attached to the plane. Our engineer is out there. We need him—we can't navigate without him," he lied.

Abdul reflected on these new problems. They were too close to success to fail now, and the penalty for failure was death. He moved the barrel of his pistol to the copilot's neck. He pushed progressively harder until Jean-Pierre Didier grimaced in pain. Abdul stared menacingly at Captain Granger.

"You will tell them to move those things. We take off now, or you will be flying this airplane alone."

"Okay, okay," replied Granger hastily, raising his hands and gesturing for Abdul to calm down. "I'll call them again. The Americans are in charge of security. We told them we need to take off. But they haven't moved the trucks."

"Do it again," warned Abdul. "And you better say the right words." He pushed harder with his pistol. Under the relentless pressure of Abdul's pistol, Didier's head was now flat against the instruments. He shut his eyes tightly and prayed silently.

Captain Granger once again called the tower and relayed Abdul's demands to the Tunisian authorities.

Meanwhile, Johnson still stood on the top step of the stairs, pistol in one hand, Motorola in the other. It was a standoff but not a good one. Johnson's man in the control tower relayed the pilot's urgent requests to take off. Johnson radioed back, "The terrorists will not be allowed to leave. If they give up, I will guarantee their safety. If they do not, they will die," he said, knowing that it was a bluff.

The Tunisian controller repeated Johnson's words in French over the cockpit radio. Captain Granger knew the terrorist behind him spoke perfect French; he winced as he heard the words coming over the radio. Abdul cursed in Arabic as he headed back to the passenger cabin. He paced back and forth, slapping his pistol up and down against the palm of his hand. Mohammed watched him in silence.

Abdul could see Johnson on the step outside staring back at him. Marie had not budged for fear that it might get her killed. She still stood at the entrance window, paralyzed with fear. She looked out at Johnson, her eyes filled with horror and panic.

Abdul placed his pistol against her temple and cocked the hammer. Johnson could see the stark terror in the young woman's pleading eyes. Abdul placed his open palm on the glass next to her face. He started counting down from five, curling one finger closed at a time. Marie knew that death was upon her.

Outside, the noise from the jet engines was nearly unbearable now. Johnson knew he was beaten. Backing away from the plane, he holstered his pistol and raised his hands, palms facing Abdul. "Okay," he mouthed.

Johnson signaled for his men to move the chocks, stairs, and trucks. His men sprang into action and removed the equipment from around the plane. The remaining agents backed away, covering their ears.

Almost immediately, the huge plane began rolling forward. It taxied rapidly toward the runway. Seconds later, at 0925 hours, it lifted gracefully up into the bright-blue Tunisian sky. Soon, only a faint, white ribbon marked the jet's path.

2

Fort Bragg, North Carolina

The cicadas in the stand of tall pines behind the house droned out a familiar reprise. The endless scratching and chirping added a sense of home to the sultry North Carolina night. The air conditioner around the side of the house contributed to the aura of peace with its slow and steady hum.

Lieutenant Colonel Steven Barclay propped his Nikes up on the picnic table bench and settled in his folding metal lawn chair. The chair creaked a bit under his weight. He rested a cold, damp can of Coors on his bare leg just below his gym shorts. On this warm southern night, the cool metal felt refreshing.

A pale summer moon peeked over the tops of the pines bordering the back yard. In the opposite direction, toward the front of the house, a few stars were still visible over the red-tile rooftops of the Fort Bragg, field-grade officers housing complex.

Sitting outside in the early-morning hours was rather pleasant, especially if one had to wait up anyway, or so Steven Barclay told himself. The oldest of his three daughters, visiting home from college, was still out on a date—and she was late.

It wasn't just his daughter, though, that was keeping him awake. He would not have been able to sleep anyway. He kept mulling over what his wife of twenty-one years had just told him only a few hours earlier. She was leaving. She had to find her own identity, her own life. Somehow, he had expected it.

His girls were nearly grown, but not quite. What would he do without them? He knew that he had spent more years deployed than he had at home. The years of absence added up after a while. He stared into the moonlit night, lost in his thoughts. Barclay sipped his beer and listened to the random sounds of the night.

At first, he was only faintly aware of a telephone ringing somewhere. Once the noise finally penetrated his consciousness, he realized that his pager was vibrating also. He sprang from his chair and headed for the kitchen phone.

"Hello?"

"Colonel Barclay, sir? This is Captain Sanders."

"Yeah, Tommy, what is it?"

"Code bravo-two, sir. I notified Colonel Sinclair. He's expecting you."

"Roger, Tommy, on my way."

Barclay replaced the receiver and hurried out of the kitchen. As he entered the living room, he heard a car pull up in front of the house, but he paid it little mind. He only briefly wondered how long his daughter would linger there.

Barclay went up the stairs two at a time. His wife was asleep. He walked softly into the bedroom with only the light from the hall.

He took off his T-shirt, put on a clean one, donned a lightweight nylon shoulder holster, and slipped a compact Walther PPK .380 into it. Barclay was not an assaulter; he was the detachment intelligence officer. The lightweight pistol was purely for self-defense. He pulled on a baggy polo and a pair of jeans, then slipped his Nikes back on.

He stood there in the cool darkness of their bedroom looking down at his sleeping wife. He didn't think he would be back here anytime soon. It could be days—or weeks—he could never tell. He sat on the edge of the bed and shook her gently.

"Dear?" he said softly, several times, until she responded. "Honey, I've got to go away for a few days."

She answered with something faintly resembling, "Yes, dear," and dropped back to sleep. He knew it was no use. He didn't have time to pursue it. Maybe that was the problem. He never had the time. *What a lousy time to get called out*, he thought.

She wouldn't even know he was gone until long after she got up. After all these years, she was accustomed to him picking up and leaving at odd hours, disappearing for days, weeks, or months. They didn't agonize over the separations anymore, there were simply too many of them. Though maybe she had agonized over them more than he had realized.

He grabbed a black nylon flight bag from the closet. It was always packed. Downstairs, his daughter was making herself a snack. He had wanted to talk to her about how late she came in. If this should turn out to be the one he didn't come back from, though, he didn't want his last words to be criticism.

He went into the kitchen.

"Oh hi, daddy."

"Hi, darling." He gave her a quick hug and a peck on the cheek.

"You going away again already? You just got back."

"Yeah, well that's how it works sometimes. Just for a few days. You take care of your mother...and remember, sweetheart, I love you. All of you." He turned to leave, then added, "And I love your mother too."

"Love you too, Daddy," she said, looking only mildly puzzled. She turned her attention back to her sandwich.

It was only a two-minute drive from Barclay's quarters to Sinclair's. He arrived just as Colonel Sinclair, Delta's commanding officer, or CO, was coming out of his front door. He had an olive drab rucksack slung over his right shoulder.

"Taking a trip, boss?" asked Barclay. The CO didn't usually deploy.

"Looks like it. Just talked to Holt," he said, referring to General Holt, commander Special Operations Command. "The White House is following this one closely."

***

Air France 622, Over the Mediterranean, 1019 Hours

Abdul leaned against the bulkhead, his back to the cramped cockpit he had been using as his command post for the past hour. Air France 622 steered east at twenty-seven thousand feet, just south of Crete.

Abdul surveyed the passengers. He could see only the heads of the first few hostages, then only seatbacks. Rows of shaking, twitching elbows jutted irregularly out into the aisles. The hostages were bent forward, their fingers interlaced behind their heads. In the rear of the cabin, some were sitting upright now. They had been bound at the wrists with plastic cable ties. Many seats, even entire rows, were empty; the plane was less than one-third full.

Abdul wiped the sweat from his brow with the back of his hand and noticed it was trembling. He lowered it, sucked in a long, deep breath, and then slowly let it out. He swiped again at the thick beads of sweat forming on his forehead.

The takeover of the aircraft had been terrifying. It was his first major operation, and it had succeeded. He knew full well, however, that it could have fallen either way without warning. Had it gone the wrong way, he knew he would either be dead or naked and in chains, undergoing a humiliating and painful interrogation at the hands of the Tunisians or Americans.

Abdul shook his head to throw off the morbid feelings, and to ease the pain in his temple. It was done now, he reminded himself sternly. His plan had worked. The operation had succeeded brilliantly, in fact. Though terrifying on the one hand, it had also been one of the most exhilarating moments of his life. His heart still pounded after more than an hour into the flight. He touched the tiny Koran in his side pants pocket. It reassured him.

He tried to calm himself, but other worries kept his tension high. He feared that Tunisian fighter jets would pursue them, thinking that the hijackers might attempt to crash the plane into something. But that was not Mustafa's plan, and Abdul was grateful for that. Mustafa wanted the plane in Beirut, for propaganda reasons.

Truth be known, Abdul did not want to die, so the plan suited him just fine. There appeared to be no contacts on the cockpit radar, *if* he could believe the pilots. Abdul tried again to relax, unsuccessfully.

He watched his three comrades busily tending to the passengers. The terrorists were brutal and efficient. Their anxiety drove them, except for that beast, Abu Hassim. He was violent by nature.

Abdul had not worked with Hassim before this operation, he had only heard of the man. He was known to be a vicious fighter. But Abdul could see something else in him, now having the opportunity to observe him closely. He wondered if the man was mentally stable.

He watched as his men searched the passengers and their possessions and then shifted them around in the plane. Mohammed carried a bag full of electronic devices and a fist full of passports.

They placed the male passengers next to windows or in the middle of the center aisle of seats. The ones who did not move fast enough were beaten. The terrorists placed women or children on either side of the men so that they would have no chance to surprise their captors.

After the reshuffling, the terrorists hastened from one hostage to the next, jerking them upright in their seat and roughly applying the cable tie to their wrists, arms in front of their body. Then they cinched the seat belt down tight. The passengers were relieved just to sit up straight again. The terrorists even bound the children.

During this process, most of the women and children, and even some of the men, wept. Fear was etched into their smudged, wet faces. Some begged. Some whimpered. A few sat stoically, defiance fixed in their hollow eyes. All feared for their lives.

Surveying his newly conquered world, it dawned on Abdul again that they had actually succeeded. Had he really doubted it so much, he wondered, that he should be so surprised? Danger still threatened, but once they reached Beirut, he told himself repeatedly, they would be safe. He had already accomplished the most difficult part of his mission, and he had the attention of the entire world. Soon, he would press his demands against Israel and the United States. They would not give in, but it would give the appearance of bringing a superpower and its minion to their knees. That was the important thing. The rest would be easy now.

His first major operation, he mused. It had gone well. This hijacking would firmly establish his reputation. Hezbollah had not managed to conduct an attack such as this in decades. Now, he had successfully done it.

Perhaps, he thought, he truly did have the makings of a combat leader. Until this moment, he had not really been sure, having only sniped at his enemies from afar or surreptitiously bombed them from a safe distance. Now, though, he had been face-to-face with the enemy, and performed well. He wanted to slow his heavy breathing and restore his normal calm, but he could not quite find the strength to do it. He felt sapped.

Taking one last look at the passengers and his comrades brutally tending to them, he turned and stepped back into the cockpit. He knew he must keep a close eye on these pilots. *Leave nothing to chance*, he thought. *Mustafa will be proud.*

***

Beirut, Lebanon, 1027 Hours

John Striker left the U.S. embassy communications center. He shoved open the heavy fire door at the end of the hall, already engrossed in fleshing out a plan that he had only just conceived. He had minutes to prepare an important and risky covert operation. He had just received instructions from the CIA's Director of Operations, Gerald Reid, to prevent the hijacked airliner from landing in Beirut at all costs.

The CIA believed that the hijackers were from the pro-Iranian, Lebanese Shiite Hezbollah. Years ago Hezbollah hijacked a plane and landed in Beirut. The hijackers savagely beat and then shot to death three Americans and dumped the bodies on the tarmac for the world to see.

Later, the terrorists dispersed the passengers throughout Beirut where the United States was helpless to act. After seventeen days of televised interviews, the Shiites released their hostages, and the terrorists escaped justice.

The intelligence community believed that an Iranian operative had masterminded the attack. It had been a clear Hezbollah victory. The media had served the terrorists' purposes well by providing near constant coverage of the drama, including interviews with the terrorists themselves.

The CIA had known for some time that the Lebanese Shiites were working in Tunisia. Now, it seemed, they were making their move. It appeared as though Hezbollah was trying for a repeat performance of their previous successful hijacking. Striker's instructions were to keep them from doing so.

Striker reached the fifth floor and strode through the fire door into the corridor. As he entered the doorway of his outer office, he pointed at his driver. "Fred, get the car ready ASAP. Local trip. Airport."

"Yes, sir," came the crisp reply. "With a security detail?"

"Bring Conrad," he replied, referring to Mark Conrad, his primary bodyguard and lead security agent. Conrad was a bear of a man with a personality to match.

"I'm on it," Fred Morgan yelled, heading out the door and already running through a mental checklist of security precautions. Beirut was dangerous territory. This would be an unscheduled trip, and the Mercedes was heavily armored. Morgan also reminded himself that the car had recently been repainted and the plates changed. Good enough for a daylight run.

Striker closed the door to his office and dropped into the chair behind his desk. He was reasonably sure that the Lebanese Army would initially close the airport to the hijackers and attempt to prevent the plane from landing. It sometimes worked and sometimes didn't. The terrorists were likely to kill one or two passengers, and the Lebanese Airport authorities would eventually cave in and open the runway. On the other hand, the terrorists might simply put a pistol to the pilot's head and order him to land.

Striker knew that Hezbollah's plan would also include a ground force. They, too, would anticipate a closure of the airport and take measures to keep it open so the hijackers could land.

Striker's immediate problem was to ensure that the Lebanese Army kept the airport closed long enough to persuade the hijackers to go elsewhere. At the same time, he had to keep U.S. involvement concealed. He didn't believe the latter would succeed, especially with such a quick operation. Normally, the CIA laid the groundwork for a covert operation with meticulous planning over a period of many months. Teams of agents would use multiple cutouts to hide U.S. involvement. Plausible deniability would be built into every step of the operation. What could he do with an hour?

Fortunately, thought Striker, he knew the airport pretty well. A Christian militia unit maintained security for the airport sector. Striker had also managed to develop a loose business association with the commander responsible for this sector, a Lebanese Army colonel named Beagea—*Pronounced ba-ja*, he reminded himself.

Striker spun around in his chair, got up, and stepped around the corner of his desk. He stared out his only window into the embassy compound below. He would prefer to remain well in the background on this operation, if possible, but he knew that he would have to go to the airport. If the Lebanese colonel showed signs of weakening, Striker might have to raise the financial stakes. He could only ensure success by being there.

At least he had a blank check to work with. He just hoped the terrorists would not start killing hostages to push their demands to land. He couldn't justify keeping the airport closed for long if they did, and his mission would fail. Nevertheless, he could not let the prospect of one or two executions deter him. He would have to get past the first one. Then perhaps the terrorists would get the message and divert to another location, maybe a location where the U.S. would have a chance to get at them, or so he hoped.

Striker considered the fact that in a situation like this, a few executed hostages would be considered 'acceptable losses.' Just who those losses were supposed to be acceptable to, he had never quite reconciled.

Striker's most pressing concern, however, was to contact Colonel Beagea, commander of the airport zone, and set things into motion. Though Striker had given money to the colonel in the past, Beagea had resisted Striker's subtle attempts at formal recruitment, so he had never established a clandestine procedure for contacting the colonel.

The only number Striker had was for the colonel's headquarters near the airport. Sitting back down, he dialed. Surprisingly, he got through on the first try. He swiveled left, then right, then back and forth as he waited for the sergeant to get the colonel.

After what seemed an eternity, Colonel Beagea came on the line. To him, Striker was known simply as John.

"Colonel Beagea, it is John."

"How are you, John?" said Beagea. "Somehow I thought I might hear from you."

"Colonel," asked Striker, "is your telephone secure?"

The colonel laughed. "But of course," he responded, as if Striker were being naive. "I have many enemies. One does not grow old in Lebanon without *much* prudence," he said, chuckling softly.

"Good. Have you heard the latest news?"

"Yes, it is on the radio. We are already planning for the arrival of the airplane."

"Then it has not yet arrived?" inquired Striker, surprised and relieved at the same time. He was taken aback because the plane was overdue, and he had been sure that it would come to Beirut.

"No," replied the Lebanese colonel matter-of-factly.

"Colonel," said Striker, pausing briefly. "What will you do if it comes here?"

"We will close the airport, of course. We do not want the Shiite terrorists to land here."

Striker let out a sigh of relief but was careful not to let the colonel hear it.

"Does this displease you, John?"

"On the contrary, Colonel, I think your judgment is excellent."

"Yes. We have enough hostage problems in Lebanon. It is bad publicity for our country. The world thinks we are all terrorists, but it is not true."

Striker knew there was some truth in the colonel's statement, but the greater truth was that it was simply part of the Christian sect's long-standing campaign to dominate the Muslims in Lebanon. The Christians had controlled the government for many years, until the Syrians muscled their way into Lebanon and the Lebanese Shiites became better organized.

"Colonel, I understand and agree with you fully," said Striker. Now he just needed to ensure that the colonel didn't lose his nerve once the pressure began to mount, but Striker felt that this man had nerves of steel and would not back down easily. Still, he might need some leverage on the colonel to see it through to the bitter end.

"Colonel Beagea?"

"Yes, John, what is it?"

"How will you do it?"

"With military trucks on the runway. And I have also set up additional security checkpoints around the airport perimeter."

"Excellent," said Striker. "I think that's wise. I would like to demonstrate my support in a…, well, a *big* way."

"That would be nice, John. Your support is welcome. What do you propose?"

"I think we should discuss it in person."

"Very well."

3

Fort Bragg

Lieutenant Colonel Barclay and Colonel Sinclair drove up to the main gate at Delta's compound on Fort Bragg. A federal police officer verified their identities and waved them through.

Delta's operations center would be alive with activity, even at this early-morning hour. Staff officers, one or two Delta operators, and a half-dozen Department of the Army civilians worked in shifts monitoring communications and satellite telemetry twenty-four hours a day. Delta had teams of operators deployed worldwide.

Barclay and Sinclair, however, were not going to the ops center. They were headed to a pre-deployment isolation area, a secure mini-compound within the larger facility, where Delta would assemble a team for deployment.

A staff officer, pulling an overnight duty shift, already had a large urn of coffee brewing when Sinclair and Barclay walked into isolation area six. Other men were beginning to arrive.

The captain handed Sinclair and Barclay each a single sheet of paper. "Latest intel summary," he said. "We've also got one photo that came in from Washington. It's a shot of one of the terrorists taken by a passenger in Tunis. View from the tarmac. Not very clear. We still don't know where the plane is," he said shrugging his shoulders.

"Any assumptions?" asked Barclay.

"CIA seems to think it's Hezbollah and that they'll be heading to Beirut, but no one knows for sure."

"Anything on deployment?"

"It's a go; a C-17 is prepping over at Pope as we speak," he said, referring to Pope Air Force Base, adjoining Fort Bragg.

The captain pointed to one corner of the large room. "Coffee's over there. It's hot." The three men moved in that direction, and the captain pulled out two Styrofoam cups. Moments later Sinclair and Barclay were huddled over a large map of the Mediterranean region, each man silently considering the various scenarios that might play out.

Sinclair picked up the photograph provided by Washington and studied it. It showed a dark-skinned, heavily-bearded, young Arab male dressed in faded khaki pants and shirt. A pistol was stuck in his pants over his stomach. His expression was fierce and determined. He stood in the open doorway of the airliner firing an Uzi submachine gun at the unseen crowd of security officers and passengers.

Sinclair tossed the picture back on the table and took a sip of coffee. Lieutenant Colonel Noah Wilson, Delta's executive officer, arrived. He was tall and broad shouldered; he wore his jet-black hair in a buzz-cut typical for Fort Bragg. Sergeant Major Scott Barrington followed close behind. He was a Delta operator, and at six foot, one hundred and seventy pounds, he was lean, wiry, and full of energy. He wore a short black beard and medium length black hair, and like the other operators on Delta, his hair was long by military standards.

"Morning guys," said Wilson.

Sinclair said, "We're gonna be loading up shortly and getting this little show on the road."

"We?" asked Wilson.

"Yeah, I'm going. I want you and Barclay along too. Benson will be acting CO here," he said, referring to the unit's deputy commander.

"Not a problem, sir. How did they know about the evacuation plan?"

Barclay responded, "CIA thinks the terrorists were coercing one of the ambassador's secretaries into providing information. She was a Tunisian national, naturalized American. Thirty years with State, and her late husband was a retired career State Department officer. She had an extensive Tunisian family. Probably trying to protect them. Cost her her life."

"What happened?" asked Sinclair.

"Tunisians just found her body in a shallow grave on the outskirts of Tunis—throat cut. The terrorists also had at least two men working at Air France."

"What kind of plane is it?" asked Barrington.

"Airbus A300," said Barclay. "Belongs to Air France. Tail number 622. Older model, but it's been retrofitted with newer engines. It's a really big plane, too. Something to keep in mind. You go in the rear door, and it's a *very* long way to the cockpit."

"Yeah, we'll have to look at going in front and rear simultaneously," replied Sergeant Major Barrington.

Wilson asked, "Any idea who we're dealing with?"

"CIA's guess is Hezbollah, out of Lebanon," replied Barclay.

"Do we have any clue as to what they might do?"

"Not yet. If it *is* Hezbollah, they'll probably go to Beirut," Barclay said, "That would only be a couple of hours flying time from Tunis. *If* they plan to land that is. If they're looking for a high profile target to crash into, then it could be anywhere in Europe. According to the CIA, they took off at 0925 alpha, Tunis time, which would put their arrival in Beirut at around noon. Within an hour or so we should have some idea where they are."

"But if they do go to Beirut, we won't be able to get at them," added Sinclair.

"No, sir. We'll just have to see where they set down. *If* they do."

"Hezbollah hasn't tried anything like this in years," said Sinclair. "Let's just pray they don't plan to crash into something."

"I have a feeling," said Barclay, "they're not going to crash it. Hezbollah is more into grandstanding."

"I hope to hell you're right," said Lieutenant Colonel Wilson.

By now, the hustle in the room had increased in tempo and volume. More of Delta's operators—tough, lean, hard-looking men—were arriving. Staff officers hurried about or worked quietly at map boards or consoles. They prepared briefings and talked with staff counterparts in Washington to coordinate deployment.

"Okay," said Barclay. "I've been thinking about a possible diversion for an assault. If Scott agrees, I want to prepare the light aircraft deception plan we've talked about, possibly one or two others."

Sinclair, and the assault team leader Sergeant Major Scott Barrington, nodded their approval. "We'll need to get the right pilot," said Sinclair.

"We've got that covered," replied Barclay.

"Okay," said Colonel Sinclair. "Do it."

Barclay said, "We should lay on a detachment of helos, too, in case we need some mobility."

"Sounds good," said Sinclair. "All right, we'll start our briefings for the team once we're airborne." Turning to Barrington, Sinclair said, "Unless you've got something else you want to cover, Scott, let's get moving."

***

Air France 622, 1138 Hours

Abdul jabbed his pistol at Captain Granger's shoulder.

"How long to Beirut?" he demanded in French.

"About one hundred and twenty-five miles, not long."

"How long?"

"Fifteen or twenty minutes," said copilot Jean-Pierre Didier.

Abdul glanced at his watch. It was shortly before noon. "Fifteen minutes," he muttered to himself.

Didier said calmly, "We must contact the tower now."

"No," Abdul retorted immediately.

"Then we can't approach the airport," warned Didier.

An angry grimace swept across Abdul's face, and he shoved the barrel of his 9mm auto against the copilot's temple, pushing Didier's head to a tilt.

"Listen," pleaded the copilot. "We must know what runway to use. There may be other aircraft coming in, or a runway might be closed for repairs, or a lot of things."

"There is only one runway," said Abdul. "The other was destroyed. But then you know that."

"There are two directions even with one runway. We could collide with another plane."

Abdul relaxed his pistol's pressure against Didier's temple. He said nothing. Captain Granger cautiously adjusted the radio and contacted Beirut tower. Didier continued talking to Abdul. "We must also let the flight attendants prepare the plane and passengers for landing."

"The passengers are prepared. Do not concern yourself with them. Just fly this airplane," replied Abdul in a sarcastic tone.

"They must also check the cabin, the doors, in case of emergency disembarkation, and other things."

"There won't be any emergency disem..., whatever. You shut up now." He waved his pistol in the copilot's general direction. Turning to the pilot, Abdul asked, "What do they say?"

Granger hesitated. Abdul nudged him hard with the barrel of his pistol.

"They say we are denied permission to land. They say we must not approach the airport."

Abdul laughed, but only briefly. "What do you think, Captain, that they would welcome us with open arms? The Army runs the airport. Of course they must say we cannot land. But we will land," he declared. "You will ignore them and land anyway. Turn off the radio," he commanded harshly.

"B-but," sputtered Captain Granger, "we *must* be in contact...."

Without warning, Abdul flicked his wrist; his pistol smacked a glancing blow across the top of Captain Granger's head. The captain reeled forward, clutching his head. Abdul clawed at him with his free hand. He jerked the communications headset from Granger's head and tossed it aside. "You too," he said to the copilot. Didier scrambled to remove his own headset and set it aside.

"You," he proclaimed, waving his pistol back and forth between the two pilots, "must do as *I* tell you. Not the tower. You will go straight and land."

They nodded and began preparations for landing.

Abdul rested his elbows on the pilot's seatback and peered out in silence from the cockpit into the hazy distance ahead. Minutes passed.

"How long now?"

"Two minutes, maybe less," answered Didier. Abdul fixed his eyes on the horizon. In the distance he could make out Beirut's jagged skyline, formed by the shattered hulks of bombed out buildings. Then he could see the distinctive shape of the airport's runways and their connecting taxiways. They created a huge, orderly scar on the Earth's surface.

The big plane descended smoothly. The airport loomed ever larger. Finally, a mile out, Jean-Pierre Didier was the first to notice. Captain Granger saw it next.

The copilot said without emotion, "There's something on the runway."

Abdul felt his skin twitch. He leaned a little more forward, hovering almost over the instruments, peering toward the airport. He could make out dark, irregular shapes on the runway. Abdul felt the blood rush to his head. He fought back an urge to panic. This, he had not anticipated. The ground unit of his team should have been in position to block this.

Only seconds remained as the runway grew larger, and the distance between the Earth and the plane shrank.

"They're trucks," advised Granger.

"Land."

"You'll kill us all," protested Didier.

"Land!"

Didier still had the controls. "I'll take it," said Granger.

"Okay," said the copilot. Captain Granger already had a firm grip on the yoke.

"Altitude," requested Granger. His copilot began to announce every two hundred feet of descent. They had already configured the plane to land—flaps, gear, airspeed, angle of approach. Jean-Pierre Didier realized what the captain was about to do. He was bleeding off altitude, getting lower, reducing the angle of attack. Then he began reconfiguring the wing surfaces. He gradually increased power. The final airspeed would be higher, but by holding a shallow approach, their rate of descent would be slower. At the last instant, he would be able to apply power and check their descent entirely.

Abdul watched in silence. Blood pounded violently against his temples. He was almost afraid to speak. He felt hot and flushed. Dark, ominous military trucks, and smaller M113 armored personnel carriers, were parked every three hundred feet or so down the entire length of the runway. Small groups of drivers dotted the low brown grass on either side of the runway.

"We're going in," said the captain. "But it's suicide. They're not going to move."

The outer runway marker slid beneath the plane.

"Eight hundred feet," said Didier, calling the altitude.

Abdul felt confused. He tried to think, but it was all coming at him too fast.

"Six hundred."

What is happening here? wondered Abdul, clenching his teeth and slamming the bottom of his fist down on the top of the pilot's seat back.

"Four hundred."

He did not want to end in failure so soon. He needed time to think. The big plane roared past the edge of the runway.

"Two hundred."

Abdul could see the drivers looking up, shielding their eyes against the haze, watching the plane coming in to land on their trucks, not understanding, just watching.

"O-okay," stammered Abdul.

Granger applied maximum power. The sudden surge caught Abdul off guard. He nearly fell backward but caught a grip on the pilot's chair. Unseen from the cockpit, truck drivers covered their ears and hid their faces from the noise and the pressure skimming past four stories above them, the enormous silver belly of the jet briefly blotting out the sky.

In the cabin, Abdul's three confederates stared incredulously through side windows at the airport speeding by below. They could not see the trucks directly underneath. They felt the sudden acceleration as the plane lurched and began to climb. They saw the outer edge of the airport grounds grow smaller once again, and they glanced back and forth at each other questioningly.

The youngest, Khalid Moussa, wearing a thick beard, his black hair cropped close, stared incomprehensibly at Abu Hassim. Hassim looked out the little window in stunned silence. The third man, Mohammed Halid, only one year the elder of Khalid, paced back and forth. Mohammed was becoming anxious. He wanted to know what was happening. He held his place, and his tongue, but his impatience was strong.

In the cockpit, Captain Granger asked where he should go, but Abdul did not respond. He paced back and forth in the small, cramped compartment. It was more like turning in circles than pacing. He slapped his pistol up and down against the palm of his hand.

"Where do we go?" echoed the copilot.

"Circle the airport," Abdul snapped at them. The pilot immediately banked left and established an orbit at five thousand feet over the Beirut International Airport.

Abdul was silent as he contemplated what to do, then Mohammed burst into the cockpit. He spoke rapidly in Arabic.

"Why did we not land?"

Abdul stopped pacing and gaped at his comrade as if he didn't recognize him. "The runway was blocked with trucks and armored vehicles."

"We must land!"

Anger flashed in Abdul's eyes. "You think I do not know this!"

"But we are supposed to meet our men on the ground. Where are they?"

"They have obviously encountered interference—as have we."

"Someone will pay!"

"Yes, someone will, but that does not help us right now."

"What will we do?"

Abdul did not answer but turned to the pilot. "Give me the radio." Captain Granger handed Abdul his headset. Abdul grabbed it from the pilot's hand and clumsily slipped it on. He called the tower and the chief controller responded.

"We will land!" he screamed into the mic. "Do you hear me? We will land, or we will fly here until we run out of fuel. Then we will crash onto your miserable tower. This I promise you."

***

Mike Elliot began to awaken, gradually. The smell of jungle-rot was everywhere. Moisture dripped from the leaves around his head, and sweat streamed down his face, burning his eyes.

He could feel the chafe from his tactical gear and the pack on his back. Something around his ribs hurt, but he couldn't tell what or why.

He could see—or sense—a large, dark-colored Burmese python slithering down a fat, fern-encrusted vine to his left. Brown patches, bordered in black, lined the length of the snake's back. Mike was not alarmed; it was not venomous. But he knew that given the chance, the monster would happily squeeze the life out of him and then attempt to swallow him whole, starting with his head, down its enormously-flexible gullet.

He slipped his Ka-Bar from its sheath, but the predator turned and slid slowly away into a strange fog of sorts, perhaps content to avoid the encounter.

Mike shook his head—but only gently because of the pain—and the interior of the Airbus began coming barely into focus.

He had a throbbing, nerve-splitting pain somewhere in the back of his head. The nauseous disorientation was overwhelming, like standing on the edge of a precipice and leaning out too far, before reeling back, head spinning.

All he could see was a blurry, jigsaw-puzzle image of light and dark. He closed his eyes, concentrated on stopping his head from spinning, and tried to ignore the pain. He slowly sucked in a long, deep breath and fought back panic.

He sensed movement. Noise. *What the hell happened?* He tried to assess his condition. Overall, he felt like he'd been run over by a truck, though somehow, he knew that was unlikely. Other than the disorientation and general stiffness, most of the pain was in the back of his head and in his ribs. He vaguely remembered coming to and going through this same process several times already. It was all a blur.

Am I still in the hospital? he briefly wondered. No, he decided, yet the painful disorientation tugging at his gut was all too familiar. He last felt this way when he was nearly blown to bits trying to save…them. He couldn't quite bring himself to say their names.

Mike gradually realized that he was in flight. There were the occasional bumps and jiggles one feels in an aircraft. He also had that hollowness in the pit of his stomach experienced when the flight was not exactly smooth. Now that he was better able to isolate his senses, he could also hear the distant roar of jet engines. Closing his tired eyes, he tried to raise a hand to touch the back of his head but discovered that his hands were tied behind his back.

He opened his eyes again and tried to focus. Near his face was a porthole window. He stared at it. At times, his sight would clear. Occasionally, though, he seemed to lose the ability to focus, and everything scurried back into a distant haze. Sometimes, he saw blue sky. At other times, as the plane leveled out, he would see the darker blue of deep water. Once or twice, he saw an almost surreal, ragged looking skyline off in the distance. For the most part, however, he could see only rocky, desert terrain scarred with meandering trails or roads.

He turned his head to look forward and gasped as he felt a sharp bolt of pain shoot through the back of his skull. He tried lifting his head off the seat back but could not quite manage it. Mike closed his eyes. He needed rest, he decided. He was exhausted. The disorientation seemed to have drained him entirely. *Sleep*, he told himself, unable to tolerate the whirlpool in his brain. *Sleep*....

***

In a third row, aisle seat in the front of the Airbus, Lynn Elliot sat thinking of her husband. Tears clouded her dark eyes. It was torture not knowing if Mike was alive or dead. She'd last seen him on the plane in Tunis, unconscious, being dragged toward the rear of the plane by two of the terrorists. His head and shirt were covered in blood, and as she thought back on it, she realized that she could not be sure if he was still alive.

At the time of the hijacking, she'd not been able to see everything that took place near the forward passenger door, but she *had* heard the deafening gunshots and terrifying screams. She didn't even know if Mike had been shot. The image of her husband's limp, bloody, unconscious body being dragged down the aisle still haunted her.

Her lip and side hurt terribly, adding to her general misery. It was difficult to breathe. She suspected that the big terrorist had broken one of her ribs when he'd punched her. As they'd dragged her husband away, she had jumped up and run to him. The big one turned on her like a vicious animal, slapping and punching her. He threw her back into her seat like a rag doll.

When she regained consciousness, her hands were bound and blood was running down her chin, dripping onto her red blouse. His punch had cut her lip. Her hands were bound in front of her body, so she was able to press her finger against the cut. For a long time, though, it continued to drip blood. She believed it would never stop.

Her hands were beginning to feel numb. A dull, tingling sensation had replaced the agonizing muscle cramps. The numbness was better, she decided. It didn't hurt quite so much that way. It seemed an eternity that she had been sitting here with her hands tied. Little did she know, but this was merely the beginning.

She knew she was not alone in her suffering. She could see passengers all around her sobbing, moaning, rocking back and forth, trying to console each other or their children. Despite the pain in her ribs, she closed her eyes and just tried to concentrate on breathing.

***

Beirut, 1203 Hours

Fred Morgan eased the armored Mercedes through the Place Chatilla and onto Avenue Jamal. Mark Conrad rode shotgun. Striker sat in the back. Above, the Mediterranean sky glowed pale blue, as usual, and faint wisps of high-altitude cirrostratus clouds streaked the heavens as if airbrushed onto an electric blue dome. On the Earth's surface, the picture was less rosy. The road unfolded in a series of potholes and bumps. Debris had tumbled down from the once elegant hotels and apartment buildings, now little more than bombed-out rubble.

Once outside Beirut and past the militia checkpoints, the armored sedan sped unimpeded past the barren landscape. Craggy, sun-bleached rocks and short, sturdy scrub brush specked the austere terrain. The trip proved uneventful and Striker's car arrived at the outer security perimeter of the airport at 1235 hours, Beirut time. It had taken only thirty minutes to cross Beirut and negotiate the various control points en route.

Morgan carefully picked his way through a maze of vehicles, barriers, and military checkpoints manned by alert troops with machine guns and rifles. His Mercedes, with its two-inch-thick windows of hardened polycarbonate, provided excellent protection. It was like a fashionable tank and could resist an attack from a medium machine gun. Just like a tank, however, it could be defeated. Its greatest protection was the fact that it could withstand an initial assault, then with its cellular rubber tires still intact, the car's powerful engine would speed it out of the kill zone—at least in theory. In this mess of cars, armored vehicles, obstacles, and machine guns, though, there would be little chance of escape.

The big car inched past the last security checkpoint, and a soldier waved them through. Striker's driver deftly maneuvered the heavy sedan through a weaving series of yellow and black I-beam anti-crash barriers protruding out from the pavement toward arriving vehicles at a forty-five-degree angle. Finally, they were inside the airport grounds.

Beirut's Airport looked like any airport under permanent siege; it had been bombed, sniped, shelled, and poorly maintained for more than three decades. Security was tight. In fact, armed security personnel seemed to outnumber the passengers. Dozens of blue-uniformed security guards, and hundreds of soldiers in camouflaged field uniforms, controlled the airport terminal and grounds.

The Mercedes came to a stop in front of the sector headquarters, the fiefdom of Colonel Beagea. At least forty armed men stood guard. They were *all* impressive, obviously handpicked. Their uniforms were crisp, and the men appeared fit. Perched on a second floor marble balcony, more sharp-eyed soldiers surveyed the scene from sandbagged machine gun positions. One unseen soldier, observing from a bunker, took particular interest in the new visitors.

The Lebanese colonel appeared through the main entrance of the headquarters before Striker had fully unfolded his large frame from the Mercedes. Colonel Beagea, in his early forties, was a tall, thin, handsome man with slight graying at the temples. Striker knew that Beagea was a Harvard graduate—top of his class. The colonel was quite distinguished looking, as well, with a European air about him. He was also obviously well off, as his impeccably tailored uniform revealed.

Of course, thought Striker, *the colonel could be well off financially simply from the contributions the U.S. government had made to him in the past.*

"Hello, Colonel," said Striker smiling.

"John, it is good to see you. You are looking well."

"And you," offered Striker. The colonel looked fit enough to have just returned from a satisfying vacation.

"John," the colonel went on, "you know the plane has arrived?"

"I assumed so. Where is it now?"

"Overhead." The colonel looked skyward. Striker followed suit but didn't see the plane.

"Any problems?"

"They are not very happy terrorists," Colonel Beagea reported, smiling. "But they have not killed anyone yet, if that's what you mean. At least not that they've announced."

Striker nodded.

"Come," said the colonel. "We will go to the tower."

Morgan remained with the car; Conrad followed Striker at a discrete distance.

The men arrived at the control tower. With a broad flourish of his hand, the colonel gestured at a flickering radar screen. It displayed a fuzzy, white blip. The numbers *7-5-0-0* glowed bright red next to it.

"Here, John," said the colonel. "Here is your airplane." The pilots had set their transponder code for hijacked, Striker knew.

A controller in military uniform seated before the console glanced up at the colonel and said in Arabic, "They are still orbiting at five thousand feet about five miles out. They insist we clear the runway immediately. They've made no other demands."

"Thank you, Assam," said the colonel, placing his hand on the man's shoulder. With a sweep of his other hand toward the airfield, the colonel looked at Striker. "As you can see, it is not possible to land." Striker could see the trucks and armored personnel carriers blocking the runway. The drivers lounged in the low grass near the runway's edge.

The two men seated themselves in the corner of the room, away from the controllers and other army officers working in the area.

"Have you received any threats?" asked Striker.

"From the militias? No, not yet. But that will certainly come. Already this morning a group of Shiites tried to infiltrate the airport grounds. We had a rather sharp confrontation but managed to dissuade them without bloodshed. This affair, though, will undoubtedly cost me several men, and I must be careful myself. In fact, I imagine that if we succeed in sending this plane away from here, the airport will undoubtedly be shelled."

Striker knew that was true. He glanced around to be sure no one was in earshot. "Colonel," said Striker, "I know you are under great pressure. There are certainly risks involved here. And because we share many of the same goals, I have, from time to time, made certain contributions to your unit." The colonel listened intently, watching Striker's every gesture, a completely detached expression on his enigmatic face.

"Colonel," continued Striker, "I would like to make a more significant contribution than usual—a more meaningful contribution of, say, two hundred and fifty thousand dollars."

"That *is* very nice," allowed Beagea. "My men and I appreciate that. You know where it should go, I believe."

"Of course." That meant the colonel's personal, numbered account in Zurich.

"But John, there will be trouble, maybe big trouble because of this affair. I will need some *real* money to spend on my soldier's salary supplements and to buy some new equipment."

The colonel, thought Striker, had deduced that this was important to the United States, and that the Americans would probably be willing to pay much more than the initial offer. He would get everything he could out of it. Striker could not blame him. It was business. The colonel had not gotten where he was by being a sloppy businessman, and if the colonel couldn't pay his men, someone else would.

"Colonel," said Striker, breaking the brief silence, "I think that's an excellent idea. I would like to provide some operational support funds for your unit as well, say an additional half-million dollars?"

Beagea's poker face betrayed his delight with Striker's offer.

"John," asked the colonel, "just how far are we prepared to go to keep the terrorists from landing here?"

Striker stared into Beagea's unflinching eyes. "Colonel, they should *not* land here."

4

Air France 622, Over Beirut, 1510 Hours

Captain Granger sighed and laid his head back against the seat to rest. He glanced at Jean-Pierre Didier at the controls. He seemed to be holding up well. *Better than I am*, thought Granger. They had held an elliptical orbit around Beirut for nearly three hours while Abdul cursed and threatened the tower and stomped around in the cramped cockpit harassing the pilots. Captain Granger was afraid, and he knew he had to do something. They could not go on like this. If nothing else, he knew, a lack of fuel would eventually put a stop to this madness.

As for Abdul, the euphoria of power and leadership had long since faded, replaced by anxiety and fear. *Incredible*, thought Abdul, *how quickly everything has turned against me. My men expect answers, and I have none. How can I make the airport move the trucks from the runway? Should we kill someone? How many? It won't work anyway*, he told himself. *These men, who have closed the airport, are Lebanese. I am not dealing with weak Westerners. These men are inured to death, torture, and threats of all kinds. Even if we did execute two or three hostages, we cannot dump the bodies on the tarmac for the world to see. No, it probably would not change their minds.*

Abdul sensed that Abu Hassim, in his own dim way, understood those facts as well. Otherwise, he would have already killed someone. The big man was an enigma. He was violent and unpredictable. Since arriving over Beirut, though, he had not so much as spoken. He sat in silence, waiting. *Waiting for what?* wondered Abdul.

Abu *appeared* to be the calm one, but Abu Hassim had a reputation for ferocity, and Abdul knew that he had not acquired such a reputation by sitting calmly and waiting. He knew the quiet facade could melt away without warning. Abdul also knew that the man's mood swings were not normal.

As for the others, they were agitated at best. Mohammed had become nervous and returned repeatedly to the cockpit to yell at Abdul. They had argued several times already. *Leadership*, Abdul realized belatedly, *is not as easy as I imagined. I must do something, but what?*

"You know," said Captain Granger, interrupting Abdul's thoughts, "we have less than one hour's fuel left."

"So what?" Abdul responded sharply.

"The nearest airport is Cyprus. Once we drop below thirty minutes of fuel we have no place to go, not even there."

"Then they must let us land here."

"I don't think they much care what happens to us here," suggested Granger. "Listen, if we go to Cyprus we can refuel and go anywhere in the Mediterranean you like."

Abdul did listen, but he did not know where to go after Cyprus. Granger pressed his point. "They will not let us land here, and crashing and dying will not serve your purpose. It will defeat you."

"Okay, be quiet now!" snapped Abdul. "I must think." But the seed had been planted. Abdul knew that he must do as the pilot had said. He really had no other choice. "Do it then," he said. "Fly there."

***

Beirut International Airport, 1512 Hours

"Well John," Beagea began, "there you have it. We have succeeded. You have what you wanted."

"It appears so, at least for the moment."

"I assume that I will see the funds in the appropriate account shortly?"

"You will."

"Excellent. Now I have several airplanes that would like to take off," announced the colonel. "And I fear there is little time. So, please excuse me for a moment."

"Of course," Striker said, signaling Conrad who was waiting in the corner of the control room. "Albert, I want you to go to the car and call the embassy. Have Andrews send a flash message to Langley. Anaconda complete. Presumed destination Cyprus."

Conrad disappeared out the door. Striker needed to talk with Director of Operations Reid soon to explain the details of the operation and to find out what else he wanted done. Striker suspected what the next step would be, and he feared the worst. Langley would probably order him to query Cupid about Hezbollah's plan, endangering one of the CIA's most valuable sources of information in the Middle East.

For the moment, though, he would wait a short while to ensure that the hijacked airliner did not double back. Striker watched as the colonel supervised the removal of the trucks. He noticed that Beagea was being cautious as well. The colonel only removed the vehicles to the edge of the runway.

After fifteen minutes or so, the air controller reported that Air France 622 had left the Beirut radar control zone on a heading of three-one-zero degrees, confirming that the plane was en route to Cyprus. As Striker was about to depart for the embassy to file his report, a Lebanese captain entered with a folded piece of paper and handed it to Colonel Beagea. They exchanged a few words. The captain fidgeted while Beagea read the message. The colonel walked to Striker, an almost sly smile on his face. He handed the paper to Striker.

Striker read the message. It was a statement in Arabic. The colonel explained that the communiqué from Hezbollah was just released to a local radio station and broadcast over the air. The colonel's signal officer had copied it and brought it directly here. Striker read it carefully. The communiqué denounced the act of violence against the Party of God by the Lebanese Army and its evil ally, the United States. It also vowed revenge—immediate retaliation against Christian and American targets throughout the Middle East.

***

Air France 622, Over the Mediterranean, 1535 Hours

Onboard the Airbus, Abdul's men vented their anger over their failure to land in Beirut. Mohammed babbled about commandos, attacks, and certain death. Martyrdom would be a fine thing, and he hoped some day to achieve this exalted status, but not today. He had not yet made the *Hajj*, the required pilgrimage to Mecca. He cursed the Christians in Beirut for closing the airport. He prayed that Hezbollah was shelling them mercilessly. He went from passenger to passenger screaming these things into their ears. He had also begun to criticize Abdul's plan.

Abu Hassim remained silent. He continued staring sullenly out the passenger window next to where he sat. He scarcely moved. The numbing mixture of thoughts, fears, and anxieties that sometimes invaded his mind had materialized once again. As the numbness invaded his body, he withdrew within himself. He sat and stared, afraid to move. He knew that if he did, he might be unable to control his actions.

Khalid, less nervous than Mohammed, stared curiously at Abu Hassim for a time. Then for lack of anything else to do, he joined Mohammed in tormenting the passengers. His heart was not really in it, but the process took his mind off their situation.

The passengers were terrified to the point of shock. Many of the children still cried, and their mothers strained to comfort them even with bound hands. They flinched each time Mohammed or Khalid swaggered past. The two terrorists continued marching along the parallel aisles of the Airbus, waving their pistols and screaming in Arabic. Occasionally, they stopped to point a pistol in a woman's face, making her cry even harder, or to slap a male passenger.

Abdul remained in the cockpit. As the Airbus neared Larnaca International Airport, he hovered over the two pilot's shoulders. He scrutinized and questioned their every move. Ten thousand feet below and fifteen miles ahead, set against the vast blue sea, was an emerald-green speck in the fading light. The island of Cyprus glimmered like a rugged yet lustrous pearl in the afternoon sun. On the western end of the island, Chionistra, more commonly referred to as Mount Olympus, cast a shadow across the island nation. The city of Nicosia was just coming into view in the far distance, beyond the town of Larnaca. Under other circumstances, the sight would have been magnificent to behold.

The copilot, Jean-Pierre Didier, contacted Larnaca tower, informed them that their fuel status was critical, and waited. Within a few minutes, a controller responded. Abdul tensed and thrust his pistol harder against the copilot's neck. The tower granted permission to land. The copilot informed Abdul.

"You tell them," said Abdul, "that you want to go to a remote place—in the open. You tell them that your life depends on it. One false move and your worthless life is sacrificed. If I see any soldiers—just one—you will be the first to die!"

Didier carefully repeated Abdul's instructions. He received an almost instantaneous response.

"There will be a small guide truck," the copilot said slowly and clearly. Abdul's pistol fully motivated Didier to avoid error at all cost. "They will take us to an open spot on the edge of the tarmac near a big field. It's about one thousand yards from the eastern fence and eight hundred or so from the main terminal building."

"Okay," said Abdul. "But do not forget what I told you."

Captain Granger and his copilot prepared the aircraft for landing. They lined up on runway two-one, as instructed by the Larnaca tower, and brought the big jet down smoothly. The pilot turned the plane onto a taxiway and spotted a small yellow truck, its lights flashing. Abdul poked his head around the cramped cockpit, scanning left and right through the small side windows. He anxiously looked for any sign of military forces.

For an instant, which seemed to Didier to last forever, Abdul leaned forward over the copilot's shoulder, his forearm resting on Didier's seat back. The heavy pistol dangled menacingly in front of Jean-Pierre Didier's face. He thought maybe he could grab the gun and kill this bastard. It was just right there in front of his face. It would be easy. The gun was so close that he could see the light coat of oil that glistened on its blued metal frame. The smell of gun oil filled his nostrils and briefly reminded him of hunting pheasant with his father's old shotgun.

For an eternity, it seemed, Didier hung there, ready to plunge headlong into the void. He imagined jerking the gun from Abdul's hand, aiming, pulling the trigger, and seeing the man's blood splash across the cockpit walls. It would be gratifying.

But what would I do about the rest of the terrorists? he wondered. He didn't even know how many there were back there. Even if he somehow managed to kill this one, he could hardly picture himself in a gun battle against several heavily armed, desperate, professional killers. With a shudder of fear, he let the idea drop almost as quickly as it had entered his head.

The Airbus followed the guide truck, which displayed a large black and yellow striped panel inscribed with *Follow Me*. In the passenger cabin, Khalid and Mohammed darted from window to window, trying to get a view of the airfield. Each time a terrorist leaned over a hostage to look out the window, the passenger would cringe, close his or her eyes, and try to sink back into the seat. None of the hijackers had been to Larnaca before. They all knew the Beirut airport. They had studied it for months. But this was unfamiliar ground.

Granger followed the truck and turned the Airbus in a tight circle. The huge starboard wing swung wide over the brown field. The plane slid into position on the edge of the tarmac and halted with a slight jerk. The copilot's hands played deftly over the console disengaging and shutting down the two turbofan engines.

One of the workers jumped out of the truck, walked to the plane, and placed a pair of chocks on one set of the jet's portside tires.

In the cockpit, Abdul lost sight of the worker. "What is doing?" he yelled at the pilots.

Granger replied, "Just putting chocks on the wheels so we don't accidentally roll."

The man hopped back in the truck, and they drove away.

When Abdul saw the men leave, he let out a sigh of relief. He scanned the immense field and vacant tarmac surrounding the plane, at least what he could see from the cockpit. He had never felt so trapped in his life. *We're not supposed to be here*, he thought. *We should be in Beirut. What do I do now? Demand a conference with the media? Ask for fuel and prepare to fly somewhere else? If so, where? Where would we be any safer than here?* For the moment, his fellow hijackers were busy ensuring that the airplane and its human cargo of misery were secure. They would want answers soon. For now, Abdul could be sure of only one thing, he needed rest and time to think.

5

Beirut, 1635 Hours

Striker returned to the embassy and proceeded directly to communications. He contacted Gerald Reid. Striker recapped the details of the operation at the airport. He also informed the director of operations about Hezbollah's communiqué vowing reprisals.

"Good work, John, keeping that plane out of Beirut. They're sitting on the ground on Cyprus. Maybe they'll sit tight there for awhile. As for reprisals, I expected retaliation from Hezbollah. That's a given," said Reid. "Now that we've managed to keep the hijackers out of Beirut, we need more information in order to deal with them. I want you to activate Cupid," said the director matter-of-factly.

Striker didn't respond.

Reid continued, "Cyprus is a good location, if they can be kept there for any length of time. Delta Force is already in the air. They'll be able to operate on Cyprus. Delta can take care of the hijackers if we take care of our end—like finding out who's running this show and what they are going to do next."

Reid paused, but Striker remained silent. "I'm sure those Hezbollah bastards are running this operation from Beirut. At least they would have, had the plane landed there. They still might be controlling it somehow. I want to know who these hijackers are, what their plans are, and especially what their weaknesses are. If we can get a lead on one of their families, we might be able to do something with it."

"You know," said Striker, "that it's dangerous to push Cupid like this. The slightest slip up, and he will be purged. Besides, I don't know if we can contact him so quickly. It's all done by dead drop."

"Listen, John," replied Reid, his voice low, "I know it's dangerous, but Cupid's all we've got right now. We have to use him. I want to make sure our military boys can take these assholes down and not have any surprises. We've been assuring the president for months that we've got a good window on Hezbollah. Well, we sure as hell didn't see this one coming, so I don't see what we have to lose. We need to know what their next move is, and Cupid seems to be the only way to do it," he said more firmly than he had intended.

"I realize we're violating every rule in the book where Cupid is concerned, but this one is important. We need to know what Hezbollah intends to do, both in Beirut and on Cyprus. Am I clear, John?"

"I think I get the message."

"Listen, John, we've been careful with Cupid. And with good reason. But as far as I'm concerned, it was for a rainy day just like this. Now we use him. If he survives, it'll be icing on the cake."

"I'll do my best."

The communications link went dead.

Striker loosened his tie and leaned back in his chair. He forced himself to relax.

In the years following the kidnapping and eventual murder of William Buckley, former CIA station chief in Beirut, the United States had suffered a devastating lack of human intelligence in the Middle East. As a direct result of Buckley's kidnapping, virtually all the U.S. sources in Lebanon, including their controllers, were compromised—either killed or forced to flee the country. It was said that Buckley produced over four hundred pages of text during his lengthy interrogation. Not only did he compromise human sources, but CIA methods and procedures as well. Striker vowed he would never be taken prisoner like Buckley.

Striker knew that the ultimate result of Buckley's capture was that it would be a long, hard road back. U.S. intelligence still had not recouped its losses in the Middle East and probably never would. There had been few important recruitments. Significant penetrations were fewer still. This was especially true for the more radical Shiite sects like Hezbollah—all with a penchant for practicing and exporting terrorism. They ran their organizations tightly. If a member was even suspected of treachery, an elite squad of internal enforcers would rapidly and ruthlessly eliminate him. As a result, potential agents, or informers, ran enormous risks by spying in Lebanon.

Striker's most valuable agent in the country, referred to only in code as Cupid, was an ordinary laborer. He was a Shiite who had been carefully recruited to penetrate Hezbollah. The group was responsible for a number of major hijackings, bombings, and other terrorist activities. They also kidnapped and murdered dozens of Westerners over the years.

Cupid was extremely important to Striker's operations. Based on information provided by this mole, the CIA had thwarted several assassination attempts against U.S. and European government officials. He was an invaluable source of information on the activities of the fanatical and shadowy terror group.

Unfortunately, though, Cupid's network was established using less than ideal tradecraft. It was a miracle, Striker believed, that Cupid had survived as long as he had. When he was sent in, they considered him just another shot in the dark, among dozens of such attempts to penetrate the Shiites. The scarred and battered bodies of most of those attempts at infiltration rapidly turned up on the streets of Beirut. Only a handful survived the initial endeavor. Only one remained today—Cupid. No one could have predicted the results.

The main problem with the setup was that the Lebanese intelligence officer who handled this vital agent was young and often less than reliable. The ironic thing, thought Striker, was that this controller, a twenty-four-year-old Maronite Christian named Akim, had the natural ability to run agents successfully. He frequently produced brilliant results. Akim had established an impressive array of informants and agents of his own, providing mundane but steady information from the Muslim sectors. Akim, though, was a bit of a wildcard and was often more interested in booze and women than his work.

Striker decided he would use Akim one more time and then replace him. After this operation, Akim would probably be compromised anyway. If he cooperated, the CIA would relocate him to the States with a new identity. If he didn't, something could always be arranged.

His mind made up, Striker returned to his office and summoned his deputy for operations, Doug Andrews, the CIA's number two in Beirut.

"How'd it go?" asked Andrews.

"I got rid of it," replied Striker, referring to the hijacked airliner. "But who the hell knows what the fallout will be," he said sitting back in his desk chair. "Did you find Akim?"

Andrews began looking for Akim as soon as the Beirut office learned of the hijacking.

"Yeah. He thinks the hijackers are Hezbollah."

Striker chewed his lip and stared at the wall as he absorbed this already stale bit of information. This was not the first indication of interference in Tunisia by the Lebanese Shiite Hezbollah. The Iranians used Hezbollah and other Shiites around the Middle East to spread their so-called Islamic revolution. The CIA believed Hezbollah had sent arms and explosives to Tunisia in the past. Now they were taking an active role in the Tunisian fundamentalist movement.

"He's guessing," said Andrews.

Striker nodded. "Yeah, but he's probably guessing pretty close to the mark. Okay, Doug, here's what I want you to do. I want to talk to Akim in person. We have to move fast if we're going to get anything on the hijacking we can work with. They went to Cyprus. Delta's en route there now. Langley wants more intel for the team to work with.

"But even if we don't stop them in their tracks, we'll still eventually want to get at whoever planned this hijacking. Set up a room at the Alfonse. Give it the works. I want the lobby, the stairways, the rear entrances, and corridors all secured. I want the place locked down tight. Get a meeting set up as quickly as you can arrange it."

"Got it, boss."

***

Air France 622, Larnaca, Cyprus, 1830 Hours

After nearly three hours on the ground, Abdul had left the cockpit only once to check on the plane's security. Both he and his men were feeling severe physical and emotional strain. In short, they were exhausted. Nevertheless, his men maintained a frenetic pace as they dashed about the plane, scanning the surrounding field and tarmac.

Abdul was trying to reason out the situation and plan their next move, but he still found himself sitting in the engineer's chair staring aimlessly out at the tarmac through the cockpit windshield.

Finally, the copilot's cautious voice dragged him back from his unproductive thoughts.

"What do you want?" he answered gruffly.

"We have to call for an auxiliary power unit. We need it to power the lights and radios, and if necessary, start the engines."

Abdul thought for a moment. He knew this was probably true, but he didn't trust the Frenchman to talk in English to the Cypriots.

"You call them," he ordered sharply. "You tell them to bring the device. But you also tell them that if there is any trickery, the pistol that will be against your head will claim its first victim. Also tell them that I will speak to them soon, and they must have someone to talk in Arabic or French. And when they come with the generator, tell them they will have three bodies to carry away."

Abdul informed Mohammed, Abu, and Khalid about the power unit. He then ordered his men to throw out the two dead American soldiers and the dead passenger.

Abdul returned to the cockpit and waved his pistol back and forth between the pilot and copilot. He watched the two Cypriots who arrived with the APU until they disappeared under the plane. Mohammed watched them from the open door. The Cypriots connected the generator, and started it. The men turned to leave.

Mohammed called for them to wait. Abu grabbed one of the Marines by his belt, dragged him to the open doorway, and dropped the body over the edge. Mohammed and Khalid did the same with the second Marine. Abu then tossed out the dead passenger. The bodies thumped the ground heavily some thirty feet below. Mohammed stepped into the doorway and gestured with his

Uzi to take the bodies and go. The two Cypriots carefully loaded the dead men onto their truck and then drove away.

"You are very lucky," Abdul said to the pilots, replacing the pistol in his belt. He retook his seat in the engineer's chair, a place that had become his refuge.

Where should I take this plane to now? he wondered again. *Where would we be safe? It will be dark in a few hours. Where can we land in the dark and be secure? Nowhere except Beirut,* he concluded. *But how?*

He carried two untraceable burner phones in his side leg pocket and could use the encryption app installed on them to communicate with Abbas Bachar, Mustafa's lieutenant. He powered up first one, and then the other, acquired a signal, and checked for messages. There were none. He assumed that Mustafa would already know that they were on Cyprus. *If he had instructions for me,* he reasoned, *there would be a message.* He considered whether he should send a report, but decided to wait until he had a clearer grasp of their situation and exactly what his next move should be.

Abdul walked back to the main cabin still contemplating his options. He stood watching the scene for a moment. Everything seemed under control, but he silently wished the hostages would not watch him with such doleful eyes. Then a young flight attendant in the front row spoke to him in French.

There were two flight attendants on Air France 622, both seated in the first row, hands bound. Marie Dubois, twenty-three, had spoken to him. Eva Martine, forty-eight, looked on anxiously.

Abdul stood in front of them, arms crossed, regarding them in disbelief.

The younger one, Marie, said to him again, "Please let me give them some water. Please," she begged with tearful eyes.

"And the bathroom," pleaded Eva. "They need to go, and those who already have, need to clean up."

"Please," Maria implored.

He looked down at them incredulously. Then he glanced back up at the hostages. Those nearby who had heard the conversation stared at Abdul with pained expressions. He looked back at the two flight attendants and said, "No!"

Then he turned and walked back into the cockpit, angry at the encounter.

Abdul's primary concern was what to do next, but he was too weary to produce any answers. His men were tired as well, but they were too anxious to rest even though they would certainly need their strength in the coming days. He felt lethargic, drained of all energy or capacity to think.

He would allow himself a few moments of rest, he reasoned, for he felt that they were in no immediate danger here. The danger would come. It would increase for as long as they remained here. For now, though, he needed a few moments just to sit quietly and think, but he couldn't concentrate. He could still see those miserable eyes staring at him.

He cursed, stood, and left the cockpit. He called the other three members of his team together.

"We will let the women attendants give them food and water, and take them to the restroom. Watch them carefully."

Abu Hassim looked as if he were about to object, but then acquiesced. Even he recognized that the odor in the cabin was becoming foul.

Abdul turned and went to the two flight attendants. He pulled out a lock-blade knife and snapped it open. They both recoiled, expressions of terror on their faces. Both of them had already endured having pistols held to their heads, their faces jammed against a window.

They both sucked in a sharp breath as if they might scream.

"Quiet!" shouted Abdul in French. He reached down and lifted Marie's arms. He sawed through the plastic strap until it cut through and fell off. Then he did the same with Eva.

They sat there for a few seconds, rubbing their wrists, unsure what was happening.

Looking at the younger, smaller woman, he said, "You will take water to the passengers. Do not use the big cart. I do not want the aisle blocked. Then some food."

Looking at the older woman, he said, "You will take the women, with their children, one at a time, to the lavatories. The doors will remain open. When they are returned to their seat, you will refasten their seatbelt. When all the women are done, one man at a time will be taken, but only with one of my men escorting you. Everyone remains bound."

Eyeing both of them, he asked, "Do you clearly understand my orders?"

They nodded yes.

"If you do not follow them exactly, you will suffer greatly. Now go."

Marie and Eva stood, almost robotically, and began their work.

***

Mike Elliot had dozed fitfully throughout the afternoon, but he hadn't gotten any real sleep. The last thing he remembered before waking up here was going into the galley. He decided that the terrorists must have dragged him, unconscious, to this seat.

He was in a window seat, among a group of passengers, toward the rear of the plane. He had figured out that his hands were bound behind his back, but he could see that the others had their hands bound in the front.

He had no way of knowing, but the beast of a man who had tried to kill him with a bear hug had also saved him. After takeoff, Abdul had ordered his men to kill Mike. "The man is dangerous," Abdul had insisted repeatedly.

Abu Hassim had refused, saying, "This man fought with honor. He will not be killed, at least not while unconscious or bound. I did not defeat him, you hit him from behind. Our destinies are still crossed."

Abdul then ordered that they bind him especially well. Mohammed and Khalid dragged him to the rear of the plane, applied two plastic cinch straps to his wrists behind his back, and then strapped him into a seat.

He knew he had not been fully conscious for much of the time, but he had seen enough to know the general situation. The terrorists had passed the remainder of the afternoon and the early evening hours alternately springing from window to window and tormenting their hostages.

Mike's head still hurt, but his vision had cleared. He felt more in control of his senses. He wasn't sure how long they'd been airborne or how long they'd been here. Wherever *here* was. Sunlight was entering the plane at a low angle, so he decided that it was late afternoon.

He could see the two flight attendants moving about serving water and taking people to the restroom. That was at least *something* of a positive development.

He thought of his wife, Lynn. He knew she was somewhere on this plane. He had watched her board. She was all he had left to hold onto in this life. Anytime she walked into a room, Mike's attention was immediately drawn to her.

She was petite with fair skin, like her French mother. She had her mother's smile, a small mouth with pouty, full lips. Her eyes, however, were those of her Vietnamese father. In fact, her eyes dominated her face and her large, seemingly black pupils held a person's gaze, fairly demanding it.

When he last saw her boarding and entering the Airbus, she wore a simple, red, satin blouse and black slacks. He had searched everywhere he could see on the plane, which wasn't much, for a hint of that red blouse, to no avail.

It was torture knowing she was here, under the control of ruthless murderers, and he could not comfort her or protect her. His old emotional wounds welled up and gripped him by the throat. He felt as though he might collapse in on himself. He had spent months in the hospital recovering from his physical wounds.

Repairing and healing the physical damage to his body was the easy part. The wound that would not heal was the emotional guilt and pain. Lynn was his nurse, and she was gradually able to reach him. She saved him. *She pulled me up from the depths of hell,* he thought, *and taught me to live and to love again. Now she might die here, and I can do nothing to save her.*

And while Mike could do nothing to help his wife right now, he knew that at least he was here with her. He couldn't see her, but he knew she was here somewhere. As long as he was alive, so probably was she.

A terrorist approached, walking slowly down the aisle on Mike's side of the plane. This was one that he had not seen before, or at least didn't remember. He could put together only bits and pieces of events, but somehow this man's size, beard, and hair seemed oddly familiar.

The diverse aspects of his appearance combined to make him seem sinister, almost ghoulish. He wore an angry scowl on his dark face, and his khaki work pants were stained with blood. *Whose blood?* Mike wondered.

Suddenly, sporadic events flooded his thoughts. It was all Mike could do to sit still and keep from flinching. The last thing he wanted was to draw the attention of the huge man walking toward him. He remembered now how this all began.

Mike had sensed something when he first saw this man, but he had not been sure what it was. Details were coming back now. He remembered another Arab worker who was holding a bottle of wine. He remembered the fight, and he cursed himself for not being able to take the big man down. Then, at some point, everything went blank. He could only vaguely remember the blinding kaleidoscope of lights that followed.

Barely peeking through his eyelids, he watched the brooding hulk of a man moving down the aisle. He looked more like a vicious, wild-eyed animal than a man. Abu Hassim moved as if in slow motion, scanning back and forth, checking each passenger as he walked toward the rear of the plane.

Mike stared at the seatback in front of him as the terrorist walked down the aisle. When the big man paused briefly to stare at him, Mike just focused straight ahead. Then the man moved on and stopped to look out the small porthole in the rear portside passenger door.

Mike could barely see between the seats, but he watched the big Arab study the door for a moment, before pulling on the lever trying to open it. He tugged clumsily on the handle. Finally, he managed to jerk the door open. He kicked at it and uttered a curse. He settled against the wall where he could see outside while remaining concealed from view. Mike wondered if this guy could be some kind of psycho.

He suddenly had the urge to finish the fight with the man. He considered how he might attack him, maybe push him out of the door. It was at least thirty feet to the pavement below. The fall would kill or seriously injure him. *But then what would I do?* Mike silently asked himself. There were other terrorists. He wasn't even sure how many, but at least three, maybe as many as five or six. *How would I get his gun before pushing him out? I'd just get everyone killed*, he decided.

Besides, until he could find a way to get himself free of whatever was binding his wrists together, he wasn't going anywhere.

6

Over the Atlantic

Delta's deployment from Pope Air Force Base went smoothly. The team had been in flight now for just under six hours. Two hours earlier, headquarters informed Barclay that Air France 622 was sitting on the tarmac at Larnaca International Airport on the Greek side of the island of Cyprus. The team's destination was now the British air base of Akrotiri on the island's southwestern coast, about forty miles by air from Larnaca. Negotiations with the Cypriot government were underway both in Washington and in Cyprus to allow Delta to operate on Cypriot soil.

The U.S. Air Force C-17 Globemaster approached the Strait of Gibraltar as it slipped through the night sky over the eastern Atlantic. Lieutenant Colonel Barclay sat at a computer console inside one of Delta's portable command posts. The box-like container was chained to the deck of the aircraft. Colonel Sinclair sat beside him and looked on.

Barclay manipulated a diagram on his laptop. The terminal linked Delta to the Pentagon's computer database via secure satellite. The two officers examined a blueprint-like sketch of Larnaca International Airport. Barclay plotted the location of the hijacked Airbus as viewed from several different angles.

In the cargo bay of the C-17, the men prepared for their arrival in Cyprus as best they could in the crowded confines of the aircraft. Barrington and his team already had the technical specs and blueprints on Air France 622 and were reviewing them now.

On Cyprus, the team would set up two command posts, or CPs. The primary CP would be at Akrotiri, but Barclay would also establish a forward, mobile command post at the hijack site using two communications and surveillance vans. The two gray,

European-manufactured, Citroen C35RD model vans were parked one behind the other only a few feet from the tail ramp of the C-17.

Barclay was satisfied with the image of the airport on the screen in front of him. He printed copies and instructed a communications specialist to deliver them to Master Sergeant Palmer and Sergeant Major Barrington. The young man scooped up the copies one at a time as they came out of the printer. When he opened the door to leave, the noise of the jet flooded the small compartment.

Next to Barclay, Colonel Sinclair leaned back in his swivel chair and stretched. Barclay glanced at his watch—five and a half hours to touchdown.

***

Air France 622, 1940 Hours

A flight attendant carrying a stack of plastic cups and a liter bottle of water, made her way down Lynn's aisle near the front of the plane. She had already spent an hour going down the opposite aisle.

She handed each person a cup and poured some water. They gulped it down and wanted more. She had to return to the galley often for a new bottle.

On the other side of the plane, under the watchful gaze of Mohammed and Khalid, her partner was still busy escorting the women, some with children, to the lavatory.

The French attendant serving water was a small woman in her twenties. Lynn watched her approach as she served the few passengers in front of her. The young woman was cute, adorable in fact, Lynn thought. And she was apparently quite strong, given the situation. Her shiny black hair was cut short, and it suited her small face perfectly. Speaking in English, she had a few consoling words for each passenger she served, touching them and trying to give them encouragement.

She finally arrived at Lynn's seat. She immediately noticed the cut on Lynn's lip. She set down her water and cups on an empty seat and hurried back to the galley. She returned to Lynn with a tube of antibiotic ointment and a cotton swab. She carefully dabbed some cream on the cut.

"There, that's better," she said softly.

Lynn whispered in French, "I'm Lynn."

The young French woman's eyes brightened. She didn't often hear an American speak French, and she had flown with many of them. She looked around. The big one was nowhere in sight, and the other two were watching her partner.

"I'm Marie," she replied softly. "Marie Dubois."

"And the other attendant?"

"Eva Martine."

"You are both very brave," Lynn added.

"No. I'm shaking terribly." She held out her hand and it was visibly trembling.

"Well, no matter, you're still very brave. I heard you both speak to the terrorist leader. Where are you from?"

Marie looked about again, and then said, "Montpellier, near the Mediterranean coast. But now I live in Paris."

"I know Montpellier. It's a lovely old city."

Lynn also scanned around cautiously, and then whispered, "Marie, my husband is on board somewhere. He was injured during the takeover of the plane. I saw them dragging him toward the back. I don't even know if he is still alive. Mid thirties, sandy colored hair. He had blood all over his head and shirt."

Lynn could immediately see the fear in Marie's eyes, and she regretted telling her about Mike.

But then Marie nodded. "I'll look for him."

"His name is Mike."

"Okay."

Lynn smiled and touched the young woman's hand. "We'll be alright, Marie."

She nodded, gave Lynn some water, and moved on to the next passenger.

***

2010 Hours

Eva Martine had finished taking all the women and children to the restroom. She was now assisting the men. Mike watched as she helped the last few men before his turn. He had let it go hours ago right where he sat. He knew most of the others had too. The smell of urine was strong.

Peeing in your pants was neither pleasant nor comfortable, but a human being can hold it only so long. He was nearly dry now and was ready to go again, though he wasn't exactly sure how he was going to do it with his hands behind his back.

The flight attendant arrived at Mike with Khalid close behind her. Mike noted her nametag: *Eva M.*

She saw that Mike's hands were bound behind his back. She turned to the terrorist and said, "He needs to go to the bathroom. Can you release his hands for just for a moment?"

"No," snarled Khalid, "if you want him to go, *you* help him."

"I will, then," she replied.

She took Mike to the aft toilet. Khalid followed, his Uzi submachine gun trained on the two of them.

With the bathroom door open, Eva unzipped Mike's pants, helped him urinate, and zipped him back up. Mike felt a little embarrassed, mostly for Eva, but he was grateful nonetheless.

"Sorry, Eva," Mike whispered to her.

"I raised two boys. There's not much I haven't seen or done," she replied.

"Shut up," snarled Khalid in French.

She returned Mike to his seat and refastened his seatbelt. Eva and Khalid moved on to another passenger.

In the process of sitting back down, Mike tried to get a glimpse of the metal bar he was using to work on his bindings, but the seat cushion concealed it. Nevertheless, once seated, he felt around with his hands, and went back to work rubbing the plastic strap against the metal bar under the seat.

***

Beirut, 2110 Hours

Striker's armored Mercedes, followed by a CIA escort car, skirted the west end of Beirut headed south. The two vehicles followed the once scenic Mediterranean coast along Avenue General de Gaulle leading to East Beirut. Just north of the Hippodrome, the avenue became Boulevard Saeb Salam.

The two sedans passed through a Muslim checkpoint, then a Phalange checkpoint, and then entered East Beirut. They proceeded along the Corniche Gemayel and past the Place du Musée. Two minutes later, Fred Morgan pulled the vehicle to a halt in front of the Hotel Alfonse just off the Corniche. The security detail halted a hundred yards back.

Mark Conrad, in the front seat, got out, stood next to the vehicle, and carefully scanned the street and surrounding buildings. Morgan stayed behind the wheel, just in case.

The Alfonse was not quite what it was in the old days when it rated four stars, but it was still in pretty good shape considering that Beirut had been ripped apart by a lengthy and brutal civil war.

Conrad saw Doug Andrews standing just inside the building's big glass doors. Hotel Alfonse was emblazoned in faded gold letters across the glass facade above the entrance. Andrews tugged once on his collar to indicate that the street was covered and the hotel was secure. Conrad walked around the car and pulled open the heavy armored door. Striker hopped out, casually bounded up the steps, and strode into the hotel.

Inside, the Alfonse was an absolute anachronism in the factious and chaotic Beirut. One glance was all it took to realize that the enigmatic Lebanese capital still held many secrets of wealth, power, and intrigue. Splendid crushed velvet in bright reds and pinks, decorated the plush lobby. Circular stuffed benches surrounded the many polished stone columns. The brilliant marble floor gleamed like wet ice. An ancient bellhop, in waistcoat and fez, waited by the desk. Younger versions moved busily about the room. African, Asian, European, and Arabian businessmen strolled about chatting. Beirut was still the crossroads of the continents, and plenty of lucrative, shady deals could still be made in war-torn Lebanon.

Striker noted his own men, Lebanese and American, placed about the lobby. Security was tight. Maintaining a safe house in Beirut was risky. Striker only created them when the need arose. The Alfonse occasionally served that purpose.

He followed Andrews up the grand staircase over a lush crimson carpet secured by shiny brass rods. They stopped on the fourth floor and proceeded to room fourteen. Striker entered alone.

"Akim," said Striker, smiling and extending his hand. "It's good to see you again."

"And you too, John. How are you?" asked the handsome young Arab. Akim was in his mid-twenties. His jet-black hair and thick moustache were closely cropped and impeccably trimmed. His clothes were casual but expensive and well cared for.

"I'm fine, Akim," replied Striker, pouring himself a drink from the bar. "We've got a problem."

"So I heard. Like I told Doug, it's got to be Hezbollah."

"That's not enough, Akim. I want more."

"Such as?" asked Akim, cautiously raising a thick eyebrow.

"I want to know exactly who is behind the hijacking. Names. Families. Addresses."

"And just where will I get such information, John?"

Striker looked Akim straight in the eyes. "Cupid, of course."

"I can't ask Cupid questions like that, John. It would get him killed for sure. Besides, if I did ask something, it could be days, or weeks, before he would leave an answer in the drop. You know I just pick up the messages he leaves, and I'm not even scheduled for a pick up soon. I don't have anyone ready to go in."

Striker already knew all this, but he had no choice. "I'm sure you can arrange something, Akim. You are quite talented in such matters. He may have left a message by now considering all that's going on. At a minimum, we have to service his drops. While that's being done there's no harm in leaving him some indication of what we're interested in. We've done it before. And in the meantime, if he leaves a name, well, we just might be able to do something with it."

"Planning something, John?"

"Nah, just want to know who we're dealing with," said Striker, keeping an air of amiability.

"I've already told you it is Hezbollah. And if it is Hezbollah, it is the Scimitar," said Akim, trying to conceal the fear in his voice at pronouncing the name aloud.

"Yes, and if it's him I want to know his next move." Striker turned and set his glass on the bar. Looking back, Striker said, "And Akim, I'll tell you something else, I want the man himself."

"John, now you're trying to get us all killed."

"We know he gets around a lot. Scimitar enjoys doing a lot of his own dirty work. All we need is one timely tip, and who knows what might be arranged. And I'll give you a little extra incentive, Akim. Get the Scimitar set up for me, and I'll send you back to the States with a half-million dollars in cash and American citizenship."

Akim's heavy eyebrows popped up briefly before settling back into a deep frown. Striker pushed the point further.

"You'd be a wealthy man, and there'd be no more looking over your shoulder."

"And what if I don't want your money and your citizenship?"

"Oh, you want it, Akim. I know you. Besides, if you left my employ and they found out that you'd been running agents in Hezbollah, the Shiites would…, well, it wouldn't be pleasant."

Akim's dark, thick brow furled even more. "And how would they find out?"

"Calm down. They won't. Just do what I want, Akim, and you'll be living in California instead of Beirut."

Akim considered Striker's words more seriously. He had guts, Striker knew. He was a product of his environment. He had been running intelligence messages for his older brothers since he was ten. Since his early teens, he had known only sectarian strife and violence. He wouldn't spook easily. It was just that where the Scimitar was involved, everybody got jittery. Rumor had it that people disappeared merely for mentioning the name in public. Striker knew, though, that Akim could not really refuse this offer.

"I will have to think about it."

"I don't have time for that crap, Akim!" said Striker with more force than he had intended.

"I said I'll think about it."

Akim was more afraid of the Scimitar than of the CIA chief.

Striker dug into his trouser pocket and fished out a tightly folded piece of paper. He extended it toward Akim. The Arab just stared back, not taking it. Striker let it drop onto the coffee table.

After a moment, Akim scooped up the note and stuffed it into his pocket. He walked to the door. "I'll have to see what I can set up. I'll call you tonight."

Striker's shoulders dropped slightly, and the tension disappeared from his voice. "Fine, Akim. Just remember, make it good. You could walk out of this with a bundle or with nothing." Striker turned to face the bar.

"If I walk out of it at all," muttered Akim, stepping into the hallway.

***

Air France 622, Larnaca, 2123 Hours

Abdul awoke suddenly. He raised his head from his arm on the small worktable before the engineer's instrument console. His arm was numb, and he had difficulty raising it. His face felt prickly and hot. How long had he been asleep? He gazed around for several seconds, uncertain of where he was. Finally, he realized that he was still in the cockpit sitting on the tarmac at Larnaca airport. The sky outside was dark, and the area around the plane was illuminated by the artificial glow of tall lamps and runway marker lights.

It was hot and stuffy. Abdul could feel that his face and hair were sticky and wet. An eerie half-light, tinted red by the instruments, bathed the cockpit. The two pilots were asleep, slouched over in their chairs. Abdul tried to rise up, but his body resisted from a million places. He forced himself to stand, and he stretched his tired and aching muscles until he could once again move them freely. The pilots stirred, awakened by Abdul's movement.

"Touch nothing," the terrorist warned in a gravelly voice. He stepped out of the tiny cockpit and walked away down the small alcove.

***

As soon as the two pilots were alone in the cockpit, Captain Granger whispered to his co-pilot, "Watch the door, Jean-Pierre." Then he began keying the mic in Morse code: *Hijackers anxious. Plan to land Beirut thwarted. They do not know next move. Bickering with each other. Believe there are 4 hijackers. What are your plans?*

The two men waited anxiously for a response, but no one in the Cypriot tower knew Morse code.

A controller called back over the radio, "Air France 622, do you have a message?"

Both men cringed, fearing Abdul might walk in at any second.

"Negative, Larnaca control, out," replied Granger hastily. He just sighed and hung his head in despair.

***

In the main cabin, Abdul watched Mohammed as he stood guard. The nervous young man seemed unusually quiet as he alternately surveyed the hostages and stared out the open passenger door.

As for the hostages, they looked pitiful. Some slept, their heads slumped forward or to one side. Most sat like zombies with vacant eyes. Tiny waves of whimpering and sobbing filled the cabin. The two female flight attendants were serving water and escorting passengers to the bathroom. Mohammed kept an eye on them from the front of the plane and Khalid from aft. Abdul looked on, trying not to see all their smudged faces.

He finally tired of watching the scene and joined Mohammed. In a few moments, Abu Hassim and Khalid Moussa came forward from the rear.

"Do we have a new plan now?" inquired Abu Hassim.

Abdul stared blankly at the big man and did not respond.

"Have you demanded fuel?"

"No," replied Abdul finally, realizing that he had wasted the remaining few daylight hours. "No, I do not want them snooping around this airplane in the darkness. We will maintain careful security throughout the night. Tomorrow morning, we will take fuel and prepare to move to a new location. We will be safe for now. The Cypriots will not be able to prepare an attack against us in only a few hours," said Abdul, hoping it was the truth.

The men nodded. They recognized the danger of soldiers camouflaged as technicians snooping around the plane in the dim light. The four terrorists stared at one another for a long moment. Abu Hassim broke the silence.

"Tomorrow we must leave here," he snorted to no one in particular as he turned and stalked away. Abdul watched until Abu finally dropped into a row of seats midway back through the plane.

Yes, thought Abdul, *tomorrow we should leave. But to where?*

He absentmindedly toyed with the two cell phones in his side pocket. He had just checked them again, and there was still no communication from Bachar. He knew he should send some kind of report to his leaders, but he needed to develop a plan before he could tell them what his next move would be.

***

Mike Elliot watched through half-closed eyelids as one of the terrorists, the nervous skinny one, worked his way down the aisle toward the rear of the plane. He paced back and forth several times as if thinking. He seemed upset. Mike sat perfectly still, scarcely breathing. The terrorist mumbled to himself. For the moment, he wasn't waving and banging his pistol around and screaming at the hostages. Finally, he went away, back up the aisle to the front of the plane.

It was dark now and much quieter on the plane. Things seemed a bit more settled, at least compared to the earlier madness they had experienced. Their captors had finally worn themselves down until they had succumbed to exhaustion. For Mike and the other passengers, it was like living through a sluggish nightmare, plodding along in slow motion, unable to wake up.

He thanked God for the two French flight attendants. Marie had brought him water several times and fed him a couple of sandwiches. Eva had taken him to the bathroom. They were courageous heroes in Mike's view.

He wondered how Lynn was holding up. He desperately wanted to see her. He had no idea, though, where she was, and he couldn't see much from his seat in the rear of the plane. He tried to remember where she had been sitting, but it was a blur. Maybe he hadn't even known. He couldn't be sure. He wanted so much to comfort her, to tell her it would be all right, that they would get out of this mess.

Mike didn't want to think about Margaret, *or* Emily. Under the circumstances, though, it was difficult not to. He loved Lynn dearly. *But you can't run from your past*, he thought, a*nd some past mistakes are worse than others.*

In his mind's eye, he could clearly see the faces of his two Irish girls. Margaret, always smiling, proudly beamed her Gaelic ancestry. Eight-year-old Emily looked just like her mother. They both had fair skin, freckles, and almost startling, flaming-red hair that demanded everyone's attention. The two of them had identical, bright-green eyes that sparkled like emeralds. To Mike, his girls had been beautiful beyond belief. He smiled, but the smile faded and tears moistened his eyes.

He thought about all the years of Special Forces deployments; operations working for the CIA in remote places around the world that most Americans had never heard of. He regretted those years. Emily had grown up so fast, and he had missed so much.

When the DIA—Defense Intelligence Agency—had offered him a position as assistant army attaché at the U.S. embassy in Brazil, he decided to hang up his guns and go. He moved Margaret and Emily to Brazil's capitol, Brasilia, with him from Fort Bragg where they had live since Emily was born.

Emily attended the American school, as all the embassy kids did. Even the ambassador's two daughters went there. And Emily loved it. Margaret did volunteer work in the embassy helping the younger State Department wives. They were finally a family, and daddy was home every evening.

He remembered that the State Department had assured him that Brazil was a low-threat environment. Still, they took all the standard security precautions when working overseas.

Mike's job was stable too, compared with his previous life roaming the earth armed to the teeth, killing people. He now did mostly analytical work, helping the DIA, CIA, and DEA coordinate drug interdiction operations against Colombian drug lords many hundreds of miles away.

"We were finally a family," he muttered to himself. "And then they vanished."

* * *

The same terrorist returned, coming down the aisle toward the rear of the plane. He checked the aft section and then wandered back up the opposite aisle.

Mike looked out the window and wondered if some military unit was out there beyond the lights preparing to storm the plane in a deadly hail of explosives and machine gun fire. The thought of it sent a cold shiver up his spine. He remembered reading about a Turkish assault against a hijacked airliner. The assault resulted in dozens of people killed. Mike had the sickening feeling that the hijackers of Air France 622 would try to take as many passengers with them as possible before they died. They had probably even wired the plane with explosives. It could all end in disaster, he knew.

He continued watching the field. The ambient light from the moon and stars, combined with the luminous glow from the lamp poles, rendered visibility generally good. *No,* thought Mike, *there are probably no commandos out there. No one could sneak up here with all that light.*

7

East Beirut, 2246 Hours

Akim and Becky sat at the small kitchen table in her apartment. She sipped hot tea, and Akim drank espresso. She had just told him a funny story, and he had gotten a good laugh from it. He needed it, given the task that awaited him.

He watched her as she talked. He thought she was pretty, in that British sort of way. Her skin was pale, and her hair long, shiny, and golden brown. She usually kept it tied up, but tonight it draped over her shoulders. Her eyes were hazel and full of intelligence. He knew she was smart; she was a doctoral candidate at the University of Beirut, studying middle-eastern history. She wrote long papers in Arabic about important historical events, most of which Akim had never heard of.

She always wanted to practice her Arabic, but he liked hearing her English accent. Becky was twenty-five and had been his girlfriend for eight months now. When they first met, she roomed with two other students. But he had helped her get this apartment, and he paid part of the rent, so they could have privacy.

It was a tiny, third-floor walk-up in an older building situated in a nice neighborhood in East Beirut. The area was filled with restaurants and cafes. Earlier, they had eaten a nice dinner at an Italian restaurant around the corner from her building, but his mind had not really been on the meal, or Becky.

He liked her a lot, but he couldn't quite figure out if he loved her, though that was not necessarily a requirement for marriage in his culture. Family ties were often more important. In this case there were none. She was a foreigner.

He felt like she loved him, but he didn't think she would just drop her studies and follow him to America—if he survived the night, that is. He realized that she was staring at him. She got up, walked around behind him, and put her arms around his neck.

"You've been distracted all evening, Akim. What's the matter, honey?"

He rubbed her hand. "Just work."

She knew he worked for the government and that he carried a gun, but that was it. He would never tell her what he really did. He pulled her around and she sat on his lap. He kissed her, and their passion soon grew. She got up and led him to the bedroom.

They made love, but Becky knew is wasn't quite the same. He seemed distant. Afterwards, they lay quietly on the bed. Akim wanted very much to stay and just sleep, but he knew he couldn't.

He got up and began to dress.

"Akim," she murmured, "where are you going at this hour? It's nearly midnight."

"I have work to do."

"Can't it wait until morning?"

Tucking his Beretta into his belt he said, "Unfortunately, no. Believe me, I would much prefer to stay here with you."

He leaned over and kissed her. "I've got to go now."

She just sighed.

Akim left, locking the entry door with his key on the way out. He went quickly down the three flights of stairs to the small, unlit foyer. He stood inside the big glass and metal door, watching the dark street for a few moments. Then he slipped out the door to the sidewalk. He paused to ensure the door closed and locked shut behind him, and then he hurried down the street toward his car parked two blocks away.

***

From the shadows of a doorway across the street, two men watched Akim exit the building and disappear down the street. They observed the quiet street for a short while, and then crossed over. Fawzi Mustafa carefully scanned the area around them while his partner took out a small flashlight and examined the door lock.

He pulled a leather wallet from his pocket and selected two picks—a torsion wrench and a hook pick. In ten more seconds he had the door open, and they slipped inside and reclosed it. They knew which apartment they wanted. The unit Akim had visited was the only one with lights on at this hour. It was on the third floor, street side.

They climbed the concrete stairs until they were standing outside number 310. The man checked the lock, pulled out another pick, and quietly opened the door. It led directly into the apartment's small living room. They stepped in and closed the door. They waited, and listened.

Lights were on in the back of the apartment. Water was running in the bathroom. Mustafa nodded to his partner and they walked toward the light. Mustafa stepped into the bathroom behind her. The young woman stood at the sink dressed only in her panties.

He stepped inside and was swiftly behind her. Startled, she shrieked. He grabbed her from behind, cupping his hand over her mouth. They struggled briefly, but he easily dragged her to the bed and threw her on it.

He was quickly over her, straddling her waist and pinning her arms under his knees. She bucked, but his weight was too much. He still held his hand over her mouth. Then she realized that another man was on the other side of the bed. He had her hair gripped tightly in both hands, pulling it like a thick, brown rope.

She could not move her head. She squealed in protest, but it was muffled by Mustafa's large hand.

"Alright now, just relax," urged Mustafa. "I only want to talk."

His English was perfect, and for a moment, she thought he might be British.

She nodded okay, what little she could move. He removed his hand.

"Good," he said, "that's better. Now, I need your help."

The man holding her hair relaxed his grip ever so slightly.

"What is your name?" he asked her.

"Becky," she managed, her voice trembling.

"That's a lovely name," said Mustafa softly. "British?"

"Yes."

"So, what I need to know, is what your contact, Akim, is up to. Tell me about him."

She shook her head. Her eyes were pools of confusion. "H-he's my boyfriend."

Mustafa remained patient. "I really do not want to hurt you, Becky. You are a nice enough looking young lady. But, I do have pressing business elsewhere, and I don't have a lot of time to spend on you. So, I need answers."

The Arab sat up straight and pulled a metal object from his shirt pocket. Iridescent patterns of tears and light clouded her eyes, and she could not quite see what he held. The object reflected light from the ceiling lamp. He shook his head ruefully as he placed the still-closed straight razor against her cheek. She sucked in a quick breath and felt his weight on her abdomen. He held the object above her eyes and turned it over in his hand. She cried as he slowly unfolded the blade, and the razor's edge flashed menacingly.

"Now, Becky, your boyfriend has been collecting information about my associates and me for the Americans. Though I'm sure you know all this already. And of course that's why I'm here, so you can tell me all about it. Fill in a few gaps, so to speak."

She just shook her head in bewilderment and sobbed. She had no idea what he was talking about. She yearned for her mother in Brighton. She wished she had never left there and that she was a little girl again, at home, playing near the park with her friends.

"I don't know what you're talking about. You're hurting me. Can't you see you're hurting me?" she pleaded. "I don't know anything."

"No, dear," said Mustafa matter-of-factly. "I am *not* hurting you. Yet."

She stared at him with wide eyes.

"I'm sure that you must help him, my dear. Are you his contact with the Americans. Or perhaps British intelligence?" He twisted the razor slightly, and a sparkle of light reflected the blade's cruel promise into her eyes. He raised his arm and shaved a patch of dark hair from his forearm. "It's very sharp, Becky," he said, grinning.

She shuddered. Mustafa's accomplice tugged on her hair and placed the palm of his hand on her forehead pressing his weight down on her. She squirmed but could scarcely move.

Mustafa slowly dragged the razor down her cheek, but only lightly. She flinched at the bite of the blade, squirming, squealing. Tears ran in rivulets down the sides of her face, stinging the painful red trace.

She sucked in a breath and was about to scream, but he said, "*If* you scream, Becky, I will cut your tongue out of your mouth. Besides, no one will hear you anyway."

He studied her in silence for a moment, and then said, "Poor Becky. All alone. You think you can come here to Beirut and play your little spy games. But as you are learning, it is not such an easy game here. The little scratch I gave you shouldn't leave a scar, but I want to impress upon you the need for urgency. I am in a hurry, and my patience is wearing thin. Things are happening as we speak that demand my attention. So, talk to me. Who is your contact in your intelligence service? Who is your boyfriend's contact? Who does he get his information from within Hezbollah?"

Her mind was in panic as he dragged the razor swiftly across the other cheek, deeper.

"I don't know anything. I'm a student," she stammered, between gasps for air.

"Who is Akim's contact in the CIA?" he demanded, cutting her again. "Who is he?"

"I don't know," she sobbed, barely able to speak, quivering uncontrollably. "Akim works for the government, and he carries a gun. That's all I really know about him. I'm a student. Check with the university."

"Of course, dear, your cover will check out. Any intelligence service worth its salt will have a fully verifiable cover identity for its agent."

"Agent? No, I'm a student."

"Who is the contact, Becky?" he repeated with more urgency in his voice. "You must work with Akim. He comes here often enough. Yes, that's right, I know all about you. And I already know who his source is in Hezbollah. So you'd better not lie to me. Of course that traitor will be dealt with soon enough. But I want your boyfriend, and you, to lead me to the CIA man who helps this traitor. Now, you really must talk to me, quickly," he said, pulling the razor across her upper lip. Her face was now streaked with a grim cross-hatching of thin crimson welts; the laceration on her lip was a gruesome red mustache.

"Unfortunately, Becky, if we have to keep this up you will soon look like an ugly old scarecrow."

She twitched under his weight and the cutting blade. Her sight was blurred and dim. She could no longer see her torturers. She mumbled incoherently.

After several more minutes, Mustafa looked up at his partner, pursed his lips, and shook his head. The partner nodded.

"Well, anyway, Becky, we're keeping a close watch on your young man. I believe he has already done considerable damage, but I also expect that he will be quite useful before we are through. I *had* hoped, though, that you would be able tell me more about his activities and contacts. I guess you *are* just a student after all." He wiped the blade clean and put it away.

"Quiet now, my darling," he said softly. "It will be all right. You can relax. I believe you. Let's clean you up a bit," said Mustafa, reaching over and pulling a pillow over her face, wiping off some of the blood. Then he reached behind his back, pulled his silenced Walther .22 caliber pistol from his belt, and pressed it down into the pillow. It rested just over her left eye. He pulled the trigger, and she went limp.

Standing, he replaced the pistol. He picked up her cell phone, quickly scanned the calls and contacts, and slipped the phone into his pocket.

"Come. We can do it without her."

8

Barclay checked his watch as the Boeing C-17 Globemaster slid down out of the black sky and landed at one of the two British bases on the island of Cyprus. It had been a long flight, and the men were anxious to begin work. Barclay sat on the flight deck looking over the pilot's shoulders as a British Air Force guide truck appeared out of the night. Yellow lights glowed atop the small cab. The little truck led the Starlifter as they moved into an isolated area of the base. In the distance, a cluster of darkened, aging aircraft hangars was silhouetted against the night sky.

They soon arrived at an old section of flight line, only used when the British air squadrons came here to train. It suited Delta's needs perfectly. The old hangars were large and would accommodate planning, preparation, and rehearsals. Several smaller, adjoining wood-frame buildings, would serve as Delta's command post. The C-17 made a final half turn and came to a stop. Its nose bounced up and down several times before coming to a complete halt.

Moments later, Barclay and Sinclair hopped down onto the tarmac. Lieutenant Colonel Wilson was close behind. The night air was warm and heavy and not particularly refreshing, but standing on solid ground again felt good. The guide truck disappeared into the night and a small sedan arrived, driving right up to the side of the aircraft. Major David Allen, a tall, slender young man, exited the car and walked briskly over to the three officers, saluting as he approached. He was gangly, with a narrow angular face and blond hair, cut short. He had a mildly adolescent appearance.

"Colonel Sinclair, sir?" inquired Allen.

Sinclair returned the salute then extended his hand.

"Sir, I'm Major Allen, the assistant military attaché. Colonel Harvey, the attaché, is over at the Cypriot International Airport in the tower. The ambassador is there, too. I've been assigned to coordinate your activities with the British here at Akrotiri and with the Cypriots at the airport over in Larnaca. There's also a British NCO who's been assigned to you. He's running around checking on something. He'll be along soon. He will coordinate any additional support you might need from the British here at Akrotiri and over at Dhekelia. For the moment, though, I believe I've already arranged for what you initially asked for. If you'll follow me, I'll give you a quick tour of the facilities."

"Sounds good, Major," said Sinclair. "But first, have there been any changes in the situation in the last thirty minutes or so?"

"No, sir. It's pretty quiet over there. They haven't made a move. We figure they're waiting for something, but we don't know what."

"Why do you think that?"

"Oh nothing, really. Just speculation."

"Have they asked for refueling?"

"No, sir, nothing."

With a gesture of his hand toward the hangars Wilson asked, "This our area?"

"Yes, sir. We sent you a diagram of the layout. Did you get it?"

"Yeah, we got it. Anyone else around here?"

"Negative. This area's deserted this time of year."

Wilson turned and nodded to a burly, camouflaged sergeant first class. He disappeared into the darkness with several other camouflaged Rangers who had gathered on the tarmac. They wore lightweight tactical assault vests and communications headsets. Night-vision goggles were strapped to one hip and binoculars to the other. They carried H&K MP5 submachine guns; a Beretta 9mm handgun was tucked into a shoulder holster on each assault vest. The Ranger security team vanished into the dark alleys in and around the old hangars.

Barclay, Allen, and Wilson took a quick tour of the facilities while Delta's operators and support personnel began unloading equipment.

"Okay, Major," said Wilson. "This is perfect. What about the light helicopter we wanted?"

"The Brits have a pilot and a Gazelle standing by on the other side of the base. They can be here in ten minutes from the time you contact them," said Allen.

"How do we contact them?"

"By Motorola, sir. I have a portable in the car I'll give you. Or you can go through the British liaison."

"Okay, that'll be fine."

"Are you aware of the other aircraft due to arrive shortly?" asked Wilson.

"Yes, sir. Four U.S. helicopters coming from Italy, a Twin Otter coming from Turkey, as well as two Lear jets from the States, I believe."

"That's correct." Wilson didn't bother to elaborate on the two jets, but the CIA would be coming in on one, and an air force test pilot was being brought in on the other. The air force pilot would fly a small, specially modified plane to create a diversion for Delta's assault. The plane he would fly, a DeHavilland Twin Otter, was being ferried in from Adana, Turkey by a CIA contract pilot.

"Yes, sir," said Allen, "I coordinated with the British. They are expecting them."

"Fine, Major," said Wilson. Satisfied that the team's immediate logistical needs were met, he nodded at Barclay.

Barclay said, "Major, I want you to pick up another portable radio from my commo sergeant on the plane—I'll take you to him—then I want you to go back to the Larnaca Airport and arrange for our two vans to be let in by the northeast gate, this one here." Barclay had a diagram of the airport and pointed out the gate.

"Yes, sir," said Allen. "I know about where it is. It should be no problem to find. My boss and the ambassador have both discussed everything with the Cypriot Airport Security Police, discreetly of course, and they have assured us that we will have their full cooperation. It's come down from pretty high up in the Cypriot government."

"Okay," began Barclay, checking his watch. "It's 0040 hours. At 0200, I'll be at the gate I showed you with these two vans." He gestured toward the two surveillance vans pulling up by the hangar. "I want to move directly to this spot near the end of the tower building and park here," he said as he pointed to the location on the diagram.

"Shouldn't be a problem, sir."

"Okay, let's pick up that radio and get you on your way."

Barclay's thoughts were already on the many tasks that he and his small team needed to accomplish—to deploy reconnaissance teams around the hijacked Airbus, to set up the surveillance vans in a secure location, to meet with the U.S. ambassador to Cyprus, and to have Dr. Hamud, Delta's negotiator, make contact with the terrorists.

Wilson would set up the Akrotiri CP. Sergeant Major Barrington, the assault team leader, would accompany Barclay to Larnaca to get the tactical lay of the land, while Barclay met with the ambassador and did the liaison work.

During the five minutes it took Barclay to see Major Allen off and return to the lead van parked next to the hangar, Master Sergeant Palmer had assembled and loaded his recon and sniper teams into the two vans. Dr. Hamud was already settled comfortably into one of the command chairs before a console.

Barclay hopped into the lead van.

Colonel Sinclair stood by the van's window near Barclay.

"All right, sir," said Barclay, "we'll report in as soon as we're set up."

Sinclair nodded and stepped back.

Turning to his driver Barclay said, "Okay, move out." The two gray vans pulled away into the night.

***

Air France 622, 0129 Hours

Marie made her way toward the rear of the plane serving water. She was just completing a second round. Hours earlier, she had given some water to the man she thought was Lynn's husband. He matched her description and was covered in blood. But she had not been able to say anything to him because one of the terrorists had been watching her.

This time, the big terrorist stood by the open door in the rear of the plane looking out, some twenty-five feet from Mike and several passengers near him. Marie was determined, though, and she cautiously approached Abu Hassim, extending a cup and the bottle of water in front of her. He nodded and she went to him, handed him the cup, and filled it. He drank, never taking his eyes off the field outside. He handed her back the cup and thanked her in Arabic, though she didn't know what he said.

She worked her way back up the opposite aisle. When she got to Mike, she poured some water, and held the cup to his lips. He drank it all and she poured some more. She had her back to Abu Hassim and the other two hijackers were near the front. She mouthed silently to Mike, "Lynn is okay."

He noticed that her uniform nametag read: *Marie D.*

Mike's eyes brightened. "Thank you, Marie," he mouthed back. "Me too." She nodded and moved away back up the aisle toward the front. She crossed over to the portside aisle, intending to relay the message to Lynn, but one of the terrorists, Mohammed, was watching her. She walked to him instead, as she had done with the big one, and offered him water. He took a cup, and she filled it.

While he drank, she glanced back at Lynn and nodded ever so slightly.

Lynn smiled—Mike was alive.

***

Larnaca International Airport, 0203 Hours

The movement of Lieutenant Colonel Barclay's team from Akrotiri to the Cypriot International Airport at Larnaca was quiet and uneventful. The two vans covered the forty-nine miles of dark, winding road in just under one hour and fifteen minutes. At this time of the morning, there was no traffic to speak of, and the convoy had made good time on the small country roads.

Barclay's van approached a T-shaped intersection and stopped. Just ahead was the airport fence. Beyond, across the gently rolling field, were the lights of Larnaca airport. Its distinctively shaped control tower was perched atop the main terminal building. At the tower's apex was a stark-white beacon that scanned the night sky. Barclay lifted a finger and pointed to the right. His driver eased onto the adjacent road. A hundred yards farther, they pulled up to an old gate. It was unguarded but locked. Grounds maintenance vehicles apparently used the gate, but judging from the lack of vehicle tracks in the sparse grass along the fence, only infrequently.

Allen soon arrived with a Cypriot police officer who opened the gate. Major Allen stuck his head in Barclay's window. "Any problems?" asked Barclay.

"No, sir. The order to open the gate had to come from the Cypriot Army colonel in charge here. Took a few minutes to find him, that's all."

"Okay, Major. We'll follow you."

The two men got back into their small car, and Allen spun it around in the short, parched grass. He pulled away toward the main airport terminal. Barclay gave a curt command into his lapel mic to van number two and motioned to Master Sergeant Palmer behind him. Before the vans pulled away, eight men slipped from the two vehicles and disappeared into the darkness. They wore Ghillie suits; green, black, and brown strips of burlap covered them from head to toe. They appeared more beast than man. They were shapeless blobs of darkness as they slipped into the night and disappeared from sight altogether.

They lay in the withered but damp grass on a small knoll not far from the fence and highway. The slight moisture from the early morning dew, practically the only precipitation the field ever received, had dampened their clothes and mixed with the dust to add new hues to their camouflage.

The four, two-man teams watched the vans and the sedan drive off down the dirt road in the direction the compact little car had come from. A dense cloud of fine dust trailed up behind each vehicle and was dimly illuminated by the three sets of taillights. Finally, they disappeared over a small rise.

The recon teams spread out in a perimeter with about fifteen yards between each two-man team. They would remain there for a few minutes, listening and acclimating themselves to their environment.

Palmer's call sign was Eagle-one. The men lay in the sparse grass on a small rise observing the field ahead and the hijacked plane. The two other two-man teams were farther back and oriented toward the road for rear security. There were two snipers in the recon element.

Through their binoculars and night-vision scopes, Palmer and his team studied the terrain and the hijacked Airbus. The plane was at least a thousand yards from their position. It sat on a corner of the airport tarmac, its starboard landing gear only a few feet from the edge of the hardstand itself. The tail hung out over the grass field, pointing toward the northeast gate and Delta's recon team.

Palmer nodded to his partner. They were sufficiently oriented to their surroundings. Palmer reached up and flipped a small switch on his radio headset to set it to voice-activated mode, then called his teams.

"Moving out," he said softly.

The two-man teams moved slowly and with great care, covering only a few yards at a time, then stopping, crouching, listening, and watching. The last two hundred yards they would cover on their stomachs, crawling and scooting along an inch at a time.

The terrain was difficult. Light from the airport's many buildings and from the expansive aircraft parking areas reflected across the field and cast long shadows out to the side of each man, even when belly to earth.

The field around the Airbus was flat and unobstructed, and the grass within two hundred yards of the target was parched and short. Palmer's men moved with care, but their task was not easy.

In the Airbus, a terrorist stood guard in one of the aircraft's doors. Delta's only advantage was that the aircraft's interior cabin was itself dimly lit, slightly degrading the terrorist's ability to see out from the plane and spot the commandos crawling across the barren terrain toward them.

Palmer scanned the field around him with his night-vision goggles. He could easily see the unearthly silhouettes of his other three teams spread out by hundreds of yards about the vast field. He also knew that if he could see them, so could the terrorists if they had similar equipment.

He lowered his goggles, checked the aircraft again with his binoculars to make sure nothing had changed, and then inched forward on his elbows.

***

Lieutenant Colonel Barclay positioned the two vans at one end of the airport terminal about eight hundred yards from Air France 622. Barrington sat in the back waiting for the driver to get the cameras up and running so he could study the aircraft and devise a tactical plan.

Barclay's driver took a seat next to Barrington in front of a console of instruments. He began setting up the surveillance cameras, communications monitoring equipment, and electronic counter-measures, such as jamming the cellular phone signals around the plane. Cellular networks used radio waves, and they were easily interrupted. The jammers on the van would produce a set of powerful directional radio waves focused directly on the Airbus, making it impossible to receive a cell signal in or around the plane. They would *not* jam the VHF civil aviation radio frequencies between 108 and 136 MHz.

Barclay and Hamud followed Major Allen to locate and confer with the U.S. ambassador and the U.S. Army's military attaché to Cyprus. Allen had already procured the necessary security passes, and they made their way to the control tower without incident, passing through a security checkpoint with ease.

Major Allen led the way as they climbed countless flights of stairs before arriving at the control tower. The lights in the room were low, but as Barclay entered the tower, he spotted a small group of men huddled over a console near one of the massive, outwardly tilting windows. The men were staring at the hijacked aircraft.

In other corners of the tower, radios crackled softly, and blips of yellow light, barely discernible as symbols and numbers, decorated glowing monitors built into consoles in the center of the room. Low-level light radiated from beneath and around the banks of radar consoles lining the perimeter of the room. Air traffic controllers stared intently at their screens, not bothering to glance up at the three men entering the room.

Barclay and Hamud followed Allen across the room to the group of men.

"Mister Ambassador," announced Allen, "this is Colonel Barclay and Dr. Hamud. They have just arrived from the States."

"Ah, yes, Colonel," began the ambassador, sounding nervous. "I'm Ambassador Anderson, Charles Anderson. We've been waiting for you."

"And this is Colonel Nathan Harvey, the attaché," continued Allen.

"Lieutenant Colonel Barclay, sir. I'll be advising you on the hostage situation." Barclay extended his hand to the ambassador, then the colonel.

"This is Dr. Hamud," said Barclay, "our negotiator."

Hamud shook hands with each of the men.

A Cypriot colonel was among the small group of men. He was a spindly, erect little man dressed in an impeccably tailored, crisply pressed Cypriot Army uniform festooned with medals and ribbons. He wore a type of Sam Browne belt, and the holster swung oddly toward the front. A nickel-plated, pearl-handled .38 caliber revolver rested in the holster. A protruding beak of a nose extended from the man's face and dominated his features. His ears stuck out and looked a bit large for his head. Despite these ungainly characteristics, he still had an air of aristocracy about him.

Barclay offered his hand and greeted the Cypriot colonel. Ambassador Anderson said, "This is Colonel Krokos. He's been appointed by President Dhimitsianos himself to assist in our efforts."

"Very good," acknowledged Barclay, smiling at the Cypriot, and thinking that the little man reminded him of a rooster.

"Well then," asked Ambassador Anderson, rocking almost imperceptibly back and forth on his heels, "what are you going to do?"

"Well, sir, Colonel Sinclair, Delta's commanding officer, is at Akrotiri at a command post we've set up there. For now, we try to buy time while we gather information and do some planning. As I said, Dr. Hamud is our negotiator, and he should do all the talking with the terrorists."

Everyone agreed.

"Once our planning is complete we will move a team here to the airport or over to Dhekelia a few miles up the coast. If we can talk them out, that would be our first option. If not, when we get clearance from the White House, we'll assault the plane and rescue the hostages."

Barclay sensed that the ambassador became uneasy at the mention of an assault. Nonetheless, he seemed pleased to have Delta on hand.

The discussion degenerated into small talk and speculation. Barclay excused himself and stepped past the ambassador to a section of the huge control tower window. It seemed to lean precariously outward. He picked up a pair of binoculars from the table and scanned the aircraft and the terrain around it for several hundred yards. As hard as he tried, and knowing almost precisely where to look, he could still see no sign of the recon teams. *Perfect*, he thought.

He could barely make out the details of people in the hijacked plane. He could tell that at least one of the plane's doors was open but could discern few other details from this distance. He returned to the other men.

"Colonel Krokos," said Barclay.

"Yes, Colonel?"

"We need to set Dr. Hamud up somewhere here with a radio console. For now, we should wait, but eventually, we will want to determine what their demands are and, if possible, their immediate plans. Please let Hamud handle the terrorists."

"Certainly," he replied.

"Yes, whatever you say, Colonel," added the ambassador, obviously relieved to have someone on hand who knew what to do.

9

Bekaa Valley, Lebanon, 0230 Hours

Akim drummed his fingers against the steering wheel of his car. His pistol—a long silencer attached—lay on his lap. He was nervous but controlled. The night was warm and the village around him dark. Few lights were on in any of the buildings. There were no street lamps in this decrepit little Shiite town of a few thousand poverty-level inhabitants.

He glanced around, checking to the rear and across the street. He was sure no one had followed him. Still, he had to be cautious. He had driven into the Bekaa Valley, deep into the Shiite Muslim sector, to the town of Zahlé. He was thirty miles east of Beirut and only three miles from the Syrian border. This was something he never did. His passes were good enough to fool most any Shiite militiaman at a checkpoint. But sitting here in the early-morning hours, not far from the Janta Shiite military barracks, would be difficult to explain.

He usually left this type of task to someone less conspicuous. This someone would come during the day, by bus or on foot, or maybe with a small wagon filled with vegetables. He came when the streets were crowded. Such a courier could pass his time chatting with local vendors and trading a few wares. Then he would service the Shiite agent's drops and wander away unnoticed. Akim had many creative ways to do what he needed done in the heart of the enemy's camp without risking his own skin. Tonight was a grudging exception.

Akim was becoming more and more excited about the prospect of living in America. The idea had fully seized him now, and he wondered why he had never thought of it before. Well, he had never really had the chance before and had never given much thought to his own vulnerability. He knew that at twenty-five years old, he had already beaten the odds for survival in the intelligence business in Lebanon.

Through the windshield, Akim detected movement in the murky shadows. His hand slid down to the Beretta resting on his lap. He scanned around him, in the car's mirrors, and out of the corners of his eyes, all the while keeping an eye on that spot before him. He saw nothing else. Then he saw the small profile of Ben Farouk slinking along the wall of the mud-brick building next to the car. He remained wary in case the boy had been followed.

Ben Farouk meant son of Farouk, who was one of Akim's brothers-in-law. The boy approached and slipped into the Mercedes. No light came on when the door opened, the bulb having long since been removed. Continuing to observe the street, Akim relaxed his hand on the pistol while the boy reached into his shirt pocket and produced a scrap of folded paper. The youngster was calm and confident, but his smooth, hairless face revealed his tender age of only thirteen summers.

"This is all? You checked both locations?"

"Yes, uncle, just as you told me."

"Where did you find this one?"

"The one at the north end of the bridge, at the place where the trail leaves the road and descends to the stream. The paper was in the crack under the edge of the village plaque right where you told me to look."

"And you left the note I gave you in the same place? And turned over the stone next to the sign post?"

"Yes, just as you instructed."

Akim slipped the small piece of paper into his shirt pocket behind his sunglasses. He glanced around one more time then started the car.

"And the other was empty? You're sure?" demanded Akim as he slipped the gearshift into first and eased out on the clutch.

"Yes, uncle. I searched exactly where you told me to look."

Akim turned on the headlights and drove out of town and onto a worn and rugged highway leading southwest to the village of Chtaura. There, he would veer west along the Bhamdoun highway and on toward Beirut. He would have to traverse the Syrian controlled zone around Qabb Elias, but that generally proved to be no problem.

For the moment, however, he was still in Hezbollah territory. He scanned the rearview mirrors but detected the presence of no other vehicles. *So far, so good*, he thought. He would feel much better once out of the Shiite zone. He never knew when a curious militiaman might ask one too many questions.

***

Larnaca, 0246 Hours

On the southeast side of the Airbus, Master Sergeant Palmer dragged himself forward the last few inches to his position behind a low marker panel. His partner eased up beside him and placed his Remington M24 sniper rifle next to the panel. He opened the spring-loaded scope covers and sighted in on the open doorway of the plane.

It had taken them over forty-five minutes of careful crawling to cover the last one hundred and fifty yards. They were as close as Palmer dared go. He reported.

"Checkpoint bravo," said Palmer into his lip mic, indicating that he and his partner had reached their observation point.

Barclay's radio operator responded and typed a note in the log.

In the tower, Barclay got Hamud settled in. He talked awhile longer with the ambassador, the attaché, and the Cypriot Army colonel. They ironed out a few more details about support from the Cypriots. The Cypriot airport police, under Colonel Krokos, would be responsible for securing the airport grounds. Delta would focus on the terrorists.

Barclay left the men staring at the hijacked aircraft just as he'd found them nearly an hour earlier and made his way down seven flights of steel and concrete stairs. He passed through a heavy fire door and out through the security checkpoints. He discovered another passageway and avoided the crowded lobby. He could see a part of the foyer through a small window in a fire door. Mobs of reporters pushed and shoved while squads of security guards held their ground. He soon found an exit near the end of the building not far from his mobile CP and arrived at the van in time to hear Master Sergeant Palmer begin his report.

Palmer had positioned himself on the northeast side of the Airbus. He reported that the starboard rear door was closed and the starboard forward door was open. He reported the number of window shades open and details about the terrorists. He transmitted digital video images to the vans. Another recon team had positioned itself on the opposite side and provided similar data.

"What do you think, Scott?" Barclay asked Sergeant Major Barrington.

"Not good. It's open terrain out there with a lot of illumination. And they're keeping regular sentry duty in the open doors. If we try to come in from the field, and the team is spotted before it gets to the plane, it could be a bloodbath," said Barrington. "Nor am I keen on trying to rush out to the plane in a vehicle. They'll take us under fire before we can even get close."

"So what are you thinking?"

"Maybe put the lead team in a Little Bird and drop them on the roof of the plane. But I've got to talk it over with the guys, and the CO. I'm gonna head back to Akrotiri."

"Okay, we'll have the British Gazelle land at Dhekelia to take you back."

"Rodg'. Hang tight."

"No choice."

***

Bekaa Valley, 0305 Hours

Akim and Ben Farouk had accomplished the most dangerous part of their trip—they had crossed out of the Shiite sector at the edge of the Bekaa valley and made it into the Syrian zone. They had one more crossing to make, their exit from the Syrian-held area before entering Christian East Beirut.

The big car hummed smoothly along even as it bounced over the unmaintained highway. Akim grinned. He liked his car and he took good care of it. He had the engine inspected weekly by one of his cousins. At times like these, he knew, you depended entirely on your car. To break down here, in the early-morning hours in the

Syrian-occupied part of Lebanon, could prove fatal. The Syrians could conceivably turn him over to the Shiites once they discovered his papers were false and saw through his ruse. The Christians were not currently in a shooting war with the Syrians but neither were they on exceptionally good terms either.

He glanced to his right at his young nephew; the boy slept. He would have the youngster home soon enough. It was only twenty more minutes to the city from here.

A quarter-mile ahead, he could see the faint glow of a lantern hanging on a pole. It was the last Syrian Army checkpoint. The relative safety of Christian East Beirut lay beyond. For the return trip, he had taken the main highway. This was a different checkpoint than the one they had passed earlier. He would also have a different story ready for these soldiers if need be. Danger would only arise if a Syrian officer was on duty, but at this hour, that was highly unlikely.

He slowed his car and turned off the headlights, leaving only the parking lights. He approached the checkpoint slowly. He had already secured his pistol under the seat in case he had to get out of the car.

Only two Syrian soldiers were visible, but Akim knew that a Syrian armored vehicle would be hidden somewhere off the side of the road. A soldier would have its heavy machine gun zeroed in on the car, thumbs resting on the iron trigger mechanism. One false move, and Akim knew that his Mercedes, himself, and his sister's precious boy would end up a flaming heap of scrap metal and blood. Caution was advised.

On this sultry North African night, his window was already down. He handed his pass and identification cards to the tired guard. The Syrian soldier glanced at them and then motioned to the trunk. Without getting out, he popped the lever to the trunk. The guard looked in, shining his flashlight. Then he closed it and flashed his light into the darkened back seat.

He stepped back and held his flashlight up to study Akim's documents. The soldier was only a corporal, and Syrian corporals rarely displayed initiative, but he seemed to be taking an unusually long time to examine the papers.

Akim's forged Syrian pass used a validation code that changed weekly. Lebanese intelligence got the code from a Syrian junior officer in exchange for money. He worked in the headquarters of the Syrian general responsible for Syria's occupation forces in eastern Lebanon. These codes had worked in the past, but there was no way of knowing if the new code was valid until someone tried to use it.

His arm lay on the window frame. He drummed his fingers against the outside of the door. He felt huge beads of sweat forming on his forehead. Glancing into the night, he considered whether to risk a getaway attempt if ordered out of the car. The clock ticked.

Finally, the corporal stepped back up to the car and with a bored look thrust the papers back into Akim's waiting hand. He waved the car through. He smiled at the soldier, switched on his headlights, and eased out on the clutch.

Another hundred yards down the road and they breezed through a Christian militia control point. They were now in East Beirut. Compared to the danger they had already survived, they were relatively safe on his home turf. He allowed himself an earthy grin. He let out a long, slow breath. A little danger now and again was invigorating for the soul. He felt alive, and his skin tingled from the adrenaline pumping through his system. He had fooled the dumb Shiite and Syrian bastards once again.

They were now in the Es Salome quarter of East Beirut, and he pulled up to a corner and shook his companion awake. "Go home, young man," he said to the sleepy boy. "You have served your family well tonight."

The boy flashed a grin and slid awkwardly from the car. He winked at the youngster and slipped him a folded bill. He reminded him one last time of his oath of silence. The boy nodded and disappeared into the shadows.

Akim removed the folded message from his pocket. He had risked his own life, and the boy's, to retrieve it. He reached into the glove box for a small penlight. Then he unfolded the note and read the message's barely-legible Arabic scrawl. It covered half a page, much longer than Cupid's usual line or two. As he read, his eyes grew steadily larger, until finally, he flipped off the flashlight and dropped his hand to his lap, his mouth hanging open.

Cupid was inside Hezbollah and high enough to hear important details about operational planning. In his message, he reported that Fawzi Mustafa—AKA the Scimitar—was headed to Cyprus.

Akim knew that John Striker wanted the Scimitar badly. The shadowy figure was a notorious Hezbollah operative believed to be responsible for dozens of executions—all done with a .22 caliber pistol. The only reason the Scimitar would be going to Cyprus, was the hijacking.

He stared out the windshield into the night until a large smile spread across his tanned face. The American will be *very* interested to have this information. He pulled away from the curb, already searching his memory for the next code word on the list he had memorized. Each word was used only once and always in sequence. Yes, he would be in America soon. He had done it. John Striker would take good care of him for providing such important information at such a critical time.

10

East Beirut, 0333 Hours

Akim's family home was located in the Karm Ez Zeitoun quarter of old East Beirut. Dozens of tiny streets formed the many mazes of blocks, circles, and zigzags. He crossed over the Nahr Beirut River. Five minutes later, he drove into a series of small alleys that made up his neighborhood. He parked the Mercedes on a side street several blocks from his family home. He never parked closer than two blocks from his destination and never in the same place twice.

He removed the silencer from his Beretta, slipped it into his back pocket, and tucked the pistol into his belt. The gun pressed reassuringly against his stomach. Other than a few stray dogs nearby, the neighborhood was quiet and still.

He arrived at the house and slipped inside with his key. He turned on several lights and reset the alarm, one of the luxuries he was able to provide his father's household. Anyone stupid enough to trip the sophisticated German manufactured alarm system would immediately face a half-dozen weapons. All his brothers and his father slept with automatic weapons nearby. That was Beirut.

The family was accustomed to him coming and going at all hours. They would not be disturbed. Even so, he was always cautious when entering his father's house at night.

He picked up the kitchen telephone and dialed a number. He didn't dare use a cell phone—he knew for a fact that his enemies listened to the entire network. Probably the landline too, so he wasn't going to take any chances.

A quiet voice answered, and he asked for extension two-five-nine. After two rings, a man said hello. Akim responded with the words, "Blue Monkey, extension three-six-five."

The man said, "Wait." After he checked a top secret code list, he dialed the extension; it rang in John Striker's quarters in the embassy compound.

"Yes," came the groggy reply.

"Blue monkey."

"Go ahead."

"I have to see you right away."

"Did you get it?"

"Yes."

Striker knew Akim had something from Cupid, and it was important. He briefly considered taking the message over the phone, but decided not to chance it. It could put Cupid at risk.

"One hour, same place as last time," said Striker, hanging up.

Akim leaned back against the kitchen counter and grinned. He reached up to a shelf next to his head, pulled down a warm can of Heineken, and popped it open. Foam frothed up and over the edge of the can. He flicked it away with his finger. He took a long, gratifying swallow, holding the warm and pleasantly bitter liquid in his mouth and throat. He had worked up a thirst tonight. He let out a long burp and wiped his mouth with the back of his hand.

He glanced down at his watch. The rendezvous with the American would be at 4:35 a.m. at the Alfonse in Christian East Beirut, not far from his home. *I have some time*, he thought, taking another gulp of beer and trying to calm his excitement. He tried to imagine life in America. *Should I ask Becky to go?* he wondered. *Should I try to take my family? Would they go? Probably not my father. Would my brothers want to go if father did not? We will just have to see.*

On a whim, Akim decided to call Becky. He dialed her cell phone. There was a click, as if someone had answered, but no one spoke.

"Becky?" he asked, but still no answer.

He disconnected and dialed again. This time her voicemail picked up.

"Hey, babe," said Akim, "just wanted to tell you that I miss you already."

He thought it odd that she didn't answer, but as he hung up the second time, his mind quickly returned to thoughts of America.

***

Larnaca, 0346 Hours

Barclay leaned forward in the pedestal-mounted chair in the back of his van. On the console before him was a video image of the hijacked Airbus. Barclay's two vans had the appearance of ordinary airport maintenance vehicles, but they were crammed with surveillance and communications equipment.

The only telltale sign that they were in fact anything more, was the large metal containers on the tops of the vans, but even those were camouflaged to resemble toolboxes mounted on a carryall rack. The containers housed an array of miniature radars, satellite dishes, telescopic video cameras, antennas, and an array of sophisticated area and directional radio frequency jammers.

Barclay fiddled with a tiny control stick on the console in front of him. On top of the van, a camera panned down the one hundred and seventy-seven foot length of the Airbus. He pondered what Sergeant Major Barrington had said about an assault plan. He twisted a small knob with his left hand and zoomed in on an open door. One of the terrorists hunkered behind the edge of the doorway.

Barclay switched to infrared, dropped down to two-power magnification, and panned right and out across the big grass field; it was open and well illuminated. The infrared produced a stark, white image of the surrounding terrain. He switched to thermal imaging and swept back across the jet.

He had digested the reconnaissance team's information and his own electronic surveillance. Barrington was right. It was too risky to walk a team carrying ladders up to the rear of the plane.

For a jet this large, Delta would need to get at least three men into the front and three into the back, simultaneously. Maybe one or two men could sneak up to the plane, but it was too dangerous to try it with an entire assault element.

Barclay continued monitoring the airbus.

***

Air France 622, 0405 Hours

It was nearing dawn on Cyprus, but Lynn Elliot had no way of knowing the time. Her watch was in her purse, and they had stuffed everyone's personal belongings into the overhead bins. She only knew that it had already been a very long night filled with a dreary, endless nightmare. They'd been sitting on the tarmac in Larnaca for nine suffocating hours. And it had been almost sixteen since they'd boarded in Tunis. She wondered just how much longer they could possibly endure this hell. Days? Weeks? Then what? Would they be released, or would they be savagely murdered by these fanatics?

The night air circulated very slowly through the two open doors. In contrast to the earlier oven-like conditions in the plane's cabin, she was now almost cold. Even so, she was grateful for the fresh air. With the coming sunrise, she knew, the temperature on this Mediterranean rock would soar back into the nineties outside, and even hotter inside.

No one spoke, at least not that could be heard. Even the children had been quick to learn that if they made too much noise these terrible, bad-smelling men with thick, dark beards would come and scream at them, or shake them till it hurt. And when mom or dad would try to intervene, they would be slapped or punched senseless. Only a very few small children still hummed or sang to themselves, not knowing just what was wrong.

Compared to the insanity of the previous hours, it was somewhat calmer now. The terrorists had exhausted themselves. For the most part, they rotated guard shifts and sat either dozing or staring out the doors or windows. She knew that it was only a matter of time, though, before the torment and harassment would begin anew.

She sighed and hoped desperately that Mike was still okay and not in pain from his injuries.

***

East Beirut, 0415 Hours

The young Arab glanced at his watch. *It was time*, thought Akim, getting up from the sofa and tossing a newspaper onto the coffee table. He reset the alarm, turned off the lights, and slipped out the door, strolling up the street toward his car.

He thought about the idea of living in America with growing excitement. He now had what the American wanted, and going there could actually become a reality. He crossed a small alley, carefully scanned left, then right, and continued straight ahead. He reflected on his time with Becky. He would miss her, he knew.

Akim liked the night and this one was sultry and quiet. A tiny animal scurried along the alley under a small, bent tree vaguely silhouetted against a distant light. The early morning air was warm but smelled fresh and clean. He had strolled about a block and a half from his home. He felt good. His future, something he had never given much thought to, began to appear bright—very bright indeed.

He would give Striker everything now—the message, Cupid's contact procedures—everything. *Then off to America*, he grinned. He had not believed it possible, but now he was safe. He had made it. Given enough time, Mustafa and the Shiites could reach out and get him, even in East Beirut, but they would not have the time. He would be in America.

***

Akrotiri CP, 0436 Hours

Delta's commanding officer stood next to Sergeant Major Barrington beside a large worktable, on which lay a diagram of Larnaca airport and a map of the surrounding area. There were also photos of the four terrorists and a variety of shots taken of the plane from varying angles. Several of Barrington's men stood nearby looking over the photos and maps.

Sinclair studied the faces of the terrorists in the photos and the shots of the Airbus perched on the corner of the tarmac. It was night in Cyprus, but the digitally enhanced pictures, taken through a telescopic lens, were extremely clear. On each photo in bold black numerals, the terrorists were prominently numbered one through four. For the time being, the numbers would serve as names.

NSA would be scanning communications, while analysts in the Pentagon, DIA, and CIA would be busy digging through data banks full of old reports, photos, and news clippings. They would attempt to match names, places, and events to those faces. The most trivial fact could sometimes turn the favor of negotiations.

Sinclair and Barrington studied the terrorist's photos in silence. Barclay had assigned #1 to Abdul. In the photo, the young Arab's eyes belied the anxiety that consumed him. Next was Mohammed Halid, tall and thin, brooding and anxious; he was labeled #2. The hulking, wild-eyed Abu Hassim was #3, and Khalid Moussa was #4.

The men stared at each photo in turn, taking in every detail. It was quiet in the command post until Barclay's radio call broke the silence. Sinclair slipped on the half headset offered by the radio operator and instructed the operator to put the transmission on the squawk box.

"Go ahead," said Sinclair over radio.

"Sir, Barclay here." A beep preceded and followed each transmission, and Barclay's voice carried that metallic sound of secure-voice satellite communications.

"Yeah, Steven," said Sinclair.

"No change on this end."

"Has there been any attempt at communication from the plane other than the radio?"

"Negative. We've got all the cell frequencies jammed for a hundred yards around it, and I haven't detected any phones powering up onboard. Do we have a plan?" ask Barclay.

"Standby," said Sinclair, nodding to Barrington.

"Colonel Barclay," began Barrington, "plan's all set. The snipers will cover. We'll fly the team in from the northeast. We'll put a two-man, lead team on top of the Airbus with a Little Bird and land the follow-up assault team under the tail of the Airbus in a Blackhawk. The topside team will toss a couple of flash bangs and be inside in three seconds or so. We'll also use the fixed-wing deception plan we discussed, and we'd like to try to get Jake up on top beforehand to prep the doors."

"Roger that," responded Barclay.

Sinclair added, "I also like the fact that once everything's in place, it can be rapidly launched. In addition, we wouldn't have to stage the assault team right at Larnaca Airport and risk discovery. The team can stage at Dhekelia."

"Sounds good," replied Barclay. "Hamud's made contact with Number One. He says the guy is reluctant, but he thinks he's making a little progress. As for the ambassador, I get the feeling he's not too keen on an assault."

"No surprise there," said Sinclair, "his job is diplomacy not combat. Let's just hope he comes around. Let us know if there are any changes. Out here," he said, terminating the radio communication.

11

Air France 622, 0445 Hours

For what seemed like the hundredth time, Mike Elliot asked himself how the terrorists could have possibly known about the flight? Even the passengers weren't told of the aircraft's time of departure; they were simply told to assemble at the embassy for an evacuation as soon as a flight was available. *And how the hell did the hijackers get through the security cordon with weapons? What did we overlook?* he asked himself. These questions had plagued him relentlessly.

Two of the terrorists walked down the twin aisles toward the rear of the plane. It was the big bastard and the nervous one. When the big one wasn't on guard or asleep, he endlessly wandered the length of the plane. The big brute stopped and stood in his customary protected position near the open rear doorway of the airplane, peering out into the night. The other one finally left.

Mike thought about his wife again. He knew Lynn would be afraid, but not for herself. She would be afraid for her husband, for the other passengers, and especially for the children. He longed to hold her. His fears for his wife's safety dredged up old memories that he would have preferred not to think about right now.

***

He tried to push the images of Margaret and Emily from his mind. He had analyzed the events leading up to their disappearance a million times over the years. He knew that his team must have been closer to finding the Colombian cartel's leadership than they had realized.

Despite a sophisticated alarm system, they had kidnapped Margaret and Emily from home, where they should have been the safest. Mike discovered they were gone when he arrived home from work to find his wife's car in the drive but his wife and daughter missing. Torturous days stretched into bleak and bitter weeks.

He could remember as if it were yesterday, as Jonas, the CIA agent that Mike worked with, had told him that they had a lead—and a location.

The CIA had been searching for three missing Americans for months, then five when Margaret and Emily disappeared. The CIA now believed all five were together at an old farm in a remote highland region some two hundred miles northwest of the capitol, in the direction of the Colombian border.

Mike closed his eyes; he could almost feel his old tactical vest and harness as he slipped it on. Even now, in his daydream, he could smell the sweat and the gunpowder on it from its many missions. He checked his .45 caliber Colt Commander and slid it into the holster across his chest.

Jonas geared-up but was more heavily armed. He carried grenades and an MP5. He handed Mike a couple of frag grenades, and he attached them to his vest. They stood on the tarmac with eighteen Brazilian Army commandos. They quickly boarded two waiting DEA Blackhawk helicopters and flew away into the night.

The sleek helicopters flew only eighty feet off the ground at well over a hundred and fifty knots. It seemed to Mike as if he could still feel the blast of cold air rushing past the open door and coursing across his face. He and Jonas sat on the helicopter's floor, their legs and feet hanging over the edge of the open door. Dark trees and rough terrain streaked by seemingly just below the soles of their boots. As they flew through the night, a rushing cascade of thoughts, fears, hopes, and possibilities streamed through Mike's tortured brain.

The big terrorist shifted his weight, and Mike involuntarily twitched as he dragged himself back from his thoughts. His eyes popped open as he was pulled back to reality. The big man still peered through the doorway. He felt a silent wave of rage swell up inside him. He had to protect Lynn, or die trying. *Never again,* Mike thought, *never again.*

***

0450 Hours

Marie stood in the galley preparing food trays for two of the terrorists, as instructed by one of them. He had ordered her to ensure that there were no swine products in the food. She didn't know their names, but she had mentally tagged them all by their behaviors and characteristics.

One of them, Mohammed, she thought of as *Moody*. The other, Khalid, she labeled *Quiet*. The big, scary one, was *Lunatic*, and the leader, *Unsure*. She carried the trays to the two men who carefully inspected the food. They took the trays and went to empty seats.

Heading back to the galley, Marie scanned over the passengers. She was doing all that she could for them, but it was still heartbreaking to look at them. She didn't know any of their names, either, but she knew them as human beings.

There was the young couple with beautiful twin girls, probably second or third graders. They were holding up amazingly well. She was impressed with the little girls. They would grow up to be strong young women, she was sure. *If* they managed to grow up.

There was a young pregnant woman, alone, her husband still at work at the embassy, she assumed. An older couple, still seated together, inspired her. The woman sobbed quietly, while her husband patiently, endlessly, tried to soothe her.

A woman and her teenage son had caught her eye. The boy was quite handsome and he looked like he should be in a fancy prep school somewhere. He had blond hair and wore a nice scarlet-red tie with a wrinkled navy-blue blazer.

She entered the galley. She had served the captain and copilot food and water, and either *Moody* or *Quiet* had escorted them several times to the restroom. Marie, though, had not had any chance to communicate with either of the pilots. Whenever she had served water in the cockpit, the terrorist leader had always watched her closely.

She searched through a drawer in the galley and found a short pencil and a stub of paper. She wasn't sure what she wanted to say, but she felt it important to try to tell the captain what she had observed. On his trips to the bathroom, she knew, he had observed the cabin. So he knew the general situation back here.

She scribbled a message on the paper: *One of them, the biggest one, seems to have mental issues. Very erratic behavior. Violent mood swings. Is there something I should do or prepare to do?*

She folded it tightly and palmed it in her left hand. She grabbed three cups and a water and walked to the cockpit. She paused at the door and Abdul motioned her forward. She handed him a cup and filled it. Then she did the same for the copilot and pilot. As she handed Granger a cup, she slipped the note to him as well.

She waited for a moment for the men to finish drinking, collected their cups, and left. She had no idea how, or if ever, she might have an opportunity to get any sort of reply from the captain.

*** *** ***

It was quiet in the van except for the soothing hum of electronic equipment and the faint vibration of the small, sound-insulated gas generator mounted on the vehicle's roof. Lieutenant Colonel Barclay's assistant, who doubled as driver, radio operator, and medic, was sleeping in the driver's seat. Barclay monitored the equipment.

He reached up to a control panel on an equipment console and twisted a small knob. The video image on the monitor in front of him shrank as the lens angle adapted in response to his command. The Airbus filled the screen from nose to tail. He released the knob and leaned back in the chair. It would be easy to drift off into a deep, much needed sleep, but he knew he could not afford it. He had to maintain surveillance of the target.

It would be light soon. Dawn came quickly on this speck of rock in the eastern Mediterranean. The recon teams had pulled back to their daytime hide positions. He could only collect information and hope that the terrorists made no abrupt or violent moves before Scott Barrington's men, and the president, were ready. Barrington's team could be ready at a moment's notice, if need be. For now, however, their biggest problem seemed to be the president.

Barclay tried to focus on the monitor, but his eyes were heavy. He felt his head nod forward, and he caught himself. He shook his head and reached for the coffee thermos. It was empty. The video monitor had a hypnotic effect. Barclay was feeling the strain of jet lag plus the stress of a live operation. He had to remain alert, he told himself. Lives depended on it.

A click of the van's radio, as it activated to receive a transmission from Delta's CP, broke his concentration.

"Tango-one, Raven-two-alpha, over," came the radio operator's call over the net.

"Tango-one, over," replied Barclay into the handset.

"Raven-six's pilot just reported in. They're airborne and expect ETA at Dhekelia Base in one-five mikes, over." Raven-six was Colonel Sinclair. He was en route via British helicopter to Dhekelia, the British sovereign base only a few miles east of Larnaca. He was due to land in fifteen minutes.

"Raven-two, Tango-one, will rendezvous at Dhekelia, out." Barclay heard the motor of the second van, parked just behind his, start up. His men would pick up Colonel Sinclair at Dhekelia.

Shortly after, Barclay heard the van as it returned behind his vehicle. He looked through the small, one-way, bulletproof window in the back of his van to verify that it was Sinclair, then popped open the rear door. The athletic colonel hopped into the van with his customary agility, followed by Sergeant Major Scott Barrington.

"Hello, Steven," said the colonel, shifting his unlit cigar from one side of his mouth to the other. After a few brief pleasantries and some shuffling to get everyone seated, they got down to business.

"Scott's team is ready. The helos have arrived, and the team has run a couple of walk-through rehearsals."

"Sounds good," said Barclay, checking the video monitor trained on the Airbus.

"What's the local security set up?" asked Sinclair.

"There's a Cypriot colonel, a guy named Krokos, a real card," said Barclay with a chuckle. "He's in charge of everything here. Quite a little rooster, if you ask me. He seems to be the Cypriot president's right hand man. Anyway, he's covering the perimeter with roving police patrols, and he's got teams on the accessible rooftops. I've got a Motorola here if I need to reach him, or vice versa."

"Good enough," said Sinclair. "What's the latest with our friends here?" he asked, pointing to the video monitor.

"Nothing really new, not since the last update. The parabolic is picking them up when they're yelling," he said, referring to the long-range directional microphone. "But I can't get any regular conversation. I'd like to get a microphone and a fisheye lens on the plane, but Palmer doesn't think it's a good idea to try to go under there."

"That's too bad," replied Sinclair. "The camera might have helped."

Barclay nodded. "Okay, sir," he continued, looking at Sinclair, "I think our big problem right now is the mental state of the terrorists. For the moment, they're calm. But that can change quickly. In a couple of hours, it's gonna start getting hot, and we could be on a short fuse."

"Yeah, I read Hamud's psych profile. Scary."

"Yes, sir. It's impossible to say just how much time we have. One minute these assholes are calm and quiet, the next they're acting like freaks. Number Three, in particular, is a real shithead, and Number Two is a close second.

"They at least have been letting the two flight attendants serve food and water," said Barclay, "and take people to the restrooms. But then one of the terrorists gets riled up and the two women have to scurry to their seats. When things calm down again, they get up and go back to work."

"That's a couple of gutsy women," said Sinclair.

"Without a doubt."

The attention of all four men turned to the video monitor as one of the terrorists began moving past the cabin portholes as he walked to the rear of the Airbus. Eagle-one reported the movement; Barclay acknowledged and typed a command into the computer console. He adjusted the camera joystick. The magnification increased on the video display until the terrorist's face appeared on the video monitor.

"That's Number Three," said Sinclair, leaning closer to the monitor.

"Yeah," grumbled Barclay. "Like I said, a real shithead. He's the one I'm worried about. Watch, I'll bet a month's pay he's getting ready to have one of his goddamn fits. He's scared the shit out of me several times. Hamud's been studying the video from upstairs. He thinks this one could be a sociopath and could go off the deep end at any time. The guy's a walking time bomb."

Barclay adjusted the little joystick to keep the camera trained on the terrorist. The men stared at the video monitor. "Watch," said Barclay.

The big terrorist moved at random up and down the aisles, slapping his pistol down on top of a passenger's seat and yelling at them. Occasionally, he bent over and put his face close to a passenger, then he would throw his arms up and move a little farther down the aisle.

"This will go on for another five or ten minutes," explained Barclay, "then he'll settle down for a while. In an hour or so he'll crank back up."

"Shit," muttered Sinclair. "We might try to take this son of a bitch out by sniper just as the assault is coming down."

"*If* we can get a shot," Barclay added. "He hasn't shown himself in the doorway."

"Okay, Steven," said Colonel Sinclair, swiveling to face Barclay, "We've got an assault plan, but the problem is, we're on hold. The president flat out denied General Holt's request for release authority. He also refused permission to give them fuel if the need arises. He wants negotiations to continue."

"Shit," said Barclay. "Why did they even bother to send us over here?"

Sinclair and Barrington shook their heads in agreement.

"What do we do when they start demanding fuel?" asked Barclay.

"Let's just hope Hamud can work his magic," replied Sinclair. "For now, we'll use the time to conduct rehearsals and hope for the best. When—*if*—the word comes down from the White House, I want to hit them just before dawn, tomorrow morning. That's twenty-four hours to give the goddamn politicians and diplomats time to get their heads out of their asses and make a decision. Hopefully."

"Got it," replied Barclay. "But how do we keep them still for twenty-four hours?"

"For the moment, we don't have much choice. Let's just hope for the best. And *if* they do give us that much time, and *if* the president makes up his damn mind, we'll send Jake in at 2400 local to climb the tail and position himself on top."

Barclay nodded.

After a pause, while the men watched Number Three settle down in a seat near the front of the Airbus, Sinclair continued, "Okay, Steven, unless you've got something else, we're heading back to the CP. Check in with you when we get there."

"Roger that," said Barclay.

***

Akrotiri CP, 0459 Hours

U.S. Air Force Captain Jim Owen sat in a passenger seat of a C-21 Lear jet as it landed on Cyprus. He had flown there from Andrews Air Force Base, Maryland. Jim was now attached to Delta. A test pilot, he would fly Delta's diversionary light aircraft rigged to appear as if it was on fire and about to crash.

The C-21 taxied off the runway and a small British Air Force guide truck appeared. The jet stopped on a ramp near a refueling truck where a passenger van awaited. Jim stepped down onto the tarmac and stretched. The air was warm, and the scent of salt on the light breeze washed over him. Jim climbed into the van and headed to the counterterrorist team's CP. Delta's executive officer was waiting at the door.

"Captain Owen," said a tall, muscular man. "I'm Lieutenant Colonel Noah Wilson, the Detachment executive officer. How was your flight?"

"Not bad, sir. Long."

"Your first name's Jim, right?"

"Yes, sir."

"Come on, Jim, we'll brief you over the map table."

Jim followed the XO down a narrow corridor. The CP was in a smaller building adjoining one of the hangars.

As they entered, Jim noted a stark contrast between the exterior of the old hangar and the high-tech command post inside. The room hummed with activity. Communications equipment, laptops, and TV screens were everywhere.

Spread out on a big worktable, a large map of Larnaca airport dominated the center of the room and attracted Jim's attention immediately.

"Is this where the hijackers are?"

"Yes," replied Wilson.

"Do you have someone out there now?"

"We do." Wilson leaned over the table. "Here, here, here, and here," he said, pointing out four markers for recon teams on the map. Two of the markers were red. "The red ones are snipers, and that's our target," said Wilson pointing to a tiny plastic model of a jetliner.

"We also have two surveillance vans at the airport providing this feed," he said, pointing to a wide-screen monitor displaying four different video images.

Owen studied the monitor for a moment.

"Want some coffee?" Wilson asked him.

"Yes, love some."

A young sergeant handed him a cup of coffee in a white Styrofoam cup. Jim waved off the sugar and took a sip of the dark, steaming liquid. It wasn't Starbucks, but it was hot. He needed it. It was nearly dawn, and he had only managed to grab a few naps during the long flight.

"I suppose you're interested in hearing the plan," said Wilson.

Jim nodded between sips of coffee.

"Jim, your role is fairly simple—create a diversion for us. We want the terrorists' attention focused entirely on you. We're going to put some smokes and flares on the wing strut to make it look like you're on fire. We'll base our assault timing on your touchdown at Larnaca airport. You'll be flying a DeHavilland Twin Otter DHC-6. Familiar with it?"

"I am."

"Great. The plane is here. It's in the hangar next door. Our technicians are working on it. We'll go have a look at it. Have you done this sort of thing before, Jim?" asked Wilson.

"Not specifically. But it seems pretty straight forward."

"Well," said Wilson, "we just want you to put on a show that will keep them occupied."

"I'll do my best," replied Jim.

"Okay, let's go have a look at your bird."

***

Beirut, 0520 Hours

Striker sat in the backseat of his armored Mercedes parked along the Rue Ghazliye opposite the Hotel Alfonse. The streets were deserted. He waited.

From a half-dozen vantage points, a dozen men covered the area around his car. Fred Morgan sat behind the wheel. Mark Conrad stood outside the car.

Striker watched the hotel. The stars overhead had disappeared, and the first diffuse, pink glow of early morning light filled the heavens above. In ten minutes, it would be full light.

A few moments slipped by as Striker stared out the window. He spied Doug Andrews coming through the big glass doors of the Alfonse and walking toward the sedan. He went around the car and slipped into the back seat.

"No sign of Akim."

"Damn," said Striker, pounding his fist against his thigh.

It was silent in the car for several minutes.

"Guys are getting edgy," said Andrews.

There was no response for a full minute. Then Striker looked at his deputy.

"They're getting edgy a little late," replied Striker with a wave of his hand. "If we were going to be hit it would have already happened. They wouldn't have given us forty minutes to sit here and think about it."

"What do we do?" asked Andrews, leaning back in the seat.

"We give him fifteen more minutes, and then we pack it in," said Striker, not looking away from the window. *Damn*, he thought, staring at the plate-glass windows of the Alfonse. *So goddamn close. Akim has a message from Cupid and it's probably related to the hijacking. Now we may never find out what it was.*

The Shiites had finally rocketed the airport as he had anticipated, but that was primarily for the benefit of Colonel Beagea and his men. *No, they're planning something special for us; and Akim, wherever the fuck he is, knows what it is.*

Andrews interrupted Striker's thoughts. "It's been fifteen minutes."

He slowly turned his head to face his deputy and stared at him for several seconds. Andrews' gaze was steady.

"Okay. Let's get the hell out of here," Striker intoned. "He's been compromised."

12

Air France 622, 0730 Hours

Abdul held the microphone by its cord and slapped it up and down against the palm of his hand as he tried to reason out his predicament. The captain and copilot sat frozen like statues, not daring to move for fear of further agitating a man they sensed was already on the verge of desperation. It was early, yet a stark and brilliant sun already stood high in the eastern sky. Sweltering heat would soon bear relentlessly down on the parked Airbus.

Throughout the seemingly endless night, he had reflected long and hard on the plight of his mission. He had talked a few times with a Cypriot Arab named Hamud that the airport had dug up from somewhere. Abdul had listened attentively to this Hamud's comforting words over the radio, but he knew their time here in Cyprus was limited.

He realized that he had not fully considered all the potential consequences of the operation beforehand. Once he had learned of the impending American evacuation from the Tunisian-American woman who worked in the American embassy, he had acted hastily.

His group had threatened the woman's Tunisian relatives, coercing her to provide information on the Americans. She had only learned of the evacuation forty-eight hours in advance. So, there had been no time for the lengthy planning and coordination that usually preceded a major operation.

It had all seemed so simple, but as he was learning, that was not the case. He had convinced Hezbollah council, and more importantly, Mustafa, of the viability of the operation. Mustafa had also stuck him with Abu Hassim, a maniac. *Mustafa must have sent him along to ensure that sufficient blood would be shed to shock the West*, he thought.

Can I still salvage the operation? he wondered. *Yes, but only from a secure location.* Unfortunately, he could not decide where that might be. Beirut was one of the few places that a hijacked airplane had never been attacked by commandos in one form or another. He cursed under his breath at his increasingly uncomfortable situation.

In Beirut, he would have had secure ground support and unlimited publicity. After all, he knew that the Americans would ignore his political demands—it was the worldwide attention, and of course making the Americans look weak, that were important. In Cyprus, they had little hope for media coverage on the scale that he had envisioned, at least not without the danger of attack from the United States or Cyprus. Only in Beirut could he have achieved all that he desired.

"We have to return there," he said aloud.

Abdul knew that he *must* confer with Mustafa or Bachar to ensure that the Beirut airport would allow him to land. He pulled one of the phones from his pocket and turned it on, but was stunned to discover it had no signal. He had not checked them since Delta began jamming in the early morning hours. He extracted the second one, and again, nothing. He cursed under his breath. He stared at the phones in disbelief, his mouth hanging open.

Abdul warned the startled pilots not to budge, left the cockpit, and stepped into the forward passageway.

***

Now alone in the cockpit, the two pilots looked at one another. Jean-Pierre Didier suddenly appeared agitated. "Albert," he said to Granger, "I don't think I can do this anymore. I feel like I'm about to lose it."

The captain gestured for him to lower his voice.

Peering over his shoulder, Granger whispered, "Jean-Pierre, we all feel that way, especially them," he said, nodding toward the cabin. "But we can make it. We have to hold it together for our passengers."

"No, you don't understand, I don't think I'm going to make it out of this alive. I had a dream."

"Of course you will. We all will. You're just tired. I've flown with you many times, and you've got nerves of steel. We'll make it out of this just fine. You'll see."

Didier just looked away out the window.

***

In the cabin, Abdul found his three comrades standing together, waiting. One grumbled about how they were doomed.

He stepped up to the group. "Don't be ridiculous," he snapped. "We are on a just and righteous cause. We will achieve our objectives. You must be patient and have faith. I have a plan."

He had their full attention. The three men stared at Abdul until he felt the weight of their eyes on him. He fidgeted but recovered. "I have decided that we will go back to Beirut and carry out our original plan," he announced.

No sooner had the words left his mouth than the other three terrorists began to mutter and curse.

"And how do you propose to do that?" snorted Abu Hassim.

His dark eyes pierced Abdul, who ignored the remark and began to outline his plan. "I will demand it from them, but we *must* return to Beirut."

"How?" asked one of the men. "How can you be sure we will be able to land in Beirut this time?"

"We will land even if we die in the process."

Abu Hassim doubted Abdul's tenacity but waited to hear the rest.

"We will concentrate all our efforts on returning to Beirut. We will insist that the Americans open the Beirut airport to us if they ever hope to have their precious citizens back alive. They must guarantee that we can safely leave this place, fly to Beirut, and land. Then we will be secure, and we can continue our mission as planned," he said, carefully watching Abu Hassim for a reaction. An icy expression slid over Abu's dark face.

"And why will they do this?" pressed Abu Hassim, shaking his head.

The smaller man shot back forcefully, "Do *you* have a better plan?"

It was quiet for a moment. The four men looked back and forth at each other.

"No," Hassim conceded, but then added, "have you communicated with Mustafa about returning there?"

"I attempted to, but there is no signal."

"How can that be?" demanded Mohammed.

"I do not know. I tried both phones. There is *no* signal. I had one earlier when I checked for messages."

The four men stared at one another for a moment, and then Abdul said, "Nevertheless, we *must* try my plan."

"Try very hard, Abdul el-Aziz. Try very hard, indeed." The big man turned and stomped away toward the rear of the plane.

Abdul was grateful that Abu had not lashed out at him further. He looked at his two comrades as they watched the large man walk away. *They seem to respect this crazy man more than me,* he thought. *I must remain strong or all hope will be lost.* "Have faith, my friends," he said, trying to sound confident. "We will succeed." He doubted his own words as he turned and marched back to the cockpit.

***

Dr. Hamud had been dozing in his chair at the radio console for only a few moments when a Cypriot controller woke him. He shook his head, gathered his senses, and responded to Abdul's radio call. The two men spoke in Arabic. Delta's translator at Akrotiri typed the English translation into a computer terminal and retransmitted it to Barclay's van. Barclay, and those in the CP, read the text almost in real time. Abdul believed he was talking to one man, but he had the full attention of many more.

"Well, Abdul, we have not talked for some time," remarked Hamud, suppressing a yawn. "I was beginning to think you would no longer converse with me."

"Yes," said Abdul dryly. "Well now I am going to talk, and you are going to listen."

"I am listening, Abdul."

"We are returning to Beirut. You will do as I say to prepare for this move."

The transcription scrolled down a dozen monitors. As the American soldiers read the text, their eyes lit up.

"What would you like me to do?" asked Hamud.

"First, you will send fuel to the plane, immediately," he said, pausing.

Hamud and Delta knew that this demand would come. It always did. They were grateful to have had this much time.

"Second, you will guarantee that the Beirut Airport is open to us. No more tricks."

In Delta's CP, soldiers exchanged uneasy glances.

In Larnaca tower, Hamud was calm; he had years of study and practice in the art of negotiation.

"I will work on it," he replied.

***

In the van, Barclay considered available courses of action. The terrorists wanted fuel and they wanted to fly to Beirut. Delta wanted to keep them still, and the president had said no fuel. Delta had to delay both demands.

Barclay called Colonel Sinclair and informed him that he had detected several unsuccessful cell phone attempts from the plane. Then he explained his idea to the colonel and got approval for his plan. They would stall.

Delta knew from a steady stream of intelligence reports that Hezbollah had fired rockets at the Beirut airport. It was closed. The Shiites had shot themselves in the foot. Convincing the terrorists of that might not be easy, but he would try.

Fifteen minutes later, Dr. Hamud crushed out his Turkish cigarette in the ashtray in front of him and slowly blew out the thick smoke. "Abdul," he said calmly into the mic, "the fuel is easy. That is no problem, you know. That aspect is entirely up to my own government, not the Americans. As far as Beirut is concerned, I was informed by my government that the American ambassador must have his people talk to the Lebanese and try to arrange for your landing there. It will take time."

"How much time?" asked Abdul.

"He cannot be sure. We were assured, however, that the ambassador will do whatever you wish. He will begin at once to start such negotiations."

Abdul wanted to believe. This man's voice was so soothing, so perfect. He sounded so credible, and he wanted to believe in something at this moment. He forced himself to be stern. "You think I am a fool, don't you?"

"Why do you say that, Abdul? I am doing the best I can to help you."

"Of course you are," he said testily, though he *did* want to trust this voice from the airwaves. He was convincing, strong, confident, almost father-like. Yes, Abdul wanted to believe him, but he knew it could prove fatal to trust this voice from afar. He sounded like a true Muslim, but Abdul suspected that he was somehow alien as well. At a minimum, this man was an expatriate Arab now of Cypriot nationality. Trust no one.

***

Sinclair and his men considered Abdul's demands. They had to delay the request for fuel, but legitimate reasons to do so were in short supply. The president had tied Sinclair's hands, and his primary concern was securing a release from the White House. Delta might conceivably stall the terrorists until dark, or even early the following morning as desired, and then have the president deny authorization to assault at the last minute.

Sinclair contacted General Holt, commander of Special Operations Command, and outlined the terrorist's demands. He strongly recommended that the president grant the authority to assault, before it was too late. General Holt told him it would have to go through the White House.

Sinclair returned the radio handset to its cradle and leaned back in his chair. He felt tired. The general had agreed with Sinclair's assessment, but the political climate was less accommodating. When word finally came back from Washington, Sinclair learned that the president, and the secretary of state, wanted the ambassador to

Cyprus to assess whether they could achieve a peaceful solution, before the White House would make a firm decision on an assault.

Sinclair passed this information to Barclay at Larnaca airport. Barclay would go upstairs to the ambassador's temporary office and discuss the subject of assault with him. All Sinclair could do was hope and wait. In the meantime, planning and rehearsals would continue.

Sergeant Major Barrington came by. "When's the next run-through?" Sinclair asked him.

He checked his watch. "In about an hour, sir. We'll review the operations order over the map board then run the rehearsal immediately after the briefing."

"Okay, holler at me. I'll watch the briefing and the run-through."

"Sure thing, sir."

Sinclair turned and started back to the CP, the president's intentions weighing heavily on his mind.

***

Hamud sat before his communications console in a secluded corner of the Larnaca airport tower. His primary tool, a microphone, rested in his right hand. He also watched a small, portable video monitor, radio-linked to Barclay's van. He could see the images, at least on one channel at a time, from Barclay's cameras. In his left hand, he held a newspaper.

When he heard Abdul's call on the radio, he rocked forward in his chair and dropped the paper. He usually waited for Abdul to initiate contact. The terrorist leader seemed slightly more manageable when not pushed. It also bought a few more minutes of delay each time by waiting.

"Hello, Abdul. I am glad you called, I have some information for you."

"Good. What about our demands? Where is the fuel?"

"I am happy to report that we are making progress. The American government will talk with the Lebanese government and try to work something out, but there is a problem. Someone fired rockets on the Beirut airport and cratered the runway. In fact, the news agencies say it was Hezbollah."

"I don't believe these lies."

"I have this morning's *Al-Anwar* before me," he said, referring to the Beirut daily the Cypriots had given him. "There is a picture of the runway."

"Send it to me. One man, alone, will bring it."

"I'll see what I can do."

"And what of the fuel?"

"The fuel is a minor thing. Frankly, it was the Beirut airport that I was most worried about, and of course, whether the Americans would cooperate. They seem to be trying, though. Now it is up to the Lebanese government. I fear, however, that even if Lebanon agrees to let you land, it is going to take some time to repair the runway."

Abdul wondered if he could really trust this man. "How much time?"

"It is difficult to say. I am just a messenger, but I imagine a few hours at least will be required for the Lebanese and American governments to work something out. The *Al-Anwar* is quite specific concerning the runway. It says at least twelve hours will be required to make the necessary repairs and reopen the airport." Hamud paused. "Abdul, my government has instructed me to relay a message to you. Will you take it?"

"Yes, what is it?"

"Since the Americans are doing what you want, would you also show a gesture of good faith?"

"Such as?"

"Would you consider releasing the women and children? You would still have many Americans under your control, and it would not jeopardize your security. In fact, it should be easier with fewer people to watch."

"What do you know about security? No. I will not consider it."

"But Abdul, at least think about it. The Americans are doing everything you ask. Please tell me, Abdul, are they all right, have they had water?" asked Hamud, knowing that they had.

"They are fine."

"Have you let them drink?"

"Yes."

"Good, but please, Abdul, consider that the Americans are doing what you ask. At least show some gesture of cooperation. At least *consider* releasing the children and their mothers."

After a moment, Abdul replied, "No."

"Okay, Abdul, but at least think about it. Such a gesture would encourage the Americans to cooperate more."

"I'll think about it."

"Thank you, Abdul. I have one more thing. We have also detected a technical problem in the APU on your plane."

"The what?"

"The power unit that keeps your radios and lights running. Also, you will need it to start the airplane engines when you are ready to leave."

"And how have you determined this?" He was no technician, but even he wondered how they could know about the generator's status.

"We have instruments in the tower that indicate the strength of the transmission from your radio. An airport technician here in the tower says that the power level on your transmission has dropped considerably. The APU may not be providing adequate amperage."

"It is working fine."

"Yes, for the moment. It will power the radios and may even start the plane, now. But in a few hours it could fail to start the jet engines. Then you will blame us. I do not want this to happen."

"And what do you propose?"

"It is easy. We just swap out the power units, and no one need come on the plane. They simply unplug the old one under the plane and plug in a new one. It will take two men, Cypriots, only five minutes."

The radio was silent for a full minute.

"Maybe. Send the *Al-Anwar*."

***

0841 Hours

Lieutenant Colonel Barclay went down the last flight of stairs in the tower and out through the Cypriot security checkpoint he had already passed a dozen times. *The guards look tired*, he thought. He could certainly empathize. He exited a door from the building just under the tower. A small airport sedan with a yellow light on top awaited him.

Barclay doubted the intel payoff would be very high for what he was about to do. He wouldn't be able to see into the plane from the ground, but it was important to delay the terrorists. The Beirut newspaper, *Al-Anwar*—meaning *The Light* in Arabic—might help accomplish this. It only mentioned the hijacking in passing since to the public, it appeared to be a Tunisian terrorist operation. It clearly demonstrated, though, that the Shiite Hezbollah militia had rocketed the Beirut airport runway. In addition, he might at least get a quick look at whoever took the paper from him. The important thing was that it got delivered.

Barclay tossed the tightly rolled Arabic newspaper onto the passenger seat next to him. He rolled up each sleeve of his shirt several turns to show he was unarmed. He had already stashed his weapon in the van. He started the little car, turned on the rotating yellow light perched atop the roof, and drove slowly out to the plane. He stopped a short distance from the front left door of the Airbus. He saw no sign of movement from within the plane, but he knew they were watching him.

The door opened. An instant later, a hand thrust past the doorway and signaled him to come forward. Barclay approached the plane, having to look upwards sharply since the passenger door to the plane was nearly thirty feet off the tarmac. The hand signaled again, and he tossed the newspaper up into the open doorway. It flew end over end like a twirling baton until it disappeared into the dimmer light of the plane's interior.

Barclay turned and walked calmly back to the car. He got in and drove off. Through the mirror, he saw the portside door on the Airbus close. He was right, there was nothing to see, but he had accomplished his mission. The Beirut newspaper was delivered— the first one he had delivered in thirty years, he mused. It wouldn't keep the terrorists still forever, but it might slow them down.

Barclay's next task was to get back to the van and report to Colonel Sinclair. Prior to delivering the newspaper, he had met with Charles Anderson, the U.S. ambassador to Cyprus. The meeting was cordial but disappointing. The ambassador had already recommended to the secretary of state that they wait, and negotiate. With the ambassador's support, plans for an assault could have probably moved forward. Without it, the mission remained on hold.

***

Abdul had watched as the man got into his car and drove away, the spinning yellow light fading into the distance toward the tower building. He picked up the newspaper and took it into the plane's galley. He removed the rubber band securing it, unrolled the paper, and spread it out on the small countertop. Mohammed peered over his shoulder.

Abdul slammed his fist down hard against the counter. On the front page, below the bold, flowing Arabic title *Al-Anwar*, read the following headline in flowery Arabic script: *Rafic Hariri Airport Closed!* Below the caption, a black and white photo depicted the cratered runway. Several clusters of men, some in hardhats, stood around the edge of one of the larger craters, staring into the hole. Unmistakably, deep in the background of the photo, was Beirut's shattered skyline.

"It is true," mumbled Abdul, over his shoulder to Mohammed. The other two terrorists had arrived, and he handed the paper to them. "It is true."

***

0915 Hours

It had finally arrived. Mike Elliot had believed it never would, but now it was a new day, and it was already getting old. It had been light for only a few hours, yet the sun was well up in the sky. It was not too hot yet, but it was already stuffy. Soon, it would be stifling. He knew that it would be a very long day, more prolonged, even, than the tedious, boring, painful night that had limped by at a snail's pace.

Barely able to peek over the seatback in front of him, he was able to see some activity up near the front of the plane. The terrorists had congregated there. He wondered what they were up to but couldn't see what they were doing.

He felt sure that the sea was nearby. He could smell it from time to time when a breeze hit the open doorway. He studied the terrain again through his small window—it was flat, open, rocky, and dull. He knew that Cyprus was only thirty minutes from Beirut; it could be where they had landed.

He wondered, though, if it might not be Beirut. Dim images of what had to be that cityscape loomed just at the fringes of his consciousness, but he could not bring it sharply into focus. He vaguely remembered seeing the uneven skyline of what was probably that war-torn city.

Could it be Libya? Mike wondered. *No, there should be more sand if it was Libya. Can't be Malta,* he decided, *too flat. Got to be Cyprus.* He had never been there, but he had studied the geography of the entire Mediterranean region.

What good would it do to know, one way or the other? he chided himself. *What possible good is such information?* He dropped it. He didn't care.

Somehow, he caught a whiff of aviation fuel on the breeze— or maybe it was just a memory. His head injury wasn't helping him keep his thoughts, or recollections, clear on anything. He knew he probably sustained some kind of concussion. Either way, real or imagined, the scent of fuel dragged his thoughts back three years to that last, fateful helicopter flight in Brazil.

***

They landed three miles from the objective, in the dark. By dawn, they had the farm under surveillance from a wooded hilltop three hundred yards away. Fifty to sixty armed men were in the camp. They eventually formed up and trekked off into the bush.

Mike, Jonas, and the Brazilian commandos moved in, easily subduing the remaining three armed men and a dozen or so women in the compound of five rotting old buildings.

In one dilapidated, barn-like structure, several of the Brazilian soldiers found the five hostages, grouped close together in the center of the structure, tied to chairs. But the commandos rapidly backed out of the building signaling not to enter.

Mike ran past them and into the building. Jonas followed close behind. In the dim light, he saw Margaret and Emily and the three other hostages, two men and a woman. They were all bound and gagged. Mike would never forget their eyes—wide with fright.

Around their feet and under their chairs were stacks of military-grade high explosives. Wires connected the stacks to a complex electronic detonator—a yellow light on the detonator flashed like a strobe.

Mike tried to run to them, but Jonas, a large and powerful man, grabbed the straps on the back of his tactical harness and dragged him toward the door. Somehow, though, maybe in sheer desperation, or perhaps hope, in those last few moments, Emily had managed to move the gag away from her mouth enough…

They were just tumbling out the door, when the last thing he heard before the detonation, was the haunting voice of his daughter when she screamed, "Daddy!"

***

Mike's agonizing recollection was shattered, but it was little relief from the misery. Shouting up front grabbed his attention. *Oh God, what are they pissed about now?* he wondered.

13

Akrotiri U.K. Base, 0930 Hours

A black, unmarked, CIA Lear jet touched down softly and taxied to an adjoining apron and an awaiting van. The three passengers, wearing civilian clothes, were transported by the British military van to Delta's CP. Lieutenant Colonel Wilson met the van.

No introductions were necessary for two of the men. From the CIA, Max Hardwick, a slightly heavyset, fortyish-looking man with prematurely graying hair, was a veteran field agent who was well known to Delta. The second man was from DIA, Steve Darnell, a Defense Department intelligence officer who frequently briefed Delta operators on various missions and hotspots around the world. At thirty, he was nearly bald, and he tended to stutter when nervous; but he was a brilliant and well-respected analyst.

The third man, Ned Bowes, was a State Department intelligence analyst. To the Lieutenant Colonel, he looked like a teen-ager who might still be in high school, but he held a doctorate from Princeton in international relations.

Wilson greeted the men, introduced himself to the officer from State, and then led them down a corridor to Colonel Sinclair's small workspace. Barrington was with the colonel.

After a brief greeting and more introductions, the six men grabbed coffees and circled up some folding metal chairs in the CP to talk.

"What do you have for us, Max?" asked Wilson.

"I think you have most of it, already. You have the Agency's assessment on the leak—the ambassador's secretary."

The Delta men nodded.

"We just wanted to tidy up a few details," Hardwick added in his thick Boston accent, a dialect he seemed to be able to change at will.

Hardwick nodded at the two men he had brought with him.

The State Department analyst, Bowes, began. Already adolescent in appearance, his high voice did little to dispel his youthful aura. "As you know, of course, State was evacuating one hundred and fifty-six employees and family members from Tunis. Seventy-two evacuees had already boarded at the time of the attack.

"Two armed Marines, trained embassy security personnel, were aboard at the time. They were killed, along with one male passenger. The terrorists dumped their bodies here on Cyprus.

"Two other Marines, sent with the catering and fuel trucks to watch over the loaders and fuelers, were found dead in the back of the catering truck—killed by brute force trauma to the neck. Obviously, by someone quite strong."

Barrington, Sinclair, and Wilson nodded at each other, knowing that it was certainly Number Three.

He continued, "In Tunis, during the takeover, we had eight serious casualties on the tarmac, including one DSS agent, plus two evacuees killed."

Sinclair and his men already knew all this from the intel briefs.

"What's the point?" asked Sinclair, starting to chew his cigar.

"Anyway," said the analyst, "we've accounted for all our personnel, the remaining passengers on the ground."

The State Department analyst nodded to the DIA officer.

Steve Darnell began, "Defense has one man unaccounted for—Major Mike Elliot."

"And why is this significant?" asked Sinclair.

"Elliot was a DIA asset assigned as the assistant army attaché at the embassy in Tunis. He wasn't scheduled to fly out—he had actually been assigned by his boss, the attaché, to coordinate the evacuation.

"So, we believe he was probably on the plane checking on something or other when it was hijacked. We don't know if he might still be alive, but since his body was not thrown out with the other three, we *assume* he is."

"Okay," said Wilson, "we're waiting for the other shoe to drop."

"Well, what you need to know is that Elliot has a lot of history."

With a flourish of his cigar, Sinclair motioned to continue.

Max Hardwick added, "Elliot was Special Forces. He spent a decade in SF working mostly with the Agency, conducting everything from raids, to high-value target extractions, renditions, assassinations, hostage rescues—you name it.

"We worked him and his team in Africa, Asia, South America, Afghanistan, Iraq—wherever—he was good. In fact, next to you boys, he's about as good as it gets. He's an accomplished martial artist and also a linguist, speaks four or five languages fluently. That made him particularly valuable as both a special operator and as a DIA asset."

The DIA rep continued, "So Elliot was a highly decorated Green Beret. Along the way, he married and had a daughter. Wife's name was Margaret, the daughter, eight years old, named Emily."

"Was?" asked Wilson.

"Dead. Anyway, at Elliot's request, DIA eventually assigned him to the embassy in Brazil. Margaret and Emily went with him. He was involved in drug interdiction, but just analytical work.

"To make a long story short, his wife and daughter were kidnapped by a Colombian cartel. Elliot and a CIA officer named Jonas Ward, and some Brazilian commandos, tried a rescue op that failed."

Hardwick interjected, "They actually found Elliot's wife and daughter, as well as three other American hostages, but they were all wired with explosives. It was a trap. Elliot tried to get to them, but Jonas Ward dragged him to the door and pushed him out just as the charges detonated. Jonas shielded Elliot with his own body and took most of the blast. The hostages were killed and Elliot and our officer were gravely wounded, Jonas more seriously."

"Okay," said Barrington, "he has a history with terrorists."

"There's more," said Hardwick, pausing. "His current wife, Lynn Elliot, is on that plane too."

"Shit," said Wilson. "This guy can't catch a break."

They all nodded agreement.

Darnell said, "We obviously don't have any idea as to his current status or his mental state. He could be injured. In fact, that's likely. It's safe to assume he was overpowered, just like the Marines, though probably not as easily."

Hardwick said, "Gentlemen, we all love the movies and the stories where the hero saves the day against all odds. But this guy tried. He failed. And his wife and little girl died. On the one hand, he's a man burdened with lots of guilt and remorse. On the other, he's also a highly trained, and very resourceful, Green Beret and Ranger. If he's alive and able, he could be an asset. But that's a *big* if."

"He could also get in the way," said Barrington flatly.

"Yep," said Hardwick, settling back in his chair.

A soldier tapped Barrington on the shoulder.

"Time for the run through," said Barrington to Sinclair.

"Let's go," replied the colonel.

***

Delta's men were gathered around a diagram of the Airbus chalked out on the concrete floor in the large hangar bay when Sinclair, Barrington, Wilson, and their three visitors entered. Some of the men joked; others studied the sketch. Other men stood waiting. They seemed relaxed, considering the task that lay before them.

Sergeant Major Barrington positioned himself in the center of the group. It was his show and Sinclair let him run it. Barrington was the assault element commander, and he was good at it—as were Barrington's men.

Sinclair often wondered if his own son might have turned out like Scott Barrington had a drunken driver not killed him. The two shared similar mannerisms, in many haunting and eerie ways, although Barrington would have no way of knowing this. Sinclair's son would have been a young man now, had he survived. He didn't want to reopen that painful, old wound, though. These men deserved his total concentration.

Nearly thirty men were present in the hangar. Staff Sergeant Jake Brady would climb onto the top of the plane in advance of the assault. He would prep the closed doors with precisely calculated cutting charges. He would also emplace short ropes over the doors for the topside team. Air Force test pilot Captain Jim Owen would fly the small diversionary aircraft rigged to look as if it were on fire. Four army helicopter pilots would deliver the operators to the jet. In addition, there were the four pilots of the backup helicopters. The remainder were operators from Barrington's team, the men who would assault the plane.

The terrorists had Uzi submachine guns, nevertheless, the Delta assaulters would use only pistols. Their weapon of choice for this type of very-close-quarter combat was the Colt .45 ACP Model 1911A1, customized by Delta's gunsmiths. The .45 offered superior stopping power compared to smaller calibers, such as the 9mm.

Barrington organized his operators into four teams.

The security team consisted of four men. They would be the first four operators out of the Blackhawk. These men would take up positions on the ground beneath each of the four Airbus passenger doors, approximately ten feet out from the plane. Their pistols would be oriented on the doors to engage any of the terrorists who showed themselves in the doorway. The security element would provide cover for the assault teams climbing the ladders and coming down from the top.

Alpha team consisted of two men; they were the lead. They would jump onto the roof of the Airbus from a hovering MH-6H Little Bird. These two operators would be the first to enter the plane, one forward, and one aft, on opposite sides.

Bravo team consisted of four men. Two would emplace and hold two assault ladders; two others would mount the ladders and enter the plane just behind the two operators coming down from the top. Barrington was on this team. He would enter forward just behind an alpha team member. While the alpha man turned right and moved toward the plane's center, Barrington would turn left and clear the galley and cockpit. Barrington would have an explosive charge in a quick-access pouch on the front of his tactical harness in the event the cockpit door was locked.

Charlie team consisted of two additional men who would climb the ladders and enter the plane directly behind bravo.

A medic would wait by each ladder until signaled aboard to treat any casualties.

Lastly, an explosives ordinance expert would stand by in the event charges were found on the plane.

Barrington reviewed the assault tasks and the overall timing. He stood over the chalk diagram of the Airbus sketched out on the hangar floor and pointed as he talked. He looked at each man, on each team, as he referred to their assault tasks.

"Okay, listen up," he began. "On in-bound, you'll be given the standard ten, two, and one minute warnings to touchdown. All right, Captain Owen's plane will touch down at H-hour—0500 hours local—initiating the assault. Owen's call sign is Condor.

"Between H+1 second and H+3 seconds, the recon team's ground snipers will eliminate any terrorists visible to them. They will call out any hits.

"At H+3, four things happen at once—Chief Smith brings the Blackhawk in close behind the tail of the Airbus; the security team exits the Blackhawk first and runs beneath the jet toward each of the four passenger doors of the Airbus; Master Sergeant Palmer, positioned near the forward landing gear, will cut the APU supplying electricity to the airliner; and from his location on the tail section of the aircraft, Jake Brady will explode two of the plane's passenger doors, forward portside and aft starboard.

"Between H+4 and H+7, the security team will take up positions around all four doors and will engage available targets in each doorway. They will call out the number of hits. The Little Bird will come to a hover above the Airbus and the two alpha team men drop onto the roof and move to their positions above the forward port and aft starboard doors. Bravo, by now, has moved the two assault ladders attached to the sides of the Blackhawk to the front port and aft starboard doors. At that time the topside men toss two, short-fuse, non-lethal concussion grenades into the plane, one forward and one aft.

"Okay, bravo and charlie are almost up the ladders. The instant the flash-bangs go, at approximately H+8, the two alpha men on top swing down into the plane's open doors using the ropes Jake installed.

"Two bravo team men are now at the top of the ladders and enter the plane immediately behind alpha, forward and aft. I will enter forward portside, I'll turn left toward the cockpit, clearing the galley as I pass it. The other bravo man, entering aft starboard, will turn left toward the tail section to clear and secure the rear of the plane.

"Charlie team's two men will come off the ladders and fall in behind alpha, moving tactical behind the alpha team man. Charlie will engage and continue the assault if an alpha operator goes down or fails to see a threat.

"Two alpha operators, each followed by a charlie team man, will move down the aisles toward each other, but on opposite aisles, one to port, one to starboard. Once bravo has cleared the cockpit and tail, we will turn and fall in behind charlie and alpha moving toward the center of the plane.

"Okay, all shots are double-tap; call out all target hits. There are four targets. We're going in from both top and bottom, so if something gets screwed up, somebody will make it in. If, for some reason, alpha's not in position, bravo goes. Same if bravo's not there, alpha doesn't wait. Go with the momentum. They just got rocked by the doors exploding, and then the flash-bangs go off. Keep them off balance. We can't let them recover.

"Everyone knows everybody else's sector. Keep it clean. No nicks or grazes like in the shooting house last year."

There were a few coughs.

"All right. If someone doesn't make his slot—adapt. You might have to clear another sector as well as your own. Also, from surveillance, we haven't seen any indication that there are explosives—but we can't rule it out, so don't give them a chance to get to a detonator. They *could* even be wearing explosives, but we think that unlikely. They were searched in Tunis, and the compartment on their truck used to conceal their weapons was very small."

Sergeant Major Barrington answered a few more questions and sent the men to get into position. Rehearsal number three would begin in ten minutes.

In essence, three operators would enter the front and three the rear, clearing in all directions and proceeding through the plane until it was secure. In all, six Delta operators would enter the plane and neutralize the four hijackers. Additional operators, waiting on the ladders, would be ready to enter the plane if necessary.

The plan seemed solid, and even with numerous rehearsals, they all knew it could go south in an instant. They were each also keenly aware that any number of them might not survive the assault. In the back of every single man's mind, ran the thought that they might be living their last hours, rehearsing their own deaths.

***

Air France 622, 1050 Hours

Lynn could feel the gnawing, burning pain in her hands and wrists as it returned—a little higher this time. The throbbing ache was moving up into her arms. She wondered if she might suffer nerve damage in her hands and arms. She forced the thought from her mind. Lynn was optimistic by nature. She came from a long line of survivors, and she refused to accept the notion that she, her husband, or any of the passengers around her, would die. *We will make it. We will all make it*, she told herself repeatedly.

The scorching heat had returned. Sweat ran down her face, stinging her lip. She had wiped her face so many times with her sleeves that they were soaking wet. The passengers she could see were suffering too. Marie had brought more water, and some food, but it was not enough.

Her thoughts turned to her captors. *What kind of animals could these men be*, she wondered, *who can so callously torture human beings like this, making them sit, bound, for hours on end?* But she knew that this, too, was negative thinking and was of no use. She was grateful for Marie and Eva. If they survived, it would be in no small part because of them.

Ignoring the pain, she took a long, slow, deep breath and closed her eyes. In her mind's eye, she visualized a gently flowing stream shaded by a giant live oak. Wonderfully colorful birds, singing enchanting melodies, filled its limbs. With all her effort, she willed herself into that joyful scene, and she felt peace. Given the circumstances, such a feeling was difficult to come by. She only knew that she had to try to stay near that tree, and hear those birds, for as long as she possibly could.

***

Larnaca, 1105 Hours

Lieutenant Colonel Barclay had just entered the airport tower and was approaching Dr. Hamud, when Abdul called.

"Yes, Abdul, how may I help you?" asked Hamud into the microphone.

"I have considered your requests."

"Yes, and what have you decided?"

"You may come and change the powering device." Hamud looked over his shoulder and winked at Barclay.

"Okay," replied Hamud. "The power unit is a small thing, but we've told the Americans that you are giving the passengers water. They see that as a very positive gesture. I am sure they will want to continue cooperating if they know that you are treating their people well. In fact, I am sure they will be more afraid now of making a false move and ruining the cooperation we have established. Is there anything else, Abdul?"

"No. That is all, except that if there are any tricks, there will be blood on your hands."

"No, no tricks, Abdul."

Hamud quickly explained to Barclay the conversation that had just transpired. Barclay was ready with a plan to exploit this opening. Changing the APU was an opportunity to get close to the plane.

If Delta could manage to emplace a microphone, and maybe a camera, they would be able to monitor the terrorists' activities more closely. The devices might warn Delta of any actions the terrorists planned.

***

After nearly ten minutes, Staff Sergeant Dwight Hayes was still sorting through a pile of coveralls in the basement of a Larnaca airport maintenance building. The clothing all seemed to be for gargantuan men. Hayes was small, barely one hundred and forty pounds, but his size was deceptive. Many an overconfident, larger man had learned this fact the hard way.

He needed a pair of coveralls like the maintenance workers at the airport wore. From the ones he could find here, most of the zippers were broken and they all smelled terrible.

"God," he said to himself, wincing. "Don't they ever wash these things?" He tossed a particularly filthy pair back into the corner.

Hayes and a Greek Cypriot airport worker would go out and change the APU. Hayes would bug the plane. He held up a large pair of green coveralls for inspection. "Maybe these'll do," he muttered. He checked the zippers. With some jerking and pulling, they reluctantly worked. He smelled them. "Shit."

With a grimace, he slipped into the coveralls and forced the uncooperative zippers upwards. He spun around and bounded up the steps, taking them three at a time. On the main floor of the maintenance building, Master Sergeant Roberts, Colonel Krokos, and the Greek Cypriot maintenance man who had volunteered to change the APU were discussing the plan.

"There you are, Hayes," said Roberts. "What took you so long? And shit, you smell like a latrine."

"Thanks, Sarge." Hayes eyed the Cypriot maintenance worker then reached out to shake the man's hand. He introduced himself.

"Hi," replied the Cypriot. "I'm Demetrius." He had no hint of an accent.

"Oh, you speak English."

"Sure, most people here do, but I grew up in Baltimore. My mother and I came back here to Cyprus to live with my grandmother when I was twelve, after my father died."

"Well, I'm glad to meet you."

"Okay, Dwight," interjected Master Sergeant Roberts, "I was just going over the plan with Demetrius here. He knows it could be dangerous, but he's volunteered to do it anyway."

Demetrius grinned shyly. Roberts continued.

"He knows the general lay of things, but Dwight, you tell him how you want things to go down. Tell him exactly what you want him to do."

"Okay," said Hayes looking at Demetrius. "First off, if they talk to us or ask us any questions you just answer in Greek."

"Okay."

"Secondly, you act like you're the boss. If they ask something, *you* answer. Don't look at me or they might suspect something. As far as we can tell, they don't speak any Greek, so when they ask you something in Arabic or French, just act like you don't understand and respond in Greek."

"That won't be difficult. I don't know a word of Arabic or French."

"All the better. Now, Demetrius, if this thing goes down easy, we'll just drive out there, change the APU, I'll do my thing, and then we'll drive back. If not, we just have to improvise.

"I want you to fiddle with the APU for a couple of extra minutes like you're adjusting something. That'll give me time to do what I need to do. I'll be working on the cable connection to the plane.

"They'll be watching us, so keep your cool and take your cues from me. You don't have any weapons or a military uniform under those coveralls, do you?"

"A uniform?"

"Yeah. No offense, pal, but do you mind if I have a look? It's important."

Demetrius shrugged and looked at Colonel Krokos, who nodded his approval. Demetrius unzipped his coveralls. He was wearing a T-shirt and boxers.

"Good. Sorry, pal, I just wanted to be sure you weren't from the Cypriot military or something. I don't want any surprises out there."

"No problem, I understand," said Demetrius.

***

1131 Hours

Hayes and Demetrius waited in the maintenance building for the order to proceed. In Barclay's van, a Delta communications specialist sat at a radio console to help with the microphone placement. Though Delta didn't expect trouble, its two snipers were carefully watching the plane.

All was ready. Hamud called Abdul.

He explained how they would change the APU. Abdul allowed him to proceed.

Within seconds, Hayes received the word to move. "Okay, Demetrius, let's do it."

Demetrius returned a nod and a weak smile. His enthusiastic manner had waned. Hayes eyed the Cypriot. It was too late to change the plan now. Hayes needed a cover, a real Greek Cypriot worker, on the off chance that one of the terrorists spoke some Greek.

They hopped into the little truck. Demetrius started the motor, and they moved off across the tarmac toward the Airbus.

"Okay, nice and easy Demetrius, slow down a bit. Let's not spook them."

Hayes noticed that Demetrius had the steering wheel in a death grip, twisting his hands nervously. He was sweating, and he looked scared. "Relax, Demetrius," urged Hayes. "It'll be okay. Just relax."

"Yeah, I'm all right."

"Okay, stop about fifteen yards from the plane. Then we'll get out, hold our hands in the air, and point to the APU."

Demetrius slowed the truck and stopped. They got out, left the doors open, and held their hands up.

There was no immediate reaction from the Airbus. Hayes and Demetrius stood by the truck, kept their hands in the air, and waited. Demetrius gave Hayes a quizzical look, raising his eyebrows. Hayes pursed his lips and shook his head. Several minutes passed.

Abu Hassim had fallen asleep. With the men now standing outside the Airbus, Mohammed woke Hassim and told him that they were about to change the APU. The huge man shot straight up from his seat with a menacing scowl on his face. Mohammed jumped back.

Abu shrieked, "Where?" Mohammed pointed to port. Abu Hassim stepped up to the closed passenger door and peered through the porthole for a moment. He stepped back and signaled for Mohammed to open the door. As he did so, Abu stepped up to the edge of the open doorway protected by the wall. He leered at Demetrius and Hayes standing by the truck with their hands in the air, their eyes wide in surprise.

Abu Hassim yelled something in Arabic. Neither man moved. He yelled again, but their only response was a shrug of the shoulders from the men on the tarmac. The terrorist twisted, twirling the Uzi hanging by its sling up into his hands.

A Delta sniper on the grass field a few hundred yards away pulled the Kevlar-graphite composite stock of his M24 up tight against his shoulder. He relaxed his body, let out a half breath, and steadied the sight picture he had formed in his ten-power scope. He centered the notched and numbered cross hairs of his Leopold-Stevens M3 sniper's scope between Abu Hassim's bushy black eyebrows.

Abu Hassim had exposed himself slightly, just enough for the sniper to get a shot. Before Delta's sniper could fire, and before Sergeant Hayes had finished his thought, Abdul stepped forward into the Airbus doorway and grabbed his comrade's arm.

"No, Abu. I told you, I let them come."

"This might be a trick," bellowed the big man.

"No, it is not. We will see. If they have weapons, you may do as you wish." He signaled the men to strip off their clothes.

Shit. It's going down the hard way, thought Hayes, as he tried to get the zipper unstuck on his coveralls. Eventually, he had to rip it open. Demetrius began taking his off. Sinclair in Delta's CP, and Barclay in the gray van, monitored the scene on video. Sinclair bit off the end of his cigar. He spat it on the floor.

Once Hayes and Demetrius had removed their coveralls, Abdul said to his accomplice, "See, they have no weapons."

"No. Tell them to take off the rest." He made motions as if ripping off his own shirt. Abdul did the same. Hayes pulled his T-shirt over his head and threw it on the ground. He kicked off his shoes and removed his jeans. He looked at Demetrius who was already down to his shorts. Both men were now standing on the tarmac in their under shorts and socks.

Abu Hassim signaled with the muzzle of his Uzi toward the hardstand. The two men lowered themselves, face first, onto the scorching tarmac wearing only their shorts. The hot concrete blistered their bare skin.

"Hell, this ain't good," mumbled Staff Sergeant Hayes through gritted teeth.

***

"Crap," shouted Colonel Sinclair, as he paced back and forth in the command post. He was chewing on a new cigar. "Dammit, Noah," he exclaimed to Lieutenant Colonel Wilson. "That son of a bitch Number Three is getting to be a real pain in the ass! The bastard is unpredictable.

"This should have been a simple, quick little operation like Barclay delivering the paper this morning. Now we have Hayes and a Cypriot civilian lying naked on the goddamn tarmac in the hot sun! Plus, the sons of bitches want fuel to leave, and the goddamn White House won't let us do a damn thing except sit on our asses. All right, Noah, any ideas?"

"We need to arrange for Hayes to complete his mission and withdraw," began Wilson, "and we need to continue stalling on the fuel. Our only chance to accomplish either is to have Hamud work on Abdul. He has to find the right buttons to push to get him to exert influence on Number Three."

"Yeah. I don't see that we have much goddamn choice. Call Steven," he said with a wave of his cigar.

***

Beirut, 1301 Hours

Sitting alone in his fifth floor embassy office, John Striker reflected on the mission the director of operations had given him— activate Cupid and determine Hezbollah's next move. Thanks to Akim, that mission was a failure.

Striker had every asset he could mobilize out looking for him, but he was nowhere to be found. Striker had no way to fulfill the director's orders without him. Akim had established Cupid's contact procedures. Only he knew them. Once Cupid had successfully penetrated Hezbollah, Akim had never given up those coded procedures, as the CIA had planned, because it bolstered his importance to both the Americans and Akim's own bosses.

Hezbollah would certainly be planning an attack somewhere in retaliation for the airport fiasco. It could even involve a maneuver directly related to the hijacking. He had to find out what that might be. Otherwise, he sensed, the American government would be at the mercy of the terrorists.

A distant explosion rumbled through the air; the shock wave rattled the windows in Striker's office. A few flakes of plaster drifted down from the ceiling. Striker hardly noticed. It happened every day in Beirut.

He thought again about his assignment. He could only get what he needed from inside Hezbollah. This would be Akim's last chance to screw up. As soon as this crisis was over, Striker would replace him, one way, or another. *If* he was still alive, of course, which Striker seriously doubted.

14

How can I lead such a maniac as Abu Hassim? wondered Abdul. *This was not what I wanted.* He had only wanted to encourage the Americans and Cypriots to do as he asked. Then this beast Hassim goes berserk, and now he had two Cypriots lying naked outside the plane. The Cypriot Army was probably lining up in front of the airport preparing their attack. What would they care if they killed a few Americans in the process? And it was all because of this fool, Hassim.

Abdul feared Abu Hassim. He hated this weakness in himself, and he detested Hassim for his size and physical strength. Nevertheless, he *was* afraid of the man, he admitted to himself, but mostly because the man was crazy and unpredictable.

Approaching Abu Hassim once again, Abdul repeated, "I told them they could come, don't you understand? I have explained it a dozen times. The Americans are doing as we ask. When the time comes to take off, we will need the new power device." His voice was strained. "It does little good to anger the Cypriots. They are not our target. But if you harm these two men, they will quickly become our mortal enemies."

"If they are doing as we ask," growled Abu Hassim, "why have they not brought fuel? We demanded it many hours ago."

"They will bring it," replied Abdul sharply, averting his eyes. "Don't forget that we asked to go to Beirut. They are working on that. There are delays because our own people rocketed the runway."

"Yes, that was stupid. But it does not prevent the Cypriots from giving us fuel."

"It will come, I tell you."

"Then make them bring it now, or I will. They are stalling for some reason, and I do not like it. Maybe they are preparing an attack," Abu Hassim screamed. "They understand force and nothing more. It is our only weapon." His eyes were bulging and fiery, and his heavy brow was furled into a harsh scowl.

Abdul paused and stared at the big man. His face was frightening. He knew that Hassim was a good fighter. He was vicious in combat. But that did not mean that he had good reasoning skills. In fact, Abdul was convinced that the man was on the verge of a complete breakdown.

He considered their security situation. He could see out the door and through two dozen small windows. He had scanned the area in front of the cockpit for hours on end. He could see nothing that posed an immediate threat. They were isolated in the middle of this huge field. They would have ample warning of any approach. With the exception of Beirut, would they have better security if they flew away to another place? He doubted it.

The big man glared at Abdul with a stare that sent a shiver down his spine.

"We will kill one of them," said Abu Hassim, pointing a large finger toward the passengers. "*Then* the Cypriots will listen."

Abdul was not above murder but only if it advanced their plans. Here, he was not sure. It could be counterproductive. An execution now might provoke an assault against them by the Cypriots where none was planned. It might cause the Americans to break off negotiations with Lebanon. He believed the soothing voice on the radio with which he had conversed so frequently in the past hours. It was his only solace.

"That may become necessary, Abu, but for now I will try again to make them listen. They will do as I say."

"If you cannot, Abdul el-Aziz, I will."

***

Abdul returned to the cockpit and issued his warning. He cautioned that he could no longer guarantee that there would not be bloodshed, and he ordered the tower to bring fuel to the plane immediately.

Colonel Sinclair and his staff considered the threat. Their options were limited. The president had not given his approval for Delta to attack, and Sinclair had kept his assault force at Akrotiri to plan and rehearse. Delta now had a new threat to evaluate.

Barrington and his men considered the pros and cons of an immediate assault. If they went in now, it would be a daylight attack. The advantage of a nighttime assault would not be with them, and they would have to modify the plan. Without darkness, the aircraft-on-fire diversion would not be possible.

In addition, without time and the cover of darkness, Jake Brady would not be able to infiltrate onto the Airbus. Without Brady's preparation of the target, the assaulting force might have to gain entry into the aircraft by other means.

The terrorists might be able to get the doors to the aircraft closed before Delta could get inside, and the commandos would have to rig a frame charge or employ a high-speed cutting torch to make an entryway—both techniques required time to employ. Neither method could get them into the plane as fast as Jake Brady would have been able to do with pre-wired explosives.

The crisis was quickly approaching a critical phase. Sinclair radioed General Holt with the new terrorist threat and requested that the president grant release authority immediately.

***

Staff Sergeant Dwight Hayes waited impatiently. *If something doesn't break soon*, he thought, *I'm gonna piss right here in my shorts.* He was sprawled on the sweltering tarmac in the hot afternoon Mediterranean sun. He wondered if he would develop skin cancer from the massive sunburn he was getting on his back and legs. He and Demetrius had been lying on the concrete for almost two hours.

Shit, he thought, *when I said the hard way, I never imagined this goddamn hard.*

Demetrius had been fidgeting more in the past thirty minutes. Hayes hoped the Cypriot didn't lose his nerve and try to bolt. Neither of them would have a chance. *Some goddamn operator I am*, he thought. *Here I am during a hostage crisis lying in my fucking underwear, sunbathing, unarmed.* He considered where he should go when and if the shooting started. He figured it wouldn't be long. He supposed he would try to grab Demetrius and dash behind the APU still attached to the truck. It was the only thing that might stop a bullet.

***

1506 Hours

Abu Hassim grew tired of staring at the two men on the tarmac. He settled down to rest, and wait. Fatigue had overcome his immediate impatience. During the past twenty-four hours, his emotional expenditure had been great. He was exhausted, angry, and worried. He closed his eyes and fell immediately asleep. The passengers who could see him let out a sigh. There would be a few brief moments of peace.

Abdul returned to the cockpit to talk with Hamud over the radio. He was the lone remaining sympathetic voice. He was, in a sense, Abdul's counselor, if a distant one.

"Abdul," said Hamud, "you must not give up your leadership role now. You are still in charge, you can still control events."

"That is easy for you to say."

"But it is true. You must continue to exert your influence over the others. The Lebanese and American governments are making progress in the Beirut negotiations, and they will eventually repair the runway. My government wants you to return to Beirut so that this is no longer our problem. Therefore, I urge you, don't risk losing everything now. I'm sure that by tomorrow we will have something."

"Tomorrow!"

"Diplomacy takes time, Abdul, and the Lebanese government is not being cooperative. That is not our fault, nor the Americans. I am told the Americans offered a considerable amount of money to the Lebanese government to accomplish what you want."

The Lebanese government, thought Abdul, *that's a joke.* "They were cooperative enough to close the airport to us."

"Abdul, the Lebanese government closed the airport, not the Americans, and it certainly wasn't the Americans who cratered the runway," said Hamud. For a few seconds Abdul was silent, and Hamud sensed an opening. "Abdul, I want you to consider what I am about to say. This whole affair can end easily, and you will have sent your message to the world. I'm sure the Cypriot government would assure your safe return to Beirut."

"No. You understand nothing. If we were to give up and return to Beirut, we would be exiled or killed." *In fact*, he thought, *if we fail in this mission, Mustafa will make us wish we were dead.*

How could one negotiate surrender, pondered Hamud, with someone whose only choices were death at the hands of the enemy, or an even more fearful death at the hands of his own people? "Abdul," he said. "You would not even have to return to Lebanon if you did not want to."

"Don't give me your useless ideas. And where is our fuel?"

"I passed your demand on to my government. I was told that they are working on it. Abdul, in the meantime, do at least one thing for me. Let the two Cypriot workers return. They are not your enemy."

"I cannot." Abdul threw the headset at the pilot. It was the truth.

15

General Holt briefed Sinclair on the results of the meeting with the president; the operation remained on hold. Holt informed Sinclair that the president had reacted poorly to the news of the Delta operator and the Cypriot national being held hostage on the tarmac.

The president had referenced Desert One and Mayaguez, two American military operations that had gone sour and resulted in American lives lost. The president had stated that he would not have a failed military operation on his watch. Holt ordered Sinclair to continue negotiations.

In a way, Sinclair understood the president's reluctance to commit to an assault. Special operations such as this one carried high risk. Any number of things could go wrong in an instant.

Still, the president's decision disappointed Sinclair. He had instructed Barrington to prepare his team for an assault. Now they would stand down. Sinclair had felt certain, based on this new threat by the terrorists, that the president would give his approval. He feared a repeat of Kuwaiti Air 422, where hijackers at this same airport had killed hostages until they received fuel, then flew away to Algiers. *How many lives is a lousy load of fuel worth?* he wondered.

***

Air France 622, 1614 Hours

Abu Hassim awoke. His sleep had been fitful and restless. Something had startled him, a dream perhaps. He surveyed the plane's cabin. It was quiet. Some passengers slumped listlessly against their neighbors, a few slept. Most just sat, silent, staring ahead with vapid eyes. They wore dull expressions of pain and fear. Abu's two comrades stood guard. The two flight attendants went about their work.

Hassim was in pain. His ears still rang, and he decided that one or more of his ribs must be broken because he was having difficulty breathing. No man had ever hurt him before in hand-to-hand combat. Even though this man was an infidel, Abu Hassim had to admit, grudgingly, a certain respect for the American who had fought him so fiercely in the galley.

Abu looked down at his watch, and a large bead of sweat dripped from his dark beard onto the watch face. He studied it as if he had never before observed such a phenomenon. Beads of perspiration dotted his dark, angular face. His clothing was soaked, and he felt sticky and wet. The mid-afternoon Mediterranean sun bore relentlessly down on the Airbus. The air inside was stifling, heavy, and foul.

He looked about for several seconds and shook his head to bring himself fully awake. It seemed that no matter how hard he shook his head, though, he could not stop the ringing and pain in his ears.

Still shaking his head, he thought, *Surely, by now, they have brought fuel for the plane.* He stood and stretched. It hurt. Every muscle protested. He was tired, sore, thirsty, in pain, and hungry. Worse, apprehension had set in. His dream had startled him, and his paranoia was building. He feared the Cypriots were stalling and that somehow a trap was being set.

Abu Hassim stretched again in a vain effort to relax his tense and overworked muscles. He slowly walked to a concealed position near the open doorway. He exchanged a few words with Mohammed by the door. The two men on the tarmac had not moved. He went to the cockpit and found Abdul. "What is our situation?"

Abdul hoped that perhaps the brief rest had done the man some good. He seemed calm. Where Abu Hassim was concerned, Abdul knew, outward appearances could be deceiving. This was a complicated and troubled man. He was aware that this tranquility was probably superficial. "No change," he finally responded. "The authorities are still working to open Beirut airport for us."

"Authorities," muttered Abu Hassim. "And the fuel?"

"Not yet, but they are working on it."

"When will they bring it?" he asked heavily, the tension already mounting in his voice.

Abdul did not answer.

"I fear that they are playing games with us."

"No," replied Abdul, less forcefully than he would have liked.

"Yes," scoffed Abu. He poked his big finger against Abdul's chest. "*We* are born into the Jihad, and *we* must die for it, gloriously, or like whimpering dogs. *We* will not die like dogs. If we must die, it will be as martyrs. I will make them listen. We will have fuel, and we will leave this place. There is danger here. I feel it. It surrounds us."

"And where will we go?"

"I do not know." He spat on the floor. "Algiers. Rabat. Malta. Anywhere away from here. It was a mistake to come here. Give me the microphone." He snatched the handset from Abdul's hand and stared into the smaller man's eyes until Abdul looked away. The pilots remained silent, staring straight ahead out the cockpit window.

"Hello, tower, hello," Abu Hassim said in Arabic. "Answer me."

***

In Delta's command post, a translator's head jerked up sharply, his eyes popping open. "A new voice," he called out as he leaned forward and began typing the English translation into the computer. In the tower at Larnaca, Hamud caught it as well.

"Yes, Air France," answered Hamud, "this is tower control."

"Why have you not brought fuel for this airplane?"

"We are simply waiting to get clearance for a landing in Beirut."

"The waiting is over. You will send fuel for this airplane before thirty minutes are up, or I will execute a hostage."

This shocked Hamud—*thirty minutes!* He had effectively stalled the hijackers without a significant violent action for over fifteen long hours. *How much longer does Colonel Sinclair expect me to keep this up?*

"But we are doing everything we can to help you. You *must* wait a little longer. You will ruin everything we've worked for."

Hamud's ploy almost worked. Even Abu Hassim hesitated. It probably would have made any other man have second thoughts, but Hassim was becoming angry.

He reflected for a moment, and then said, "You speak like an Arab, but I feel that you are not. What are you?"

This shook Hamud even more. *Who is this man? He's mentally unbalanced, a ruthless murderer; but he possesses piercing instincts, like he can reach across the airwaves and see into my soul. Nonsense,* he thought. *I'm just tired. He is only a man. I am Doctor Hamud, a professional, the best negotiator available. I've ended more hostage situations through negotiation than the next ten negotiators combined. I must not give into to my own feelings. I must remain detached and professional. Lives depend on it.*

Hamud called the terrorist again, but precious seconds had been lost. Abu Hassim would have no more discussion. He had left the cockpit.

In Delta's CP, Sinclair felt that it may already be too late. The chain of command, in Sinclair's opinion, followed a cumbersome route. It wound circuitously through special operations command and the office of the deputy chief of staff for operations; then the chairman of the joint chiefs and the secretary of defense would have their say. Finally, the chain wound its way into the White House national security staff and ultimately to the president. It was more streamlined than in the early days of special ops, but even so, this chain of command had already proven ponderous. Sinclair notified the Pentagon again, and Hamud continued his attempts to restore contact with Abdul.

***

Onboard Air France 622, the fear was palpable. Abu Hassim's rage grew. He could never control it. At times like these, it seemed to consume him altogether. Now, he yearned for its blinding effects to help him carry out the ugly task he knew he must perform. He walked into the galley, lowered himself onto a small stool that folded down from the wall, and hung his head.

Marie and Eva cautiously backed out of the galley and went to their seats.

After a few minutes, he slowly stood, unfolding his large frame one section at a time. Then he moved into the passenger cabin and began to roam the aisles. He would work himself into a fit of rage. It was his only escape.

He stalked the aisles of Air France 622. He muttered to himself and waved his pistol back and forth. He screamed at his hostages with all the energy he could muster. Occasionally, he viciously shook one. All the while, he searched for a victim.

Soon, Abu Hassim stopped dead in his tracks. He fixed his uncomely eyes on a young man, a boy who looked barely eighteen. Dean Bradford looked away. He had already witnessed the rage of this man numerous times. The boy's mother was sitting next to him, but his father had remained at work in the embassy. The mother's intuition urged her to ignore the terrorist's stare, but it would not go away. Instead, it hardened.

Dean Bradford's bright-blond hair stood in sharp contrast to his expensive, yet wrinkled, navy-blue blazer. He shifted, but the menacing stare remained. *Perfect*, thought Abu Hassim. In the Middle East, psychological warfare played an important role in daily affairs. *The Cypriots are weak*, he reminded himself. *One lifeless body like this young boy*, he thought, *and there will be no further questions or hesitation when we give instructions.*

Abu Hassim tucked his pistol into his belt. He reached down and wrapped his thick fingers around the boy's scarlet, silk tie. With the other, he unsnapped the seat belt. Horror consumed Martha Bradford's face. A scream tried in vain to escape her lungs, but she seemed incapable of movement. Hassim jerked the youth from his seat. Only then did the mother's panicky scream finally emerge. She unbuckled her seatbelt and tried to lunge at the big terrorist, but Khalid was standing over her. He pressed his hand to her shoulder, holding her down. She could not move.

She helplessly watched the huge man drag her son up the aisle. Her screams turned to hysterical sobs. Mascara streamed down her cheeks and onto her neck and white blouse in thick, black lines. Then Khalid snapped open a knife and cut her bindings. He pushed her head forward, jerked her arms behind her back, and fastened her wrists with another cinch strap. He pushed her back into her seat as she screamed from both physical and emotional pain. He fastened her seatbelt and cinched it tight.

Up front, the big man signaled for Mohammed to open the forward, portside passenger door. Abu Hassim pushed the boy to the door, spun him around, and shoved the frightened young man down onto his knees in the open doorway. Below, Hayes and Demetrius looked on. The violent drop to the floor hurt Dean's knees so badly that he started to cry. Only hours before, he had been dreaming about college in the fall. Now he was kneeling in the doorway of this godforsaken plane on this rock of an island somewhere in the middle of nowhere. He was confused and afraid.

Abu Hassim leaned over, very close, and whispered into Dean Bradford's ear. "Not move," he growled in his rudimentary English. The boy squirmed as he felt the terrorist's scruffy beard against his ear. The man's fetid breath made him flinch. He jerked his head away, but the terrorist grabbed him by the back of the neck, digging his fingers into the flesh. He twisted the boy's head and repeated his words. Dean grimaced. Finally, the big Arab went away.

Relieved that the man had at least moved away, Dean looked out the door. In the distance, shimmering waves of heat rose lazily from the tarmac. Just in front of him was a small yellow truck with a trailer of some sort. Two men lay in their underwear on the pavement to either side of the vehicle. Sergeant Hayes was looking up at the terrified boy, who was weeping and sucking in heaving gulps of air, his body shuddering each time he did so.

Hayes knew that his teammates were probably maneuvering into position. He pondered the actions he should take when Delta assaulted and the shooting began. He was unarmed. *Best just to stay out of the way, take cover, get Demetrius behind something,* he thought. Still, the horrid vision of these men executing this boy was more than he could bear. He even considered climbing the wing and rushing the plane—but for what? He was unarmed. *Shit,* he thought, *I wish I had some kind of goddamn weapon.* He glanced back up at the boy.

"Crap," he mumbled to himself, lowering his forehead to the tarmac. *Please God, don't let them hurt him. He's just a kid.*

***

Though Lynn Elliot had no idea that someone named Hayes even existed, she was sharing nearly the same thought as he, along with many other hostages—*Please don't let them hurt that boy.*

She couldn't see Dean Bradford kneeling in the doorway for the seatbacks in front of her, but she *had* witnessed the big terrorist drag him there and shove him down. Tears ran down Lynn's cheeks as she tried to hold back the flood of emotions overwhelming her. She wanted to be strong and not totally lose it. But the feelings cascaded over her in uncontrollable rolling waves—fear, loathing, anger, sadness, helplessness, hope.

Is there anything I can do? she wondered. *Should I try something? What? Run over and push him out? No, that would just kill or maim him. What good would that do? Volunteer to take his place? That would not be fair to Mike, though that's probably what he would do if he could.*

Lynn closed her eyes tightly and took several deep breaths. Her rib felt a little better. Maybe it wasn't broken after all. At least that was some good news.

But for the moment, she just wanted to calm herself and her emotions.

***

Seated in the front row not far from Lynn, Marie, unfortunately, had a perfectly clear view of the sobbing young man kneeling in the open doorway just fifteen feet to her left. Sitting next to her, Eva cried as well.

Marie wanted to get up and go to the galley and be busy again, but after all this, she was just too terrified to move. She was also very afraid for this poor boy and his mother.

Would they really harm him? Even murder him? she asked herself. *Is that even possible?*

Marie simply refused to believe that even this beast of a man who had put him there, could harm this innocent, beautiful young boy. This was all just a big bluff to get attention, or to get *something* they wanted.

The terrorists still yelled and intimidated everybody occasionally, especially the big one, but once they had let her and Eva move about and see to everyone's needs, it made them seem a little more human.

She had begun to truly believe that this nightmare would end peacefully, and they would all walk off of this plane and go home.

That will still happen! she told herself. *It will all end soon, and peacefully.*

Praying that she would not fall victim to one of the terrorist's rage, she got up, went to Mrs. Bradford, put her arms around the wailing woman, and tried her best to comfort the distraught mother.

*** *** ***

Sinclair turned away from the video monitor. The thought of them killing this boy scared him to death, too, but the president of the United States had denied him permission to assault. His hands were tied.

If he moved against the plane now, without the president's authorization, and was successful, they probably wouldn't court martial him. He would just quietly retire. If, on the other hand, even one hostage was killed, he would be held responsible, both professionally and criminally. There would likely be a court martial and prison.

Wilson walked up to Colonel Sinclair. "Sir, we have to give Barclay and Palmer some guidance, there's only fifteen minutes left."

Sinclair watched the video monitor above the communications console. He had stared at the handsome young boy's face for nearly fifteen minutes, thinking of his own son. *The boy is so damn close*, he thought, *I could almost reach out and touch him. What would I do if it were my boy? Would I order an assault, even without permission? Is this boy's life worth a career? Is it worth a load of fuel? Is it worth going to Leavenworth for?*

Sinclair could have assaulted, before, but now he had wasted the past hour on the Pentagon—time he could have used to launch the birds and have them in orbit within striking distance of the airport. If he moved now, there would not be enough time to get the choppers on station.

Sinclair looked up at Wilson. "We can't sit here and watch them kill that boy, and if we take out Number Three without following up with an assault, it'll cause a bloodbath. Then they'll just fly away without enough fuel to get anywhere. Noah, get with Steven and have him get a truck ready. We're giving them the goddamn fuel. Have him tell Hamud to let the bastards know it's on the way. Just have him tell them we don't know about Beirut yet. And Noah, put the snipers on hold."

"Yes, sir," he replied, already on the move. Wilson knew that once the plane flew away, his commander, and probably he as well, would pay the price for disobeying the president, but Wilson followed his colonel's orders. He also silently vowed to ensure that Barclay and Barrington were absolved of any wrongdoing.

Wilson returned. "Sir, I've informed Steven to give them the fuel. He's moving now to get a truck out to the plane. Hamud's going to tell them to put the boy back in his seat and calm down."

"Okay," said Sinclair, lowering his head to his hands. "They've fucking won."

"We did all we could, sir. It stinks, but if the White House isn't ready, there's not much we can do about it."

Sinclair said, "And Noah, when the shit hits the fan back home, this is on me."

Wilson didn't respond; he just walked away. He had every intention of standing firm beside his commander.

Sinclair looked back up at the live video transmission of Dean Bradford kneeling in the doorway. The boy was crying.

***

Sinclair's thoughts drifted back to that dreadful night nine years ago. He was a young lieutenant colonel then, just selected for battalion command. His career was about to take off. His son was doing well in school. They were happy at Fort Bragg.

He was watching TV. His twelve-year old boy had gone to a ballgame. Sinclair usually went too, but he had worked late and missed the game.

He heard a knock on the door but paid it no mind, sure that it was one of the neighbors dropping by for gossip. His wife answered it. The next thing he heard was his wife as she collapsed to the floor. He ran to the door. A military police officer, a new second lieutenant, was bending over her, looking dumbfounded, his mouth hanging open. He was mumbling, "I'm sorry, sir. I'm sorry."

Sinclair scooped up his wife and carried her to the couch. The lieutenant followed. Somewhere outside, he could hear a dispatcher's voice on a radio blaring out across the housing area.

"I'm sorry, sir," he was still muttering as Sinclair stood and clasped the young officer firmly by the shoulders.

"Calm down. Calm down. What the hell's going on, Lieutenant?"

The young man's eyes were misty. He had to swallow hard before he could speak. "I shouldn't have just told her like that. But I didn't...I..."

Sinclair shook him. "Told her what?"

He calmed down and looked into Sinclair's eyes. "I'm sorry, sir. It's your boy. We just got a call from the North Carolina state police. A drunk in a pickup truck out on the interstate hit the Jackson's car head-on. He was headed east in the westbound lane. He hit them head-on," he repeated, now mumbling.

Sinclair felt weak. He was suddenly trembling.

"All three of them, sir. Instantly. Mrs. Jackson, her son, and your son. They didn't have a chance."

Sinclair staggered back. He heard his wife moaning on the couch. The room seemed a blur. He felt confused. Sick.

***

Sinclair shook his head and focused on the video monitor. Dean Bradford was still kneeling in the doorway of the hijacked airplane.

Sinclair watched him for a moment, wondering what the kid might be thinking. He glanced at his watch. "Noah," he called out, "we've only got five minutes left. Check with Steven and see if everything's going all right." Before Wilson could get to the secure radio handset, Barclay called.

"Colonel Sinclair, Barclay here."

"Go ahead, Steven," said Wilson. "He's listening."

"Sir, we've got a problem. The Cypriots won't give them any fuel."

Sinclair jumped from his chair and snatched the handset from Wilson.

"Dammit, why?" he cried into the mic.

"Sir, they refuse to give in to the terrorists' demands."

"What the hell happened to this *full cooperation* bullshit?" yelled Sinclair. "Can you commandeer a truck?" He knew as soon as the words left his mouth that it was a stupid suggestion, an act of desperation.

"I could, sir," was Barclay's calm reply. "But some Cypriot security people might get seriously hurt in the process."

"Forget it, Steven, I didn't mean it."

"Understood, sir. Our time's about up. Hamud's working on it, but we've stalled them so many hours already, he's getting real worried."

"What are the chances Number Three's bluffing, Steven?"

"Not good."

"Standby."

Only a few years back, Sinclair recalled, the Cypriots had let Arab terrorists murder four passengers before they finally relented and gave them fuel. *How many would it take this time?* he wondered.

"Steven."

"Sir?"

"What's Palmer's position?"

"We moved them up a bit when we were asking for an assault. He could move in a little closer, but he'll be pretty exposed."

"Steven," said Sinclair again, pausing to glance up at the video monitor and look at young Dean Bradford one more time.

"Sir?" responded Barclay.

"Tell Hamud to buy thirty more minutes. Promise them anything. I don't want any goddamn excuses from him. Tell him to do it. Keep working on the fuel. That's my first choice. But if it doesn't work, I'm sending Scott in."

"Wilco."

Sinclair turned to Wilson. "Tell Palmer to be ready. If they start to shoot the boy, tell him sniper weapons are free, and Eagle moves out on the first shot. They're to take out as many terrorists as possible. Tell Palmer I'm launching the birds, instructions to follow."

"Yes, sir." Wilson turned to give Barrington the order to move out, but he was already on the run. Sinclair knew that the president had not given his permission for either the fuel or an assault. He thought only briefly about the military retirement he would never see. He knew his wife would understand.

Sinclair reasoned that if he could get ten more minutes, Master Sergeant Palmer would be in position closer to the plane— if they were not spotted first. If the terrorists would give them twenty more minutes, he could fly Barrington's team in and hit them with the primary assault element. Either way was risky. He had to act, and he knew his men felt the same way. He also knew that he alone would bear full responsibility for his actions—not his men.

***

1715 Hours

Abu Hassim spoke into the microphone. "Your time is up."

"Listen to me. I implore you," urged Hamud. "My government has agreed to give you your fuel. Just give us time to organize it."

"How much time?"

"A few minutes, it's coming."

"You want time to organize your attack. We are not stupid," shouted Abu Hassim. "This is a big airport. I know you have many trucks. You only need to drive one to this plane."

"No, the fuel handlers are afraid. They don't want to do it. We are bringing a supervisor in from off duty. Just give us a few minutes."

Abu Hassim paused to absorb this information. "No," he said finally. "You are stalling. There will be no more of it."

He tossed the mic over the pilot's shoulder and stomped around in the cramped cockpit. He heard Hamud calling over the radio. Abu Hassim knew he must decide. He was tired of games.

***

In a nearby maintenance hangar, Lieutenant Colonel Barclay wanted to throttle the little Cypriot colonel. Krokos, though, was tougher than first impressions revealed; his hawkish features were void of expression.

"My government decided from the beginning that it would not furnish fuel. Maybe your president didn't bother to tell you, but *no fuel* was part of the agreement between our two countries. Cyprus has long since replaced Beirut as the Middle Eastern center for drug trafficking, espionage, slavery, and a host of other sordid enterprises. These activities interfere with our tourism industries.

"The only reason my government turned this affair over to you in the first place was because we assumed that you Americans would attack the hijackers and quickly resolve the crisis. You have not, and my government might soon reassert its sovereignty in the matter. We will give the terrorists nothing! This will be a firm signal to would-be hijackers not to come to Cyprus—and if you Americans won't take care of this matter, maybe the Cypriot security forces will."

Barclay, almost blue in the face, just starred at the little Cypriot colonel. There was going to be no reasoning with him. Barclay relayed this new information about the agreement to Colonel Sinclair.

***

Dean Bradford's knees hurt badly, and his legs were starting to cramp. His face was wet with tears. He wished his hands weren't tied. He could swing down through the doorway, drop to the ground, and run. He knew, though, that he couldn't abandon his mother. Peeping over his shoulder, Dean could see the four terrorists huddled together about ten feet behind him. He wanted to block everything out, but he was afraid and couldn't quite manage it.

Abu Hassim glanced from his comrades to the boy. Abu did not fear his own death, or killing. He had spilled the blood of his enemies on countless occasions. He did not kill for pleasure, however, as did many men he knew. He would only take a life when necessary.

"We have passed the deadline," he said to the other three men. They were silent, but they nodded. Abdul returned to the cockpit. Mohammed and Khalid moved to their customary guard positions in the front and rear of the plane. Abu Hassim turned to face the boy, whose back was to him. Dean Bradford stared vacantly out the open door.

Abu Hassim removed the pistol from his belt and pulled the slide back until he saw the brassy glint of a 9mm round seated in the chamber. Mrs. Bradford saw the pistol, too, along with Marie, Lynn, and the hostages seated near the front. Dean's mother sucked in a deep breath and her nostrils flared; her eyes registered shock.

In the tower, unable to talk to the terrorists, Hamud was on the verge of desperation. Finally, after what seemed an eternity of trying, he reached Abdul in the cockpit.

"Abdul, what are you going to do? Please, do not do anything rash. Give us just a few more minutes. I swear to you we are preparing the fuel."

Over the cockpit radio, Abdul said to Hamud, "No, it is too late. You will have time before the second execution."

Abu Hassim turned and took the first of ten steps to young Dean Bradford. Mrs. Bradford let out an ear-shattering scream. She howled at the top of her lungs and thrashed in her seat. Khalid went over to her and slapped her into silence. Other passengers began screaming. Some looked around in dazed confusion. Others cried through hoarse, dry voices. Some hid their faces.

Back in the van, Barclay spoke calmly into the mic, "Eagle-one, engage target Number Three, weapons free." One of Master Sergeant Palmer's snipers, lying in the grass not four hundred yards from where Dean Bradford knelt, had already trained the cross hairs of his riflescope precisely six inches above Dean Bradford's head. He flipped off the safety, steadied his breath, and waited for the target to walk into position behind the boy.

From the tarmac outside the Airbus, Dwight Hayes heard screams coming from within the plane. He looked up and met the boy's searching eyes. Inside them, Hayes saw confusion and fear. He felt a sadness he had never before experienced. He wanted to move, to do something. He wanted to rush forward, wave his arms, and yell for the boy to jump. He was sure, however, that an assault was seconds away. He kept his discipline to avoid alerting the terrorists and putting his teammates in danger.

Abu Hassim stepped up behind and to the side of the boy. He remained concealed. The sniper could see only a pistol and a hand, just as those watching the video display could see. The sniper spoke urgently into his lip mic, "Eagle, negative target, negative target, over."

Abu Hassim did not hesitate. He mouthed a silent prayer and pulled the trigger.

On the tarmac, Dwight Hayes recoiled at the sound of the shot. It was as if he had been the one shot. It felt to him like he was outside his own body, hovering above the tarmac. In this detached state, he saw himself, his own body, the body of Staff Sergeant Dwight Hayes, lying on the scorching tarmac. He was looking up and watching this boy just above him as he went limp and then tumbled seemingly in slow motion out the door of the plane. Dwight Hayes felt as if his nerves were on fire. He suddenly returned to his own body. He let his head drop to the tarmac, and he began to cry.

U.S. military men from Larnaca to the Pentagon stared, mouths agape, at the video transmission from Barclay's van via satellite. They watched the crumpled, lifeless body of Dean Bradford, the son of the State Department's political affairs officer in Tunisia, thump against the hard tarmac thirty feet below Air France 622. A puff of dust swirled up around the misshapen body.

In the CP, Sinclair stared for a moment at the video display in disbelief; then he dropped his head into his hands. It was too late. He could no longer help young Dean Bradford. Sinclair felt that old familiar surge of pain. He had worked hard at burying those emotional scars, but he could never bury them deep enough. He ordered a recall of Barrington's helicopters. They would wait.

Abu Hassim went into the cockpit, grabbed the copilot, and dragged him down the small corridor to the open passenger door. He told him in French to instruct the two men lying on the tarmac to take the body and go. Didier did so in English.

Hayes and Demetrius got up, unaware of the stiffness in their bodies. They walked slowly to Dean Bradford's corpse. Hayes gently picked up the boy's body and cradled it in his arms. Blood and tissue oozed over his arm. He didn't notice. He carried the boy to their truck. Demetrius opened the passenger door, and Hayes slid in, still holding the boy's body. They drove away.

Abu Hassim pulled the passenger door of the Airbus closed and stared at the two men through its porthole. Several minutes passed while Abu Hassim stood motionless behind the edge of the passenger doorway, the pistol in his limp hand. He lowered the hammer and replaced the weapon in his belt. He turned and said to Khalid, "Now, they will listen."

16

Air France 622

Mike was already alert and on edge from all the screaming up front. Then the shock wave from the 9mm cartridge reverberated through the cabin, jolting him like a lightning bolt. The pistol shot had electrified every nerve in his body. He sat frozen, eyes now wide, waiting. Others did the same.

Then the whispers started. A hushed murmur swept through the Airbus. "They killed him, oh my God. They killed him." Some passengers cried openly; some sobbed softly. A few moaned as they rocked back and forth in a mournful rhythm. Others sat motionless. From somewhere near the front of the plane, a mother's piercing wail renewed itself.

From his location in the rear of the plane, Mike could not be sure what had happened, but he assumed the worst. Death was no longer a distant fear. It had arrived.

Mike was still searching for a plan. There were at least four heavily armed, vicious, desperate terrorists. He would have to take out all of them to succeed. He had thought through various scenarios, but it was difficult to imagine one that would work. He knew, though, that he would have to try, and soon.

He could only do so, however, if he could free his hands. He felt around in the crack between the seat cushions behind his back and found the metal bar again. It was part of the seat frame. He also managed to touch the strap binding his wrists with one finger. It seemed to be plastic—a cable tie perhaps, maybe even two.

For hours, as the hijackers patrolled the aisles, he cautiously and quietly tried to rub the strap around his wrists against that metal bar in the seat, but it was awkward and painful. He could not even be sure that he was making good contact between the strap and the metal bar, but he continued trying.

***

Akrotiri CP

For the second time in only a few short hours, circumstances forced Sinclair to secure his team from immediate strike alert. He had been prepared to commit his forces without authorization, but it had been an emotional decision to send Barrington and his men to attack the plane—not cold calculating military logic, or even good tactics.

It was too late to help Dean Bradford. It would be better to conduct a planned assault, he reasoned. He decided, though, that there would not be a second execution. The president's reluctance to commit Delta to an assault had resulted in an unnecessary death. They had warned the president this would happen.

Sinclair jerked up the handset from the console in front of him and called General Holt in the Pentagon. "Sir, did you receive the transmission of the video?"

"Yes, Sam, we did. I'm sorry," said the general.

"Tell it to the boy's mother. Hell, sir, he was seventeen, eighteen at most. We could have prevented it. And why wasn't I told that the U.S. had agreed from the beginning not to give fuel?"

"Sam, we feel as badly about this as you do, I assure you. The secretary and the chairman have both seen the tape. We're sick about it. As for the fuel, we had no choice. The Cypriots wouldn't give us authorization unless we agreed. The president wanted to keep it close hold."

"Well, sir," replied Sinclair, "I suggest you take the tape to the White House and tell the president we can't do our jobs here with our hands tied. I plan to assault that aircraft and rescue those hostages at 0500 hours unless you relieve me of command here and now. I also plan to mount an immediate assault if the bastards put another hostage in the door."

"Sam," the general responded. "The first thing I want you to do is to calm down. You know we're behind you on this."

Sinclair took a long, deep breath and slowly let it out. He knew the military leadership's hands were tied just like his. They were just following orders, but Sinclair was a little rougher around the edges than these general officers. That was why he would never be one. It was a given. Sinclair spoke his mind when it suited him and took risks that the more refined elite might be reluctant to take. He was the unpolished warrior, a valuable but ultimately expendable breed of soldier.

Holt continued, "Sam, I understand your plans, and we're going to the president with the video. Hopefully I'll get you a release."

"Fine, sir," said Sinclair more calmly, but then he added in a deliberate tone, "and sir, if the president is not ready to do this, he can get someone else to sit over here on his ass and watch these bastards execute young American boys." He hung up the receiver.

Sinclair turned to his exec, Wilson. "I want Hamud talking to Abdul again. We're going to try a new tact. We'll tell them there will be no fuel for now."

Stalling them had not worked, and since he didn't have much choice with the Cypriots controlling the fuel, Sinclair decided to seize the initiative and take the direct approach. They would tell the terrorists that for now, there would be no fuel, no matter how many hostages they executed. There were obvious risks, but Sinclair was betting on the fact that Arabs respected authority and power over persuasion. He had no choice but to try.

***

Air France 622

Marie was standing in the galley when the gunshot had shattered the still air. She had turned to face the wall, her back to Dean Bradford, fearful of what was about to happen, once the terrorists had gathered in the cabin near the galley.

Then the shot, and she jumped. Her heart thumped brutally in her chest, and blood pounded viciously in her ears. It was a long moment before she sucked in another breath. Then the mother's wails, and the passengers' screams, began anew. She stood there, frozen in place like a statue, afraid that if she moved she would shatter like glass.

She took several more deep breaths, turned, walked out of the galley, and went to the mother. Marie knelt and put her arms around the rocking, sobbing woman. She tried to soothe her, but there was no comfort for this grieving mother. Her world had just ended.

At this moment, Marie didn't really care if the terrorists turned on her and attacked her. She stroked the mother's hair and talked softly to her.

***

Lynn sat perfectly still, her eyes closed. The ear-shattering gunshot, only three rows in front of her seat, had stunned her completely. Somehow, the massive flood of emotions that had overwhelmed her earlier had vanished. Now she just felt numb.

She had watched Marie face death by going to the mother of the dead boy. Lynn was in complete awe of her selfless bravery. She had continued to watch for a while as Marie knelt by the woman, embraced her, and rocked with her, stroking the woman's hair, talking to her, even as Marie cried too.

Lynn couldn't bear it any longer. She had to close her eyes and struggle not to keep hearing that gunshot repeatedly in her imagination. But it wouldn't go away, and each time she heard it again in her mind, her skinned jumped.

Then the tears came.

***

Abdul sat in the cockpit trying to make sense of the events that had swarmed past him during the last few days. Had it been an error to push so aggressively for this mission? He had convinced Mustafa that he, Abdul, was the only possible choice to lead such a mission. After all, he had successfully spearheaded the Tunisian campaign. *What ignorance. Now look at the mess I'm in*, he thought. He was not even in charge any longer. Abu was, or the Cypriots were. *And*, he thought, *Mustafa is not lenient with failures.*

A familiar voice pulled Abdul from his dismal soul-searching. "Abdul? Abdul, are you there?" It was Hamud's voice coming over the cockpit loudspeaker. The two pilots ignored it and stared dumbly at the lifeless instruments. Hamud called several more times before Abdul reached for the microphone hanging by its cord over the back of the pilot's chair.

"I am here."

"You are back," replied Hamud with unconcealed elation. "We must talk again."

"The only thing we need to discuss is the fuel that you have failed to bring to us."

The radio was silent for several seconds before Hamud responded. "Abdul, listen carefully to me for a minute, and let me explain the details before you get upset," he said, pausing only briefly. "I have just been informed by my government that our president, Mr. Dhimitsianos, has reserved the authority to give you fuel only for himself. No one here at the airport, or elsewhere in the government, can give it to you. And for now, he will not authorize it."

Abdul's chest began to swell with air, but Hamud quickly went on. "But, Abdul, before you go into a rage let me explain to you the situation. All is not lost. Let me tell you why."

There was no reply.

"Abdul? Do you hear me?"

"Yes, I hear you. And I will give *you* something to hear. You will have another body to carry away from this plane."

"Abdul, do you not at least want to hear another way?"

After nearly a minute, Abdul responded. "Yes then," he muttered angrily into the microphone. "Please, do tell me why all is not lost."

"For now, there is no military threat against you. My government instructed me to assure you of this fact. It comes directly from our president. My government does not want to provoke any more violence. As I understand the situation, my president is waiting to see the results of the American administration's negotiations with Beirut. I am told that progress is being made in that area, and we believe that our president will give you fuel and let you fly away to Beirut.

"Don't you see, Abdul, in that manner it would be the Americans, not the Cypriots, who give in? Our president will never bow to threats of violence. If you kill again, you could provoke the Cypriot government into unleashing its military against you. The military would love nothing more. You would just be playing into the generals' hands and worsening your own situation. Not improving it."

Hamud paused, and then continued while he had momentum. "The reports that we have here indicate that the runway in Beirut will finally be repaired and open to traffic sometime this evening. I believe that the Americans will produce an agreement tonight, and I think that by early tomorrow morning you will be able to have your fuel and fly away from here to your home. The Cypriot political leadership would like nothing better than to be rid of this problem with no further bloodshed, and they would be able to blame it on the Americans. This is the truth, Abdul," he said solemnly. "Abdul? Are you listening to me?"

Abdul was indeed listening, and he, too, believed. It was all so logical, so clear now. He could already taste the sweet victory of a triumphant landing in Beirut and a joyous reunion with their Shiite brothers. The Shiite ground commander in Beirut had sown the seeds of failure when he failed to keep the airport runway open. When all was said and done, he, Abdul el-Aziz, would have successfully held out in Cyprus against all odds, ultimately to return to Beirut a hero.

His main problem was Abu Hassim. He somehow had to convince the brute not to kill again and to let Abdul handle this situation.

"Abdul?" repeated Hamud.

"Yes, yes, I am here."

"Did you hear everything I said?"

"Yes, I heard."

"I know it was your comrade's voice on the radio just before the execution, and I assume that it was he who shot the passenger. Abdul, you are the leader. You must set the course. I only want to see this thing end, eventually, with no more bloodshed. But only you can ensure your own victory by avoiding additional violence. Do you not think that this is so, Abdul?"

"Yes," he admitted. "Perhaps we will talk later. I must think now."

"As you like, Abdul. I will be here when you are ready."

The terrorist leader slumped down into the engineer's chair and rested his elbows on the small worktable. Before him was an instrument panel of incomprehensible gauges, buttons, and switches that ran together in a bizarre, multicolored, electronic patchwork.

He had long since gotten over his hesitation to send a message to Mustafa. Now, he desperately wanted to contact him. If only he could. He had repeatedly attempted to get a signal on both of his phones, to no avail.

If only I could contact him, thought Abdul, *and get his instructions. He would know the best course to take and could advise me about conditions in Beirut.*

Abdul felt exhausted. He could not remember ever feeling this drained. He would have to summon enormous strength from somewhere, though, because the task ahead was daunting. He needed to reassert his authority over Abu Hassim. That would be the only way to avoid an attack by the Cypriot Army and ultimately to reach Beirut and success.

The problem, however, was Abu Hassim's mental state. Abdul had suspected for some time that the man had mental problems. Those suspicions were proving correct—he was mentally unbalanced, and his behavior was totally unpredictable. Nevertheless, Abdul had to reassert control. It was their only hope.

First, though, he needed just a few minutes to gather his strength, and his courage.

Abdul reached down and felt the small book in the side leg pocket of his trousers. After a moment, he slipped it out and turned it over in his hands, tracing the fine cover with his finger before thumbing through several pages. The delicate vellum sheets were trimmed in gold colored ink. Intricate designs of vines and leaves decorated the edges of each page. The Arabic print was of extremely high quality. This book was Abdul's life, and it was his only family heirloom.

Abdul held it in the palm of his left hand. He opened it and read passages at random. It comforted him.

***

1736 Hours

Abdul could not see Abu Hassim, but he knew that the big man was pacing around, fuming over their situation. He knew that he had waited long enough, too long, in fact. He would have to go out there now and make them listen to his plan. If he showed the slightest weakness, the slightest doubt about the plan or his own leadership, Abu Hassim would laugh in his face and select another hostage for execution.

He sucked in a deep breath, raised himself up slowly from the chair, and exited the cockpit. He ordered Khalid to assemble the men in the galley. He stepped into the small kitchen near the aisle. As he waited, he watched Khalid, the youngest of the four, march to the rear of the plane to fetch Hassim. Mohammed, on guard near the forward door, eased nearer to Abdul, whose face was set. It was time.

"What is our situation now?" demanded Abu Hassim.

"That is precisely why I have called you together. To inform you of our situation, and our plan," said Abdul firmly. He held his calm. Abdul had decided that fate would guide his course. If destiny allowed, he would win this contest of wills with Abu Hassim. "There are those," he said slowly, looking at each of the other three men in turn, "who would take the role of leader and who would make our plans and issue the orders." He fixed his eyes on Abu Hassim. "This hostage execution has served its purpose. It has demonstrated our resolve. But now the situation has changed." He paused, but his gaze did not waver from the men.

"Now, here is our situation. Only the Cypriot president can say whether we shall have fuel, and for now he will not give it to us."

The three men burst into anxious chatter. Abu Hassim's voice soon rose above the din.

"You will all listen to me!" exploded Abdul. "I am still the leader here! You *will* listen to me. You *will* hear my plan, and you *will* obey it." Abdul's outburst left his comrades with their mouths agape. Mohammed Halid fidgeted. Khalid Moussa said nothing. Abu Hassim glared at him, but Abdul did not waver.

"This is our plan." Again, he looked firmly from one man to the next. "The Beirut airport runway will be repaired and reopened to traffic this evening. The Americans will reach an agreement tonight with the Christians to reopen the airport to us. Once this is accomplished, the Cypriot president will give us fuel. And tomorrow morning we will fly to Beirut."

"And they told you this?" scoffed Abu Hassim, pointing toward the cockpit.

Abdul barely hesitated. "It is what I know," he retorted. "I was chosen to lead this mission because I have the capability to reason and to plan based on such deductions of reason. And you, Abu Hassim," he said, looking unwaveringly into Hassim's eyes, "are a soldier, nothing more. It is not your destiny to plan the way of others. It is your destiny to follow. If not, our superiors would have made you the leader. But they did not, did they?"

The big man's stare melted. He knew that he was not in possession of the mental capacity to make intricate or detailed plans, to understand complex, confusing situations fraught with conflicting information. He never had and never would have such abilities. He knew that Abdul was right. Rage, fear, and emotion drove him, not brains. He never really understood what was taking place behind the scenes. Perhaps, though, Abdul understood these things better.

Hassim looked at Abdul, and his glare softened. "All right then, what must we do?"

Abdul's eyes became moist, and he had to choke back a burst of emotion. He put all his energies into maintaining his facade. He was the leader once again.

"As I said, we will wait through tonight for a satisfactory response from the Americans and the Cypriots. To kill another hostage now, would force the Cypriot president to release his military on us. If we wait, just a few more hours, we can gain everything. We *will* win this battle." Abdul paused and looked squarely at each of the men.

"We can see far around the plane. Our security is good. Nevertheless, we will remain vigilant. At the slightest hint of danger, we will fly away, even without the fuel. If by tomorrow there is no change, then they force us to resort to further violence, and we will dump one body after another from that door until they bring fuel, or until we run out of hostages to kill. But for now, we wait. Is that understood?"

The three men looked at each other, then back at Abdul and nodded.

"Good," he beamed. "Now return to your posts."

The men made their way back to their positions. Abdul watched Abu Hassim walk down the aisle to the rear of the plane. It was almost too much to believe that he had reasserted his influence over that monster. Abdul suspected Hassim would slip into more fits of rage. The man's mental state was precarious at best. For the moment, Abdul was happy to have won this contest of wills. With that matter temporarily resolved, he began to wonder if his plan really would prove to be the right one. Without fuel, though, he really had no choice but to wait.

17

El Mina, Lebanon, 1740 Hours

Though it was already late afternoon in the Lebanese port village of El Mina, some thirty-seven miles to the north of Beirut, the sun was still a bright yellow orb in the sky. It would have been warm but for the slight breeze from the sea. A trawler prepared to depart while Fawzi Mustafa waited on the quay. Nets were piled everywhere, leaving little room to walk along the wooden planks of the pier. The smell of fish permeated the air, and swarms of soaring gulls filled the sky overhead. They cawed and squealed impatiently for a morsel of fish.

A black Mercedes arrived with three men. A short, heavy-set man exited the vehicle and strode out onto the dock. Abbas Bachar was slightly bow-legged, and he bore a jagged scar across his large, sun-toughened jowl. In a vengeful fit, Mustafa had given him the scar with a rusty old sword when they were both twelve. Bachar had referred to his friend ever since as the Scimitar.

Mustafa hugged and kissed his trusted lieutenant as he would a brother. Only then did they speak.

"It is as you predicted, Fawzi," said the newly arrived man in Arabic, "Massoud Faoud is a tough little man. He has given very little. We did learn, however, that the Americans call him Cupid."

"We trusted Massoud," said Mustafa shaking his head with disdain. "We advanced him, protected him." He shot a sideways glance at his long time lieutenant. "One never really knows who one can trust."

Abbas Bachar squirmed under Fawzi Mustafa's gaze. He had been with Fawzi since childhood, but he knew that even the mere suspicion of treachery could lead to a slow and painful interrogation and death.

"Do you have everything you need?"

"Yes, if it plays out as we expect."

"It will," replied Mustafa, a languid grin arriving at his lips.

Bachar continued, "We also have a report from our man in Beagea's headquarters at the airport. It was the American who went there and met with Beagea."

"Yes," said Fawzi Mustafa, nodding and glancing at the men preparing the trawler. "I knew the good colonel would not do such a thing all alone. I expected him to make a show of it, but then it would have been much more logical, not to mention safer, for him to let the plane land. No, as I suspected, someone paid him a large sum of money. He will not live to spend it, though," he said, looking over his shoulder to survey the chaos of the busy fishing port. "Very well. And the plan is set?"

"Yes," replied Bachar. "It will not be easy."

"That is why you will see to this personally. Do not fail me, Abbas. This may all work out much better than I dared hope."

The smaller man nodded.

"Anything from Abdul?"

"No. I sent him an encrypted message instructing him to report his plans hours ago. I have heard nothing in return."

"That's to be expected. Someone, the Cypriots or the Americans, are jamming the signals. But I'm sure the plane is still sitting in Cyprus. If the Cypriots had stormed the plane, or if it had landed elsewhere, the media would have reported it. I also suspect that they *cannot* leave because the Cypriots have denied them refueling."

Glancing over his shoulder at the trawler behind him, Mustafa said, "I must go now. I will arrive in six hours time."

"What can you hope to accomplish there alone?" asked Abbas Bachar.

"Ah, but alone is the only way. We cannot invade Cyprus with a battalion of men. But one man, the right man, can do marvelous things."

"It is dangerous."

"Of course it is. Perhaps I can do nothing. If that is the case, then so be it. There will be other American targets to pursue. Perhaps not as grand as this one, but there will always be others. At any rate, do not worry, my friend. I will not sacrifice myself for this mission.

"I may be able, though, to help them hold it together long enough to get back to Beirut. Or, perhaps, ensure their deaths. But I must know if the Americans are there and if they will attack. If so, I will see what I can do. Maybe nothing," he said, with a shrug.

"We cannot let the Americans win. It makes them feel powerful and potent, and it defeats our efforts to humiliate them. Besides, my own reputation is at stake, the reputation of the Scimitar," he said with a wry grin.

"*Inshallah*," replied Bachar.

***

Akrotiri CP, 2015 Hours

The long awaited release authority had finally arrived. The president had reviewed the videotaped execution of young Dean Bradford. He was horrified. He had reluctantly agreed that such men were unlikely to surrender. He gave the word to go whenever Delta was ready.

Sinclair had feared that they might have to move quickly to prevent a second execution, but so far, that was not the case. Delta could not be sure, but Sinclair's plan appeared to be working. Three hours after Dean Bradford's execution, there had been no new threats or demands from the terrorists. Number Three was quiet. They could only hope he was asleep.

Now that Delta had the authorization to assault, Delta's men had much to do—provided the terrorists remained quiet. Sergeant Major Barrington wanted one more rehearsal. Then, it would be time to deploy the assault helicopters and his team of commandos to Dhekelia, the other British base on Cyprus, just up the coast from Larnaca airport. Once there, they would be only a few minutes striking distance by helicopter from the hijacked Airbus. Sinclair also wanted to get Staff Sergeant Jake Brady up on top of the plane to wire at least one of the closed doors with explosives, but preferably both.

If all went well, and if Delta could keep the terrorists quiet through the night, Sergeant Brady would be able to complete his mission ensuring that Delta would be able to gain access to the plane. Then at 0500 hours local, earlier if necessary, the assault would begin and end. It would last a mere handful of seconds.

***

Several hours had crawled slowly past since the death of Dean Bradford. For the hostages aboard Air France 622, those hours had seemed without end. The sun had set, and darkness crept over the field, but the heat of day had not yet dissipated. Along with the unbearable temperature, tension hung heavy in the putrid cabin air. Each moment dragged by like an eternity. A collective anxiety, stark and foreboding, had replaced the previous hours of naked terror. By now, most of the passengers had resigned themselves to the fact that the hijacking would end in violence, one way or another. With the death of Dean Bradford, their drama had taken a turn for the worse, if that was possible.

From Mike's location in the back of the plane, he couldn't see whether the big terrorist was asleep. He knew only that it was quiet. Abu Hassim had slumped into a passenger seat and collapsed from sheer exhaustion. He appeared dead to those who could see him. The other two hijackers constantly patrolled the aisles.

Mike continued to work on his bindings, glancing toward the front of the plane to ensure that the terrorists weren't moving in his direction. One of them would soon return. They always did. Through the door, off in the distance, he could see some light. At the edge of the doorway near the ground, though, the light was dim. It was inviting. If he could not attack the terrorists himself, he thought, maybe he could sneak over to the door, hang from the bottom of the doorway, and drop to the tarmac below. He could provide valuable intelligence about the terrorists to the assault force—*if* there was one.

In the end, he rejected any thought of an escape plan. Not so much out of fear for his own safety, but out of a greater fear, that his beautiful and loving wife could die aboard this ghastly airplane and he would live.

After the explosion that killed Margaret and Emily, and nearly killed Mike and Jonas too, Lynn had saved him. Mike awoke from a coma at Walter Reed, twenty-seven days after the explosion that nearly crippled him—emotionally as well as physically.

Mike spent the next eight months learning to walk, and even talk, again. Lynn was his nurse. Besides his physical recovery, she had also helped him learn to live again—and to love.

A year later, they were married. He had not forgotten Margaret and Emily, and Lynn understood that. Now, though, Lynn was his life. When the position in Tunis came up, Mike at first wasn't interested, but Lynn had insisted. It seemed safe enough in the beginning, and then Tunis exploded into the flames of a Muslim Brotherhood revolution.

I couldn't save Margaret and Emily, he thought, *am I now going to fail Lynn as well?*

***

Akrotiri Airfield, 2239 Hours

Chief Smith scanned the dimly lit cockpit instruments arrayed before him as his copilot read off the Blackhawk's start-up checklist.

"Battery switch, on."

"Volt meter, check."

"Emergency hydraulic pump, check...." They continued for a few minutes, then Smith held down a button and cranked off the Blackhawk's internal APU, an engine the size of a car motor used to start the Blackhawk's twin turbine engines.

Finally, the copilot said, "Okay Chief, all electronics and hydraulics off-line. Engine start."

"Ignition starter switch on," said Smith, casually into his mic, "pedals even, collective down, cyclic centered." To the crew chief standing just outside the helicopter, he said, "Coming hot, Henry." Smith engaged the number one engine and the huge, four-bladed rotor began to churn. It cut a fifty-four-foot diameter swath in the air, slowly at first, then quickly accelerating to a blur. Outside, the Blackhawk's crew chief, fire extinguisher in hand, moved about the exterior of the sleek aircraft, searching intently for the slightest spark or hint of electrical or fuel related fire during the start-up procedure.

Inside the old hangar, Sergeant Major Barrington continued down the small line of men, carefully inspecting each one. Captain Owen, Colonel Sinclair, and Lieutenant Colonel Wilson watched from a short distance. This was the final inspection.

All communications gear had been thoroughly tested and retested. The weapons were test fired, cleaned, and oiled, but not disassembled. Barrington checked the two flash-bang grenades attached to a commando's assault vest. The safety pins were bent flat, but before landing, the two men throwing them would straighten the pins out slightly to ensure that one quick jerk on the safety ring would be sufficient to arm the grenade. Barrington watched the man slide three magazines into small, quick access pouches aligned horizontally across the front of his assault vest before moving to the next man.

The commandos wore black jungle fatigues and boots with soft rubber soles. Even the protective masks were solid black. The only non-subdued item to be found was a three-by-five inch, red, white, and blue flag of the United States of America, attached by Velcro to each man's left shoulder.

Sinclair and Wilson watched the inspection and discussed last-minute command and control details. Sinclair would be located with Barclay in the surveillance van at Larnaca Airport. Wilson would remain in the main CP to monitor the overall operation and ensure that Captain Owen departed from Akrotiri on time. Finally, he would maintain a continuous communications link between the team in Cyprus and the Pentagon.

"Well, sir," said Barrington, to Colonel Sinclair, "that's it. We're as ready as we're gonna get."

"Okay, Scott," said Sinclair, "let's get aboard. Noah, you plan the evacuation from here. The instant that plane is secure I want a C17 on final approach with the med team. There's going to be some seriously dehydrated folks on that Airbus."

"No problem, sir," said Wilson with a wave of his hand. "Just give me some passengers to put on that bird. We'll be ready."

***

Beirut, 2310 Hours

Striker had finally called off the search for Akim. He knew there was no point in continuing. Lebanese intelligence had found the young Arab's Mercedes abandoned in the Karm Ez Zeitoun area of East Beirut, not far from his home. They were keeping the car under surveillance, but nothing had turned up. It appeared more and more likely that Akim had been kidnapped. Under torture, he would expose Cupid, and the U.S. would be back to square one for human intelligence in Shiite Lebanon. Plus, whatever Akim already knew about Hezbollah's current plans, went with him to the grave, or to the torture chamber.

Striker leaned back in his creaky desk chair in his office in the U.S. embassy and propped his feet up on the corner of the desk. He stared absentmindedly into the cheap tumbler he held between his thick fingers as he swirled its contents. Doug Andrews sat across from him, sipping his own drink. On the desk between the two men was a near empty bottle of Chivas Regal.

The door to Striker's office swung open, and the night CIA duty officer entered with a single tap on the door.

"Got an interesting message here, sir," he said, crossing the room and handing Striker a handwritten note on a single sheet torn from a steno pad.

Striker sat forward in his chair and took the message. The duty officer explained as Striker read in silence. "It was an old guy by the sound of his voice. He wouldn't stay on the line. Just read it off and hung up. We have it on tape."

Striker tossed the paper to Doug Andrews, jumped up, and strode toward the door. "Let's hear it," he said, passing through the door with the two men in trail. Striker listened to the recording several times, and each time, he became more excited.

The old man had given his message in English. He stammered a few times, but it was quite understandable. "This is a message from my nephew, Akim. The code word is Green Giraffe. I was attacked, likely Hezbollah. Barely escaped. I *have* the information you want, but you *must* pull me out and get me out of the country. Contact point Rachiine village, eleven miles northeast of Beirut, 5:00 a.m."

Striker reflected in silence. He knew he would have to go up there and get Akim.

"Do you think Akim's really behind this message, John?" asked Andrews.

"No way to know for sure except to go up there and find out."

"Smells like a trap to me," said Andrews. "Besides, the code word's invalid if it doesn't come from Akim himself."

"They could have forced Akim to call in the message just as well."

"*If* he's still alive."

"I'd be more suspicious if he *had* personally called. Using the little old man, though, is just Akim's touch. He's a shrewd operator."

"John, just a few minutes ago you were convinced he was dead."

"Maybe not," said Striker. "Akim suddenly disappeared. Then we found his car. We naturally concluded that they grabbed him. Maybe they tried and botched it. If Akim managed to detect their surveillance and escape, as he says in the message, then he's alive and can tell us what Hezbollah plans to do. And more importantly, without Akim, we permanently lose Cupid, because we don't know his contact procedures.

"Besides, my gut says it really is Akim. He spotted a trap and took off. He's holed up somewhere near that village in the Christian zone where he feels safe. Not *in* the village, but near it. Anyway, it's our only lead," said Striker, standing again.

"I found it, sir," shouted the duty officer from his desk in another corner of the room. "I found the village."

He crossed the room and shoved a large map between Striker and Andrews. With his finger, he traced the thin, black, squiggly line depicting the road leading out of Jounié, just up the coast from Beirut. The little road pointed to the northeast and twisted up through the hills until it ended in the tiny hamlet of Rachiine. "It's nothing but a few huts and ruins," said Clyde.

"Its rugged terrain out that way," Andrews added.

"That's why it's stayed so isolated all these years," offered Clyde. "The road heading up there runs through the *Radab Allah* gorge, which means *God's Wrath*."

"Yes, it's rugged terrain," said Striker, "but it's in the Christian zone. Hezbollah wouldn't likely operate there."

"What do you plan to do with him?"

"Pump him on the way back. I want whatever Cupid provided—I'm sure it will have some bearing on the hijacking, and hopefully, on the Scimitar as well. I'll take a satcom set and transmit it directly to Langley. We've lost a lot of time already."

"But if the Shiites know their plan is compromised, they may have already changed it," added Andrews.

"Maybe. Or maybe they just figure there's nothing we can do about it. I'll bring him back here. We'll keep him until we're sure we've got everything we need to set up a new handler for Cupid. Then we'll get Akim out of the country."

Striker rubbed his chin and paced the room for a few minutes. "He's gonna be edgy. He won't trust anyone but me to get close to him, and I know I can handle him. I think once I've made contact with him, he'll be more than willing to play ball. What other choice does he have? He can't stay up there forever, and he's a marked man in Beirut."

"All right then," said Andrews. "You want me to go with you?"

"No, get things ready here. *If* he is cooperative, it will be a debriefing. If not, I want to have a place to hold him. Have Conrad prepare the move to the village. I want to leave in time to get there by 4:30."

"John, are you going to tell Langley about this before you go?"

Striker reflected for a moment. "Yeah, you can tell them that before dawn, we'll know what Hezbollah is planning."

18

Off the Coast of Larnaca, Cyprus, 2340 Hours

The night-cloaked trawler rolled gently in the swells just offshore and about a mile south of Larnaca airport. Mustafa stood on the curved wooden deck, watching the tower's beacon paint circles in the night sky. He was dressed in black, and on his back, he carried a soft container the size of a briefcase. His men silently prepared a small, black, rubber boat.

Mustafa's plan was simple and direct. He would carefully approach the airport grounds, alone. If security was lax, he would penetrate the perimeter and attempt to observe the hijacked Airbus. If not, he would backtrack and depart. In any case, he would return to sea before dawn, and his crew would innocently deploy their fishing nets while he scanned the radio waves and observed the airport through binoculars.

Mustafa turned and stepped over the slippery railing and into the bobbing dinghy. Two men steadied the small craft while he took a seat. The men cast off and began to paddle the hundred yards to the flat, rocky shore. After depositing Mustafa on the island, the two men would return to the trawler. The larger vessel would then move out to sea until one hour before dawn.

Mustafa studied the rugged and murky shoreline ahead. It was perfect terrain for such an infiltration. Easy, in fact, compared to the training the former Czech secret police, and other so-called terrorist masters, had put him through in his early years. He had learned his trade well in a half-dozen such espionage training camps, from the Libyan Desert to the Bulgarian highlands. He had rapidly mastered the technical aspects of his trade—demolitions, electronics, infiltration, intelligence, surveillance, the silent kill, martial arts. In nearly every discipline, he had quickly eclipsed his instructors, even the Russian GRU and the former East German Stasi officers. He had quickly earned their respect and admiration.

He possessed much more than natural talent. He had a passion for the work, and he was ruthlessly cunning. Within only a few years, he was a legend among operatives and governments alike. He had become a shadowy, much-feared master of the tenebrous arts. His physical characteristics even supported his chosen career. He was of medium height and build, with nondescript features. He was handsome enough to charm women when he wanted but not so good looking as to be remarkable. Such physical characteristics had served him well.

The rubber boat arrived a few yards offshore, and Mustafa's two men slowed their pace, carefully approaching the dark ground as quietly as shadows. Tiny waves slapped against the dinghy and the low rocks which dotted the sandy shore.

Mustafa left his two men with the boat. They would return for him before dawn. He made his way northeast along the shore toward Larnaca airport. He moved silently, systematically, concentrating on the sights, sounds, and smells of the night. He was alert to every detail as his feet sensed the ground for the surest and quietest footing. He heard frogs chattering, even the tiniest rodent's scurrying dash. He saw the occasional bat flit across the horizon. He smelled the seaweed and salt air from the bay. He would smell or hear a man well in advance of encountering him. Mustafa was merely another shadow in the night.

He arrived at the airport perimeter fence where it intersected the sea in the airport's southeastern quadrant. It was barely chest high, only designed to keep animals from the runways. It was unguarded, and he deftly swung around the last pole supporting the rusting chain-link barrier and crouched inside, listening. He moved forward a few yards more and caught the faint hint of men talking, their voices floating on the night's warm breath. He lowered himself flat against the uneven ground.

He lay as still as death itself in the midst of brambles and rocks. He watched the shadowy outlines of two approaching Cypriot police officers making their rounds. They paid little attention to their environment, he noted. In low voices, they chatted in Greek, concerned more with the long, boring night than with the security of the airport grounds. They carried flashlights that only illuminated where they put their feet. Mustafa let the dark silhouettes pass.

He studied the terrain. Over the years, he had been to this airport a hundred times. It was often a mandatory transit point when flying circuitous routes to clandestine meetings throughout the world, each time with a different passport and a new identity. He raised small but powerful binoculars and carefully scanned the airport's tower, hangars, and maintenance buildings situated several hundred yards inland to the north.

The buildings appeared somber and quiet. Beyond these structures lay the taxiways and runways, as well as the object of his interest, Air France 622, not visible from his current location. He considered his courses of action. He knew he dared not approach the big field from behind the Airbus, opposite the buildings from this position. If the Americans had come, they would be lurking there in the shadows. From here, he could neither confirm nor deny his suspicion that the Americans were even on the island. He would have to proceed with extreme caution, he decided, as he began methodically evaluating the terrain directly ahead. Maybe there was a way.

***

Larnaca, 0001 Hours, Day Three

Colonel Sinclair's van approached the airport at about the same time Staff Sergeant Jake Brady was beginning his ground approach toward the tail of the Air France jet.

Sinclair joined Barclay in the surveillance van. "What are they doing, Steven?"

"They're quiet. Abdul is in the cockpit. Number Three seems to be asleep. The other two are wandering around off and on."

As they talked, Barclay manipulated a camera and scanned the length of the Airbus at close magnification. Looking at the monitor was almost like looking at the Airbus in daylight. The camera system employed infrared and thermal imaging observation devices in tandem. Coordinated by a computer, the two sights produced a crisp black and white image at night.

"Is Eagle positioned to move if Jake gets into trouble?"

"Yes, sir."

Sinclair stared at the monitor. "What's your recommendation, Steven?"

"I think we should go."

"The deception plan ready?"

"Yes, sir. A Cypriot jetliner will taxi out and take off during Jake's approach and climb. Hamud will be talking to Abdul."

Sinclair looked at Barclay, hesitating only briefly. "Okay, let's do it."

***

Staff Sergeant Jake Brady, an operator from Sergeant Major Barrington's team, crept toward the Airbus. Master Sergeant Palmer was near his side. Along with the snipers, Palmer would cover Jake as he climbed to the tail section of the aircraft.

Brady and Palmer eased up under the rear of the plane where the tail curved sharply upward. Palmer clasped his hands together, and Jake stood up on one foot in Sergeant Palmer's hands.

He reached up, affixed a rubber suction cup to the bottom of the plane, and flipped a lever on the cup. A five-foot long rope with a loop on the end hung down from the back of the cup. He tested it to ensure it would support his weight. It was solid. He slipped his foot into the loop and lifted himself up. He nodded at Palmer, who crouched down and slipped away. Palmer lay down in the grass with his silenced pistol oriented on the open passenger door above.

As Jake worked, a jet taxied toward the distant runways. It would provide noise cover, as well as give the hijackers something to look at.

Jake attached a second cup and rope farther up on the fuselage. He cautiously switched his weight up to the second rope. Then he moved the first cup two feet higher. Jake was climbing the underside of the plane, up toward the tail, using basic mountain climbing techniques used for scaling the underside of a rock overhang. Instead of pitons, however, he used suction cups. He moved slowly, ensuring the plane's tail didn't bounce as he shifted his weight upward.

***

Lynn had been unable to take advantage of the relative quiet. She could not sleep. She had tried desperately to escape into slumber, even if only for a few moments, but she couldn't. Across the plane, she caught glimpses through the windows of a large jet taxiing out toward the runways. She had no idea what type of plane it was, or what country it was bound for, but it gave her mind something else to ponder. She wondered if they knew she was here. Lynn shifted her weight again, but it didn't ease the agony from sitting so long.

The departing Cypriot airliner began to test its engines. They rumbled in the distance. She caught glimpses of the plane's rotating anti-collision lights. Lynn just tried to concentrate on those lights and pushed everything else from her mind.

***

"Okay, okay," groaned Abdul, "enough chatter. What other news do you have?"

"Wait just a minute, Abdul. Some sort of message has just arrived. Yes, I have good news," said Hamud with glee. "According to the Americans, the Beirut airport, at great expense to the American taxpayers they tell me, will accept your arrival at nine o'clock this morning."

Abdul listened intently.

"They prefer," continued Hamud, "to wait until daylight for your arrival. As you know the Beirut airport is not always secure in the dark. They indicated that sometimes they find obstacles on the runway that someone placed there during the night."

"Yes, I know. And the rest?"

"As I predicted, our president has agreed to a request by the American government to give you fuel. Our day maintenance crews arrive at six. We will quickly refuel your plane at that time, and you will take off for Beirut as you like."

"Very well. This is good."

Abdul sat back, and for the first time in many hours, he allowed a faint smile to slip across his thin lips. He would enjoy the triumphant announcement of this news to his comrades.

***

0033 Hours

Jake reached the portside vertical stabilizer and sat down. The diversion jet had taken off and flown away. It was quiet once again. Jake sat perfectly still, concentrating on controlling his breathing and slowing his heart. He had a lot of work to do, he told himself.

In the van, Colonel Sinclair sat back in his chair and let out a long breath. He had watched Jake's climb on Barclay's video monitor. He leaned back in his chair and turned to look at Barclay who was already grinning.

"Alright," muttered Sinclair. "He did it."

***

0045 Hours

Mustafa lay silent in the brush for some time assessing the situation around the sprawling airfield. An unlit, concealed route ran the length of the fence line. It would carry him up to the rear of a cluster of hangars and maintenance buildings. After a few minutes of observation, he decided that it would be a rather simple task to make his way to one of those buildings unseen. If someone there spotted him, however, he would need an edge. He would need something to distract the casual observer long enough for Mustafa to kill him, or simply to walk away and disappear. He needed a Cypriot police officer's uniform.

Mustafa had already observed two police patrols in this remote and darkened area of the airport grounds—a two-man patrol and a one-man patrol, on a fifteen-minute interval. He chose his victim. Mustafa remained as still as the night itself, and waited. The two-man patrol came and went, chattering away, a flashlight beam bouncing about their feet. They quickly receded into the night farther up the shore.

Soon, Mustafa heard the sound of a man whistling as he approached. *Perhaps*, thought Mustafa, *he fears the dark, and he is whistling to console himself. If this is so, then his worst nightmare is about to come true.* The man walked slowly along the edge of the field where cut grass turned to scrub brush; Mustafa lay just inside the line of brambles and bushes.

The police officer approached. He was more alert than the other two. Mustafa readied himself. His target was only a few feet away now, then one step past, his back to his attacker. The intruder sprang from his hiding place, and before the Cypriot could make a sound, Mustafa had slammed the man to the ground. He shoved the Cypriot's face into the dirt. The officer suddenly felt someone sitting on his back and whispering into his ear.

"Be still, and I won't hurt you," said Mustafa in English. The man stopped wiggling and lay still. Holding the man's hair and pushing his face down, Mustafa looked around and listened. The night was undisturbed.

"That's a good boy," he said to the Cypriot, removing the man's police cap and setting it aside. He reached behind his back and produced his pistol. He placed the end of the Warp 3 sound suppressor on the back of the Cypriot's head. Nine inches of death rested against the man's skull.

The Cypriot sensed the meaning of the deadly object pressing against his hairline and began to squirm. The gun made a barely audible pop, and the man was still. "Now, my friend," whispered Mustafa, "let's hope that your badge and uniform will do me some good so that you will not have perished for naught."

***

Delta was hopeful that all would remain calm. The announcement that fuel would arrive at 6 a.m., and that Beirut would welcome them shortly thereafter, seemed to have appeased the terrorists. Number Three was awake and moving about, though, so the possibility of an earlier assault was real.

With the main assault element in position at Dhekelia and ready, however, Sinclair intended to attack the Airbus at the slightest hint that another passenger might be shot—and, Delta now had a man in place. If the counterterrorist team needed to move quickly, Jake Brady was in position to provide support.

Jake whispered, and his throat mic transmitted. He reported that he was in position and continuing with his mission. Jake's first order of business was to prepare a safety anchor in case the terrorists decided to takeoff. He pulled out a small packet, opened it, and unfolded a four-inch wide, two-foot long piece of material. It resembled a large Band-Aid with a metal ring attached to the non-sticky side. He peeled off the backing, applied the tape over the leading edge of the vertical stabilizer, and pressed it firmly into place.

He then attached a quick-release snap link into the metal O-ring and affixed a rope to it. He laid the coil of rope on the horizontal stabilizer. Jake's escape plan was now in place. He could fast-rope down should the plane begin to move. Once he was safely off the plane, he could detach the high-tech snap link with the push of a button on a small remote in his shirt pocket, and the rope would fall to the ground.

Jake was now ready to install ropes for the topside assault team. The top of the aircraft curved down sharply above the plane's doors, so Jake would affix glue pads, with short, knotted ropes attached, just above the two doors he was going to prep with explosives. He would add a third rope over the open rear portside door just in case it might be needed. The topside assault men would use the ropes to drop quickly from the roof, through the blown doors, and into the plane.

Once Jake completed those tasks, he would rig explosives around the outside of the two closed doors. He began to crawl forward, slowly, on top of the Airbus.

***

0105 Hours

Wearing the dead Cypriot police officer's shirt, the saucer-like police cap atop his head, Mustafa slipped along the fence heading northward. He had not actually walked this particular piece of terrain before, but he knew the sprawling airport in general quite well.

The fence ran directly behind a row of hangars and a smaller maintenance building. The light was dim in this area, but he was able to pick his way along a well-worn path running behind the buildings. Piles of old, rusting parts, cables, oil drums, and other discarded junk lay on both sides of the trail. It was a convenient, out-of-sight dumping ground for mechanics and grounds keepers.

Mustafa quickly arrived at the building of his choice. It was a flat-roofed, two-story maintenance building. The roof appeared to have a solid ledge around its perimeter that would provide concealment. It was the only one with such a roof. The hangars were all aluminum and steel frame with high arching ceilings that offered no protection and no level platform on which to sit or stand. This building, though, was perfect.

Checking the building's rear windows, he verified that no lights were on inside. He forced the lock on the back door and slipped in. Using a small flashlight, he inspected the building's first floor. He located a steep wooden staircase, without railings, that led up one wall to the second level. He carefully eased up the steps to a metal access door to the roof. A key was in the lock. He twisted the key and determined that the door was unlocked. He turned the knob and gently pushed.

Mustafa froze. He had the door open only an inch, but he heard a noise—a low cough and a slight shuffling. He detected the distinct sound of a man snoring. Mustafa cursed, but only in his thoughts. Someone was on the roof.

He opened the door enough to peek through it. The scene was only dimly illuminated, but he could see the silhouette of one man leaning against the low wall encircling the roof on the side facing the tarmac. Another man slouched against this same wall; he had some sort of cap pulled down over his eyes.

The building was better for his purposes than he had thought. The Cypriots, or the Americans, had apparently chosen it for nearly the same purpose—a concealed position from which to observe the hijacked Airbus and the tarmac.

Mustafa evaluated the situation. He decided that it was probably the Cypriots because he doubted an American commando would be asleep and snoring. Plus, he thought he could make out the dark outlines of the same type of cap he now wore.

What would be the odds, he wondered, of more Cypriots coming here to check on these two? Did they have a radio? He could hear none, but he could not be sure. Then he decided. The presence of the two men complicated his plan, but this was the only building he could infiltrate and have good observation of the plane and surrounding field. He would have to make do. If someone came to check on these two, he would deal with him, or them, and then leave. He had come too far just to slip back out without even seeing the plane.

He pushed on the door slowly and carefully. He soon had it open just enough to step through. He pulled his pistol from his belt and let it hang by his side.

He stepped through the door and walked at a normal pace the few steps separating him and the two men. As he approached, he could tell they were Cypriots. The officer watching the field jerked around, but he spotted the outlines of a police cap in the dim light.

"Damn," he said in Greek, starting to chuckle, "you scared the hell out of me."

Mustafa halted at the man's feet, raised his pistol, and fired one silenced round. The police officer's smirk barely had time to change to an expression of surprise before the .22 caliber, forty-grain bullet entered his forehead. The other officer stirred, and Mustafa dispatched him with a single shot through the top of his cap. His head drooped back down as if he had never awakened.

Mustafa returned to the door, took the key, and locked it from his side. He checked the two dead Cypriots for a radio. He found a portable Motorola, but it was not on. Maybe they had instructions to turn it on if they had something to report, to preserve its charge. On the other hand, maybe they were required to check in at regular intervals. He could only hope it was the former.

He took up a position next to the low wall and scanned the tarmac and field. He could plainly see the Airbus some nine hundred yards away. He could discern little detail. At this distance, the dimly illuminated field beyond the plane offered no details to the naked eye. He slipped the pack off his back, opened it, and removed a long, thick scope. He flipped a switch and peered through the optical lens. The scope glowed a glaucous green and brought the gloomy field immediately to life.

A first quick scan of the field revealed no obvious anomalies. He twisted the rear bezel ring and zoomed up to ten-power magnification. Still, there was nothing really out of the ordinary to the untrained eye, only a few small mounds of dirt grown over with grass.

Mustafa was suspicious, though. He was an expert in the art of camouflage, and he decided he would study those mounds more closely later.

He ran his scope across the hijacked Airbus and immediately spotted Staff Sergeant Jake Brady near the aircraft's tail. The image was green-tinted but clear. He placed the scope's cross hairs between the eyes of the unsuspecting young man he was observing before panning forward to the illuminated cockpit. The two pilots sat, heads slumped over, seemingly asleep. Behind them, Abdul held a microphone and was talking.

Mustafa lowered the scope and dug into his bag for his portable radio scanner. He plugged a small earpiece into the device and affixed the other end in his ear. Then he set the scanner to VHF and flipped it on. It began to hop rapidly from frequency to frequency, stopping once or twice to lock onto some aircraft somewhere in the sky overhead. Each time, after three seconds, it continued its scan. Finally, it locked onto a frequency that made Mustafa blink.

He heard the Arabic language, reached down, and hit a button locking the scanner to that frequency. He immediately recognized Abdul's voice. He was talking to someone in Arabic. Mustafa's annoyance over the hijacking turned to rage. Abdul was chatting away with this fellow as if they were old friends—the stranger was telling him how everything would work out as he had planned—while a commando crawled around on top of the plane.

Mustafa almost wished that he had brought a transmitter. He had expressly not, for very specific operational security reasons. The risks of transmitting a radio message to Abdul far outweighed any potential gains. The man on the plane was probably an American, and he knew that the Americans possessed advanced technology. If he transmitted, they would rapidly detect it and locate him, whether here or back out at sea.

He also knew it would be useless to try to contact Abdul via encrypted text. He had checked his own phone, and he had a full signal. He knew, though, that Abdul would not. He also knew that any jamming would involve sophisticated equipment and would be directional only. It would be focused on the airplane and not affect the surrounding area.

The signals near the Airbus were certainly jammed. It was standard military and police procedure. Mustafa could not see the two vans from his location. They were parked around the corner of the terminal. If he had been able to, he would have certainly deduced the source of the jamming.

So, he could only listen, but he *could* influence the situation. He began to pull rifle components from his bag and assemble them. *I will certainly influence the situation*, he told himself again, *but patience will be required.*

19

Beirut, 0120 hours

The CIA arms and equipment rooms were located in a secure area in the basement of the U.S. embassy. This area remained under constant electronic surveillance from Striker's suite of offices. In one of those rooms, a group of men dressed in dark, civilian clothing, busily inspected weapons, radios, and other equipment.

"Hustle it up," grumbled Conrad in his gruff voice. He was a bear of a man, with broad, thick shoulders and a deep, reverberating voice. When the occasion demanded, Mark Conrad could be quietly refined. When it did not, he paid little attention to social convention. The crass mannerisms with which he was infinitely more comfortable simmered to the surface.

"What do you think of this move tonight?" Robert Erwin asked him casually, setting down a Heckler and Koch MP5 and picking up a thirty-round magazine of 9mm ammunition. He began tapping the magazine against the palm of his hand to seat the shell rims firmly against the back of the magazine to avoid hang-ups when fired. Erwin was the team leader for the lead vehicle and its three-man security team. Fred Morgan prepped his own weapons and watched Conrad for his response.

"I think we do what we're told," Conrad replied sourly, as he inspected his .45 caliber Ingram Mac 10.

"You wearing a vest, big guy?" Fred Morgan asked Conrad.

"No. Too hot. Makes me itch."

"I am," replied Erwin. "Got a bad feeling about tonight."

"Bad feeling, my ass," snapped Conrad. "Go check your goddamn cars and quit your bitching. I don't want any mechanical problems tonight. The old man says this is a big one. We do it right."

"They were just serviced," protested Morgan.

"Check them again," growled the big man through clenched teeth, a malicious scowl on his broad face.

"Okay, okay, calm down. We're going."

***

Larnaca, 0220 Hours

Colonel Sinclair stepped back into the cramped van after taking his fourth stretch in the past hour.

"Wilson relayed a message from the Pentagon while you were out," said Barclay. "Everything's okay in Washington. The current plan is for the White House crisis management team to monitor from the Situation Room. General Holt wishes us luck."

"Luck," said Sinclair. He let the word roll off his tongue. He glanced at the monitor focused on the Airbus. Would the terrorists allow Delta that luxury?

Several minutes passed as the two men sat quietly.

"How's Jake doing?" asked Sinclair.

"Can't see him. He's working on the other side of the plane. Eagle-two is keeping an eye on him. He's okay. He'll be finished soon. Once he gets back into position on the tail, the hard part will be over for him. All he'll have to do is wire up his backup detonator and stay under cover—and push the button at the right time."

"He's done a hell of a job."

"Yes he has."

It was quiet in the van for a few moments as both men watched the video monitors. They could now see Jake as he eased back up to the top of the plane just over the door he had been working on.

***

Beirut, 0338 Hours

The two armored Mercedes departed the U.S. embassy and headed north up the Mediterranean coast. Fred Morgan drove the second car carrying Striker. Albert Conrad rode shotgun next to Morgan. Robert Erwin rode shotgun in the lead vehicle. Conrad and Erwin conversed from time-to-time over their radio headsets between the two cars. Otherwise, they proceeded in silence toward their rendezvous with Akim.

***

Akrotiri CP, 0320 Hours

Captain Jim Owen was sitting in the CP reviewing his part of the plan with the XO when one of the mechanics working on Jim's plane clambered into the CP, clumsily banging his steel-toed boot against the leg of a wooden table. "Cap'n Owen, sir," said the mechanic, slightly embarrassed. "Chief Rodney is ready to go over the final checklist with you on the bird, sir."

"On my way, Sergeant."

Wilson checked his watch. "Okay, Jim, it's 0338. You'll take off in an hour. Your personal gear all squared away?"

"Yes, sir. Survival vest, LPUs, flares, helmet, all on the plane. Checked everything about a dozen times now, including the commo. If that little airplane starts and runs long enough to get me to Larnaca, we'll be squared away."

"It'll crank, sir," said the mechanic, regaining his composure and his Tennessee backwoods grin. Jim followed the young man out to the hangar bay. He found Chief Warrant Officer Rodney standing by the plane, clipboard in hand. Captain Owen could have been Rodney's grandson, and while a captain technically outranked a chief warrant officer, everyone knew who was in charge.

"Okay, sir, I just wanted to go over these modifications with you one more time. You're sort of my responsibility, you know, *sir*," added the crusty old warrant officer.

"And the emergency procedures," Jim said grinning.

"*Especially* the emergency procedures, sir."

***

Air France 622, 0346 Hours

Besides his physical discomfort, Mike Elliot felt only despair, loneliness, and a burning fear for his wife's safety. It appeared that no one outside this plane knew or cared about their miserable existence on this sweltering tarmac. He knew he had to make a move. No one else was going to do anything.

He had already carefully analyzed the pros and cons of his decision many times. He had tried to examine his plan as a straightforward military problem. He coldly weighed the advantages and disadvantages of each potential course of action he had devised. This situation, though, always seemed to transcend the formal military decision-making process. It always boiled down to a very personal level and the distinct possibility of deep personal loss—something he understood all too well.

If he did nothing, the terrorists could possibly release them in a few days. On the other hand, they might just as well shoot their hostages one at a time, or they could all be massacred at once in a miscalculated assault from some third-world military playing commando. The terrorists might even intend to take off and crash somewhere.

If he attacked one of the terrorists, and failed, he would be signing his own death warrant. They would surely execute him. He would be leaving Lynn to face this terror as a widow.

What trap might I be walking into here, Mike asked himself.

He knew that he and Jonas had walked blindly into a trap in Brazil, and it had cost him his wife and daughter, as well as the lives of three other innocent people.

Someone in the Brazilian security services, someone who worked closely with the Americans, probably someone Mike had even called friend, had sold them out to the Colombian cartel.

That's how they knew exactly how, when, and where to take Margaret and Emily. That's how they knew we were coming to rescue the hostages, he thought. *It was all done to send a message.*

So, what unforeseen trap might I be walking into here? he wondered for the hundredth time.

When one of them had come back and stood guard near the open door, Mike had tried repeatedly to visualize how he could take the terrorist by surprise and get a weapon from him without alerting the others. He could think of no sure way to do it quietly.

They were nearing the end of their second night of captivity. The third day was approaching. He knew he had to do it, and soon, while he still had the strength—if he still did. The flight attendant,

Marie, had given him some water several times, and even fed him a couple of sandwiches, but it wasn't nearly enough. He could feel his stomach shrinking in on itself. It was a feeling he had known many times during military operations.

All he knew for sure, was that he could not fail again. Despite the blood he could feel running down his wrists and fingers, he worked on his bindings with a renewed sense of urgency.

***

0414 Hours

Mustafa peered through his scope, aligning its fine cross hairs against the side of Jake Brady's head. *It would be so easy to kill this man now and be done with it*, thought Mustafa. Unfortunately, the consequences were all too unpredictable. His rifle was silenced, and he could certainly do it and withdraw before anyone could determine how the man had been killed.

When he did shoot, however, he could not remain in place afterwards. Killing the man would provoke a search of the grounds, so he would be forced to flee without really being sure of accomplishing his mission. He feared that the commando might fall to the tarmac, unnoticed by Abdul or his men. The authorities would be forewarned, and Abdul would continue to sit there unaware of the menace lurking outside his door.

It was 0415, and Mustafa knew that he should soon be withdrawing. The first, soft rays of dawn would arrive promptly at 0530, and soon thereafter, his night cloak would vanish in the mists of the new morning. To be on the safe side, he needed a minimum of thirty minutes to make it to the shoreline and his boat. He knew, though, that if an assault was planned for this night, it would be launched soon. *It must be tonight*, he thought. *Why else would they put this man on top of the plane and leave him there?*

Also, he reflected, *it is now the traditional hour of attack—the last hour before dawn*. A major of *Spetsnaz* troops had once told him that it was written in an American military document of some sort from the eighteenth century that the French and Indians attack just before dawn. "The Americans still quote it," he had said with a wry grin and a fair amount of reverence. "So always keep that firmly in mind when dealing with the Americans," he had said. Mustafa always had.

If he could catch the commandos in the actual assault, he could cut down enough attacking soldiers to sow panic in their ranks. The assault would wither and die. Even better, they might believe they were taking fire from within the plane and use heavier than planned firepower, ensuring the deaths of numerous hostages.

In fact, if he could dupe the Americans into killing their own citizens, it would be even better than getting the plane back to Beirut. Then, while everyone's attention was glued to the carnage in and around the aircraft, he could easily slip away under the veil of confusion and make good his escape. His actions might just give Abdul time to rally his forces and escape with the plane, or to destroy it. Either way would serve his purposes at this point, just so the Americans were not successful in their attack.

Mustafa continued monitoring the conversations of Abdul and Hamud. He had to admit, the man who had so thoroughly charmed Abdul was quite an engaging character. His Arabic, high and of noble blood it seemed, was flawless—all the more reason to suspect that he was more than just an innocent airport official called in to talk with the terrorists because he spoke the language. He was just too confident and too convincing to be true. He had to be a specialist in this type of affair, and perhaps an American.

Abdul should never have stayed in one place so long, thought Mustafa. *He was briefed on western counterterrorist procedures and should know to keep moving. The only logical reason he has not moved to another location, is because the Cypriots have denied him fuel, as they have done in the past with hijackings.*

Mustafa checked his watch again. It was 0425. He had barely thirty minutes to remain. He continued observing the plane and the field while listening to the scanner with one ear and trying to stay alert to his immediate surroundings with the other.

He detected a movement on the field, several hundred yards beyond the tail of the plane. Mustafa felt his adrenaline surge. Something was happening. A man was moving. He studied the shadowy figure. The man moved like a phantom. He was quite talented, observed Mustafa. This man was certainly an expert.

Yes, something will surely happen soon.

20

John Striker's two sedans reached the coastal city of Jounié. From there, they turned northeast onto a small road leading to the mountain village of Rachiine. Striker sat in the backseat of the second sedan. He had not uttered a word since leaving the embassy. He was lost in thought, planning for the possibilities that might come from this meeting with Akim.

They turned onto an unpaved mountain road. A few miles later, they reached the deserted village of Aachqout. Conrad figured the village they were looking for should be only a half mile farther. He could see the lead sedan about two hundred yards ahead. Clouds of dust swirled up from its tires.

The serpentine gravel and rock road ran uphill and curved right in a wide arc. To the left of the car's headlights, the edge of the road gave way to nothing but a dark abyss, though one couldn't tell how deep it was. Judging from their increasing elevation, it was probably quite deep. It didn't rain here often, but when it did, it came down all at once and washed out huge sections of earth forming deep wadis or ravines.

On the right, the ground rose sharply and created a wall of brownish-black rocks, loose dirt, and thorny scrub brush. The vehicles had nowhere to go but straight up the road. The night was so dark in this hellish desert terrain, that the lights on the lead car, already much higher up the hill than Conrad's sedan, appeared to fly through the star-studded sky on an undulating brown carpet of dirt, dust, and sand.

Robert Erwin, in the lead car, peered through a small monocular night scope out the side window of his car as the dry, rocky terrain sped by. The scope magnified the ambient light, but there was little to amplify. He spoke softly into his lip mic, "Hey, Conrad," called Erwin over the radio.

Conrad reached up and pressed his earpiece a little closer. "What?"

"Can't see shit up here."

"I know. Stay alert." He saw the taillights of Erwin's car take a curve to the right and disappear around a bend in the road. He could barely make out the outline of a rocky bluff directly ahead that was now concealing the lead car. The bluff stood silhouetted against the night sky.

Seconds passed.

Striker's car approached the bend in the road under the rocky outcropping. From somewhere on the hill to the right, a lightning-like streak of light, trailing sparks and flame, reached out and disappeared behind the rocky bluff to their front. Conrad knew instantly what it was—someone had fired a rocket-propelled, antitank grenade at the lead car.

Before he could open his mouth, he heard Erwin through his radio headset shouting. His warning was stifled when a tremendous fireball of bright orange and black roiled up from the opposite side of the little knoll. At the same time, Conrad saw a second bright flash from the hill. This time the trajectory was vertical. A projectile shot up into the sky and then burst into sparks and light. It was a parachute flare.

He felt himself pressing against his seat belt as Morgan stood on the brake pedal trying to stop the heavily-armored Mercedes. In the back, the sudden change in direction caught Striker off guard, and he slammed hard against the driver's seat back.

Fred Morgan had already crammed the automatic gearshift into reverse. The car's powerful engine spun the tires in the opposite direction as the car slowed to a stop and then started picking up speed in reverse. The heavy, cellular rubber tires squealed in protest. A dense cloud of smoke and dust welled up around the two spinning rear tires as the rubber heated against the rocky surface of the road.

On the hillside above, a prone figure verified his sights and tightened his grip on the trigger mechanism of his weapon. The standard two-kilogram warhead, such as the one that had destroyed the lead vehicle, had been reduced to one kilogram on this rocket. If it hit the right spot, it would disable the big car but not destroy it.

The gunner pulled the long, slightly unbalanced tube closer to his shoulder. He was sweating. He could feel his hands shaking. He took a deep breath. His target was moving rapidly and swerving in the confines of the narrow road. *This driver is a madman*, he thought. *Be patient.* The car was returning to him just as Abbas Bachar had said it would. *Wait.*

***

Akrotiri Airfield, 0440 Hours

Jim Owen taxied down the ramp in his small plane heading for runway one-six. It was time. He swerved left and stopped on the end of the long runway. The parallel rows of runway marker lights stretched out before him until they seemed to collide in the distance. The runway was all his. Nothing else was moving on the sprawling military airfield at this time of the early morning.

He pushed hard on the tops of the two rudder pedals to apply the brakes. Then he eased the throttle knob all the way out to perform a power check. The engine noise increased in intensity. He did a magneto check by switching from the primary to standby electrical system. He reduced power and then pushed and twisted the pedals and yoke while observing the control surfaces on the wings and tail. He checked the instruments—oil pressure, temperature gauge, fuel level. He made a quick call to the CP on each of his radios.

Finally, he rechecked his safety harness. He felt under his seat for the third time to touch the two chemical fire extinguishers the Delta engineers had secured to the seat frame just on the outside of Jim's legs.

They had also rigged high-intensity signal flares and long-duration smoke grenades in an array down the left wing strut of the small airplane. When activated, they would simulate a fire in flight and provide the diversion for Delta's assault.

All he had to do was push the newly-installed little red button thirty seconds out from the runway and Delta's diversion would be underway. The technicians had reminded Jim several times not to look at the flares. It would be blinding.

As a safety precaution, the left wing fuel tank was empty, so the plane would be unbalanced and heavy to the right side. Jim would have to compensate.

Fire trucks would race out onto the runway as part of the show. Jim was not disappointed that Delta considered the fire trucks necessary to make it look like a real emergency landing.

If all went well, between Jim's simulated crash, the noise of the sirens, and the tower talking to the terrorists on the radio, their attention should be fixed. They wouldn't know what hit them.

Owen released the brakes and applied power. The small plane began picking up speed, slowly at first, then the acceleration began to build. He pushed alternately back and forth on the two rudder pedals to maintain a straight course down the middle of the runway. As he approached takeoff speed, he eased gently back on the yoke until it felt right. Within a few seconds, the nose lifted smoothly from the runway. He banked slightly left and headed out to sea.

***

Lebanon, 0441 Hours

Striker's armored sedan accelerated in reverse. Only seconds had passed since the initial attack. Morgan gripped the steering wheel with his left hand and flung his right arm over the seat back, twisting himself around to look out the rear window. The car's custom brake lights would have provided sufficient light to the rear had it been necessary—but it was not. The magnesium parachute flare drifting overhead lit up the small strip of dirt road like day.

Even over the roar of the car's powerful engine, straining to accelerate the heavy car, Striker could hear the pinging sounds of small arms fire impacting the right side of the car. Then heavier thuds, one after another in rapid succession, pounded the Mercedes as machine gun rounds found their mark. The bullets made slight dents in the body of the car before flattening themselves against the armor plating or zinging away as ricochets.

Tracer rounds streaked through the night like short bolts of fire. Those that missed their mark zinged off the rocks around the car. The sedan's side windows became opaque as the outer layers of polycarbonate absorbed and dissipated the kinetic energy of each bullet.

The car raced back down the hill. The rocky wall and hillside to the right sped by. The seemingly bottomless ravine loomed to the left. One false move and Morgan would lose it all. Striker's driver was executing a brilliant escape maneuver—he was an expert at it. He zigzagged and struggled to increase his speed while maintaining control of the heavy car on the narrow road.

Striker realized that the small arms fire was just for show, to let them think they were escaping while directing the sedan to a desired location. "We're still in the kill zone!" he yelled. "There'll be another RPG!" Striker scanned the illuminated hillside zooming rapidly by. "When it fires," he shouted to Morgan, "hit the brakes." Striker groped blindly under his feet for his H&K MP5. He found it and pulled it in close to his left side.

A sharp curve to the rear forced Morgan to slow the vehicle. He decelerated quickly. In that instant, from off to the right, a bright flash caught Striker's eye. The launcher was still farther back down the hill in the direction they had come from. They were backing right into the secondary kill zone. *Hell of a trap*, thought Striker. The antitank grenade seared a yellow-white streak on his retinas. There was no time to breathe.

Morgan saw the flash of light, too. He hit the brakes and tried to jig the big car in the narrow road, but the gunner was an expert, the range short, and his aim nearly perfect. Morgan's evasive maneuvers caused the grenade to impact a glancing blow on the right side passenger door, only inches from Conrad's right shoulder, instead of against the right front fender as the gunner had intended. Conrad never felt a thing.

The detonating, Iranian-made, 85-millimeter antitank round easily penetrated the side door armor plate and sprayed shrapnel throughout the car. Searing pain shot through Striker's right leg, and the side of his face felt as if it were on fire. Morgan, only lightly wounded, worked to control the heavy sedan as it continued down the narrow road in reverse.

The Mercedes spun around in the small road and hit the rocky embankment with a sickening crash, rear end first. The rear armor plate crumpled under the impact and the vehicle bounced off the embankment and rocked several times before finally settling down near the center of the road, facing uphill.

Striker and Morgan sat stunned for an instant, badly shaken. It took them several seconds to determine that most of the blood covering their bodies was from Conrad. Nevertheless, both men were wounded, Striker worse than Morgan. Striker did not yet realize that his right femur was broken at mid-thigh, and his right leg nearly severed above the ankle. He was also unaware that he was rapidly losing blood.

Morgan hit the ignition. Nothing. "They'll be coming," he yelled over his shoulder. "Move!" He reached down between his legs near the base of the driver's seat and extracted an MP5, attached to the seat by Velcro.

Striker found his submachine gun, raked it in with his right arm, and tucked it under his left armpit. He shoved hard against the heavy passenger door, but the movement caused pain to radiate from his thigh in all directions. His body stiffened, and he winced.

Morgan pushed open his door and rolled out onto the dirt. Another parachute flare rocketed into the night sky with a loud swoosh and pop. The car was under a spotlight. A hail of small arms fire descended on Morgan as he tugged on Striker's door. He jumped up and sprayed a ragged burst of 9mm over the top of the car in the general direction of the hillside.

The incoming fire intensified. Rounds flickered off the car and road. They wanted to keep him away from Striker, he realized, as the first bullets tore into his legs, knocking him to the ground. They knew the man they wanted would be in the back seat.

In pain, bleeding badly, and under a hail of fire, Morgan reached up and tugged on Striker's door until it finally swung open. Dropping back down under the open door and looking under the body of the car, he saw two men running up the road. He aimed and the short barrel of his MP5 spit out a burst of rounds, clipping them in the shins. They fell and rolled, screaming. Morgan fired again and the last round was gone.

Striker watched helplessly as machine gun fire hammered Morgan repeatedly. Striker clutched his MP5 with his left hand.

Dragging his right leg with his right arm, he managed to get out of the door. With a final, superhuman effort, he hopped twice and lunged toward the edge of the road. He was aware that the firing had waned as he hobbled for the ravine only a few feet away. Voices replaced the sound of gunfire. They of course wanted him alive.

The overhead flare died as Striker dove over the edge. The abyss swallowed him up. Images of pain and confusion swirled in his brain as he tumbled head over heels down the steep gully. Rocks, briars, and brush tore into his skin. He could faintly hear his own muffled screams as he fell.

***

0442 Hours

Through his scope, Mustafa carefully followed Master Sergeant Palmer as the commando crept in from the field and made his way under the belly of the plane. He paused near the center of the plane for a moment, then cautiously made his way forward until he was under the cockpit. Now, the man crouched near the front landing gear next to the APU, waiting.

Mustafa had also watched what seemed to be small mounds of dirt out on the field, as they had eased closer to the plane, perhaps to a pre-assault position. Their movement had been impeccable. Mustafa was thoroughly impressed. These men were good, and he was sure now that they were not Cypriots. He had watched the commando on the plane crawl to the tail of the aircraft and sit down. His work apparently complete, the commando sat waiting.

Mustafa's normally cool demeanor was beginning to fray. He had barely fifty minutes of darkness remaining, and he was cutting his escape very close. If the Americans did not assault this night, his own direct participation would be finished. With the trail of bodies he had left behind, there would be no way he could return a second night. The authorities would be ready, and a trap would be set.

Of course, if things developed as he believed they would, it would not be necessary to return. Abdul might survive, and if he somehow managed to return to Beirut during the coming day, they would have beaten the Americans anyway.

Mustafa glanced at his watch. *I wonder how that Striker fellow is doing about now,* he mused. *It will be a pleasure to discover if the CIA man is as tough as his reputation belies.* He doubted it. In any case, he would soon be meeting the CIA legend face-to-face. The Arab realigned his riflescope and waited, but not patiently. Too many of his plans were approaching their climax for patience.

***

0444 Hours

When his tumbling had finally ceased, Striker lay flat on his back, frozen in pain. Was he thirty, forty, fifty yards down the ravine? He had no idea. He had landed in a shallow ditch. His heart pounded in his throat, and he gasped feverishly for the air that had been expelled from his lungs during the violent descent down the rocky slope. After a few seconds, he tried to move. Pain gripped him. He lay still.

Above the fierce ringing in his ears, he heard voices and then the pop of another parachute flare as it launched and ignited. It was daylight again. The intense illumination nearly blinded him. He barely managed to sit up. He looked around, struggling to see despite the multicolored spots imprinted on his eyes. There was no cover, only precious little scrub brush. He thought of his submachine gun and searched frantically as far around him as he could reach. It was not there.

He looked at his right leg; it was a twisted mess. He lay back down. Small, jagged stones pierced his scalp, but he was too tired to care. He felt dizzy. The pain that had gripped him by the throat during his rolling, pounding descent seemed to dim. He felt weak and knew that he was losing consciousness, or going into shock, or both.

He felt an intense rage well up inside him, and he slowly forced himself to sit up again, grimacing in pain as he did so. "No," he told himself, through gritted his teeth. He would not give up so damn easily. He was John Striker. The bastards would have to pay to get him. He forced himself to concentrate. He had to think. What could he do?

Striker felt his right leg. It was mangled. He knew he was losing a lot of blood. With great effort he managed to get his belt off and wrapped around his right calf, but he couldn't get it cinched tight and tied off with only one hand. He had difficulty moving his left arm, but he forced it anyway, wincing at the excruciating pain. He somehow managed to get what seemed to be a decent tourniquet in place.

He looked around again and then lay back down. He knew that if he could remain concealed long enough, eventually a Christian militia reaction team would come to investigate the firefight on their territory. The parachute flares could be seen for miles around. But how long would it take?

He knew his attackers were gutsy and determined. To hit him in the Christian sector, then to hang around for this long, they must want him badly, perhaps more than they valued their own lives.

Striker was startled out of his thoughts by more shouting from up the hill. Painfully, he forced himself onto his left side and tried to see up the hillside, but the flare had died out. Only the brilliant, blinding spots from the flare's intense light remained emblazoned on his eyes. He didn't have to see; he knew his attackers were clearing and searching the kill zone. It was standard ambush procedure.

He heard several pistol shots fired in quick succession, then several more—the *coup de grâce*. They were firing a few extra rounds into the skulls of his men. Surely they were already dead. Still, it infuriated him. He knew that a bullet to the head would not be his fate.

Doug was right, he thought ruefully. *Nice trap, all for one man—me—and I was only too obliging. I wanted so much to believe that Akim was alive and still had Cupid's goddamn message that I walked right into it.*

***

Over Larnaca Bay, 0445 Hours

It felt good to be airborne again after the long, confined, and relatively tense hours of waiting and rehearsing back in the hangar. The cloud cover had moved out hours before. The air was smooth and the stars bright. Jim Owen spotted the outline of a ship vaguely silhouetted against the ominously black waters of Larnaca Bay. The bright moon cast an eerie glow across the uneven surface of the water.

He scanned his instruments. Heading one-zero-two degrees—destination Cape Greco Point, a peninsula jutting awkwardly out into the Mediterranean Sea on the southeastern edge of Cyprus. It created a landmass that formed part of Larnaca Bay to the west. It was also the location of a large lighthouse, easily identifiable from the air at night. Once there, he would assume a holding pattern for several minutes then turn north toward checkpoint four and a rendezvous with Delta's two assault helicopters.

Jim spotted the dimly glowing halo of Larnaca Town many miles off to his left. He again verified his location, heading, altitude, and airspeed. The early morning Mediterranean sky was dazzling. He peered through the overhead window at the illuminated heavens.

Straight ahead, he could just make out the lighthouse on Cape Greco. Far off to his left, the rotating airport beacon light at Larnaca scanned the night sky. It flashed brightly each time it revolved in his direction.

He checked his watch again. He was almost to Cape Greco where he would set up a holding pattern at twenty-five hundred feet. Then, a few more minutes, and he would proceed on a heading of three-five-five degrees to checkpoint four. He checked the stopwatch on the panel before him. He reviewed the timing to checkpoint four and beyond one more time.

He banked left to assume a racetrack holding pattern. He was nearly vertical over the lighthouse. He checked his watch again. It was 0446. "Seven minutes holding, one to check point four, then six to the target—and its Miller time, baby. They better have some beer," he said chuckling.

***

0446 Hours

Striker laughed, but it made him cough, so he stopped and tried to lie still. A jumble of thoughts raced through his mind. He assumed that his attackers were Shiites from Hezbollah. They could have easily killed him up on the road. A second antitank round would have finished him off, or they could have gunned him down when he lunged from the car.

They wanted him alive, and if they captured him, they would patch him up and nurse him back to health. Once he recovered, the months of torture and interrogation would begin, followed by the humiliating videotapes of his statements released to the West. It would show a broken CIA spymaster indicting the United States and revealing all the CIA's nefarious plots against the Muslim world, real or imagined. He would be fuel for the Lebanese and Iranian Shiite propaganda machines.

"Where is the damn Christian militia?" he grumbled again, clenching his fists. Maybe there weren't even any Christian units in the area. Maybe the Shiites had caused trouble elsewhere to draw off units that normally patrolled this zone. Maybe they didn't even bother to patrol this wasteland sector.

He heard shouting, voices issuing orders in Arabic. They had finished searching the cars and bodies. Striker clawed and elbowed at the rocky dirt, but he couldn't move himself more than a few inches. He was either already at the bottom or on some type of flat ledge. In any case, he no longer had gravity to propel him along. When he tried to move, the pain was so great that he feared he might pass out—something he could not afford to do.

Striker thought briefly about the satellite phone in his left leg pocket but immediately dismissed it. Even if he managed to reach someone on the sat-phone, they could never get to him in time.

The voices were growing louder, as if oriented in his direction. Another illumination flare rocketed up into the sky and burst into a ball of light. The murk disappeared, and it was like day again, except that the shadows of the rocks and brush moved rapidly as the parachute flare drifted overhead. The ever-shifting shadows danced over Striker's pain-wracked body, immobile except for his heaving chest.

He twisted his neck and head, grimacing at the pain and squinting to focus his eyes. He looked up to the edge of the road. One man gave a signal, and a dozen others started over the rim and down into the ravine, slipping and sliding down the steep slope. Several cursed as they lost their footing in the loose rocks and slid or tumbled.

It was difficult to see through the sweat, blood, and dirt that covered his face and eyes, but he had seen enough. The image of the big, sweeping gesture of the leader's hand, as he sent his men over the edge, lingered in his mind.

He clutched at his left side but couldn't locate his pistol. Finally, he found his shoulder holster strap and painfully followed it around. It had slid farther back under his arm. The pistol was still there, but before he could pull it out, he heard voices and the sounds of scuffling feet. Another flare was aloft before the first had burned out.

They would surely see him any minute, he knew. *Goddamn you, Akim. You bastard,* he thought, but he knew Akim was either dead or wishing he was. *What did Cupid tell you? Was the message worth dying for? Maybe you never even had a real message.*

Striker struggled to extract his pistol. He pulled the Smith and Wesson 9mm, 459 automatic from its holster and almost dropped it. It weighed a ton. He grabbed it again with a more solid grip. He looked around once more for additional cover. The flare was drifting farther away, and the shadows were growing longer. He saw a fleeting movement in front of him. Striker froze.

***

Dhekelia, Cyprus, 0447 Hours

The MH-60M Blackhawk and the smaller MH-6H Little Bird sat side-by-side on the British base near Larnaca. Their main rotors whirred in an odd blur highlighted by red anti-collision lights. The crews worked methodically through their checklists. In the Blackhawk's cockpit, the red and yellow illuminated digital instruments pulsated in rhythm with the engine's vibrations. The pilot called his crew chief on the intercom.

"How we doing back there, Henry?" inquired Chief Warrant Officer Smith.

"We've about got 'em all in, Chief."

"Okay, we're good to go up here."

"Roger, Chief."

Chief Smith reviewed the timing again. It was a four-minute flight to checkpoint four, then six to the target. It was 0447. He would take off in two minutes and have sixty seconds to spare in case of head winds at altitude.

The spinning main rotor caused the cool, moist early morning air to swirl down over the last couple of Delta men checking the quick-release attachments on the assault ladders. Though the engines were at full operating RPM, and the noise deafening, the helicopter created only a relatively gentle turbulence. Once Chief Smith applied collective for takeoff, however, the rotor wash could knock a man off his feet.

Team leaders checked their teams one last time. Sergeant Major Barrington checked everyone. They scanned for obstacles on the floor of the helicopter that might trip someone. Then they verified the exact seating arrangement that would allow the teams to spring from the helicopter in the proper order—security team first, ladder men second, assault element next, medics and EOD last.

Sergeant Major Scott Barrington walked the few steps over to the Little Bird. The two men of the forced-entry team would be the first to enter the hijacked Airbus from atop the plane. They sat patiently on the rear seat of their helicopter. The side doors on the chopper had been removed. Just before hovering over the Airbus, the two operators would step out onto a small platform over each of the skids. The men would be secured by a single, quick-release safety strap. They would need only pop the quick-release and hop onto the roof of the airliner.

Barrington gave each man a grin and a thumbs up. The sentiment was returned. He walked back to the Blackhawk just as the crew chief reported to Barrington.

"We're ready."

"Let's do it."

Barrington sat on the floor of the sleek helicopter and buckled in. The crew chief made one last visual sweep of the exterior of the Blackhawk and then climbed into his seat behind the pilot. The other passenger seats had been removed. "Okay, Chief. We're ready back here."

"Roger," was the reply. "Okay, Stan," Chief Smith said to his copilot, "let's get this here show on the road. We ain't getting any younger."

"Roger that." The copilot's left hand danced across the instruments, touching each one as he made a final verification of each critical system. "Okay, Chief, looking good. Blade RPMs steady at three hundred."

"Roger."

The crew chief piped in. "Clear to the rear, Chief."

"Roger. Coming up."

Chief Smith slowly applied collective with his left hand. He controlled the cyclic between the thumb and forefinger of his right hand. For an instant, the Blackhawk's thirteen-thousand-pound mass resisted. More collective and it lifted effortlessly up to a hover. Smith applied a little left pedal to steady the yaw; he eased right and forward a bit on the cyclic.

The smaller helicopter popped up like a hummingbird. The pilot adjusted for the rotor wash coming his way from the Blackhawk. Chief Smith rotated his helicopter and pointed her nose into the wind. As he added collective and eased the stick forward, the nose dropped like a charging bull. The Blackhawk, with the Little Bird in trail, slid gracefully up into the night sky toward their rendezvous with destiny.

***

0449 Hours

Striker rolled over onto his stomach, flinching at the sickening, gut wrenching pain. He heard a man slip and fall in the gloom just in front of him. The man cursed in Arabic and got up slowly, rubbing his right hand against his pants. An AK-47 dangled loosely from his left hand by his side.

He was a young man with a short, scraggly beard and loose-fitting, earth-colored garments typical of the *Mujahedeen*. He was fifteen feet in front of Striker. He turned and looked straight at Striker's prone figure. The man wasn't sure what he saw. The drifting flare and the moving shadows played tricks on his eyes.

He yelled over his shoulder. When he looked back, Striker squeezed the trigger. He had not cocked the pistol, and the double-action trigger was harder to pull than he had anticipated. It didn't fire.

Then the light from the last aerial flare faded, but Striker knew that the young Shiite fighter was nearly on top of him. Striker felt calmer. At least now, he knew for sure what had happened to Akim. Striker knew that Akim had been captured, tortured, and murdered.

"Sorry," Striker said to no one, "but you bastards won't have John Striker's goddamn secrets."

He raised the gun to his mouth and cocked the hammer, but before he could pull the trigger, out of nowhere, a hand snatched the pistol away.

21

On the tail of the Airbus at Larnaca, Cyprus, Jake Brady sat on the starboard horizontal stabilizer, his back against the vertical tailfin. The cool predawn air crawled across the surface of the jet. He readied himself for the explosion he was about to initiate and the quick, sharp, violent action that would immediately follow. Jake was tired and hungry, but he kept such thoughts neatly tucked away in his subconscious.

He glanced at his watch. In eight more minutes, it would be over. All he had to do was flip the switch on his detonator and blow the two closed aircraft doors off their hinges.

The choppers were inbound. His team was on those birds. The thought flashed through his mind that Delta could lose someone in the next few minutes. *No matter how fucking hard you work at it, there's always some shit to mess up your plans*, he reminded himself. Jake and his teammates had been through a lot together. He knew that any one of them would give their life for him as he would for them.

Earlier, Jake had watched Master Sergeant Palmer sneak past the tail section of the jet on his way to the APU. Palmer would cut the APU's power to the plane at H plus three seconds—the precise instant Jake would detonate the doors. Then the Blackhawk would land close behind the tail section and the Little Bird would come to a hover over the Airbus just in front of him.

He heard Colonel Barclay give the code word that the mission was a go. The sniper teams reported their new positions closer to the aircraft. He knew they could see him with their starlight scopes, though he couldn't make them out in the field surrounding the Airbus.

Jake checked his watch—seven minutes. For the fifth time, he conducted a circuit check and a detonator self-test. The circuit was complete, the detonator ready. Jake had also affixed an electronic homing beacon up high on the huge vertical stabilizer fin towering above him. He glanced up to ensure that it was functioning. He saw the faint, greenish glow of the beacon's tiny light as it pulsated. With each pulse, it sent a directional radio wave skyward. The Blackhawk would home in on the beacon and ride it right down to the big jet.

Only minutes now. He reviewed the timing one more time.

***

Striker was dazed, but within a few seconds he realized what had happened. He had been too slow, and now he was doomed. He knew the Shiites would ultimately torture him to death.

A man kneeled over him, but Striker couldn't make out his captor's face. The man raised his arm straight out. In his hand was a pistol with a long silencer attached to the muzzle. He fired twice, but Striker heard no sound. Unseen by Striker, the Shiite fighter closing in on him dropped to the ground, dead.

Just as another flare streaked up into the night sky and popped, two more men ran up to Striker's position from below. He barely noticed the other men as he looked up in astonishment at the one hovering over him—Akim carefully scanned the terrain around them, his pistol sweeping left, then right, searching for another threat.

***

Aboard Air France 622, sleep was difficult. The fortunate ones had finally succumbed to sheer exhaustion and found a dreary half-sleep. The hostages suffered from numerous physical and emotional ailments. Many moaned. A few still sobbed quietly. Some jerked spasmodically as they startled themselves awake from time-to-time with their own tormented dreams, only to settle back into the gloomy yet welcome semi-consciousness.

Mike Elliot did not sleep.

He stared into the night through the porthole window by his seat as he continued scraping his bindings against the seat frame. Amid the sickening odors of the foul cabin air, the early-morning hours had brought a faint hint of fresh breeze. It was a little cooler, and more quiet, than the previous day. Mike knew, however, that this brief respite would not last.

The worst was yet to come. With the coming light, a torturous new day would begin. It would be a day of scorching heat and short tempers. It would be a day he was sure none of them, neither the passengers nor the terrorists, could endure with their sanity intact.

Mike had now begun to question their very survival. Either the terrorists would fly the plane away and the drama would renew itself elsewhere, or another passenger, maybe several, would almost certainly be killed. Something had to give. They were all near the breaking point.

His thoughts returned to his plan. Just pushing a terrorist out the door would not work. He needed a weapon. If he could free his hands, he felt he could take one of the smaller terrorists as he stood guard in the doorway. He had carefully visualized the exact techniques and moves he would use to takedown and disable the terrorist. He would kill him and take his weapons. It would be a desperate move, but the situation demanded it. So far, though, he could not be sure if he had managed to cut through his bindings at all.

All he could do for now, was keep scraping.

***

Akim nodded at the two men with him. They quickly slung their weapons over their backs and scooped Striker up from the ground. One man gripped him under the armpits; the other grabbed his legs. Striker's vision dimmed, and he stifled a scream.

His right leg was barely attached just above the ankle; it dangled from a few ligaments and some thin strands of raw muscle. Akim produced a switchblade from somewhere, snapped it open, and with one clean swipe, he sliced through the tissue letting the foot drop to the sand. He picked it up and flung it farther down the hill and over a ledge. He checked Striker's tourniquet. It was tight.

Akim nodded again, and the two men ran toward a ditch a short distance away. He kept his pistol oriented to the rear. They all entered a narrow but deep ravine that ran northeast out of the enemy's search zone.

The men ran through the dark of the ravine, stumbling occasionally. To the rear, Akim ran backwards, his pistol trained in the direction they had come. With each bouncing step the men took, Striker gritted his teeth and fought to remain conscious.

***

Captain Owen banked his small, fixed-wing aircraft in a left-hand circle for the last time. Verifying the stopwatch mounted on the cockpit instrument panel, he leveled out on a heading of three-five-five degrees. He scanned his instruments—altitude twenty-five hundred feet, airspeed one hundred knots. One minute remained to checkpoint four and link up.

Several miles to the northeast, the two U.S. Army helicopters flying in tight formation, had just reached altitude. They were also closing on that point in the sky twenty-five hundred feet over the lighted buoy designated as checkpoint four. Chief Warrant Officer Smith located Owen's small plane on his cockpit radar display.

"Condor, this is Hammerhead, radar contact, two-two-zero degrees, over," said Smith.

"Roger, Hammerhead, I have you visual, thirty seconds to checkpoint four, over," said Captain Owen.

Owen could see the two helicopter's flashing anti-collision lights several miles to his right. Their lights would remain on until linkup. From checkpoint four to the ground, the two army helicopters would fly in blackout mode. Only Owen's lights would remain on.

In Lieutenant Colonel Barclay's van, he and Colonel Sinclair observed the target and monitored the progress of the approaching assault element. At the main CP on Akrotiri, Lieutenant Colonel Wilson, and a deathly silent staff, stared at the video monitors and waited.

Captain Owen banked slightly left as he crossed over checkpoint four. Chief Warrant Officer Smith banked right and fell in line behind Owen at an interval of three hundred yards. *Perfect,* thought Smith. *Six minutes to target.* He extinguished the rotating anti-collision lights. The Little Bird pilot followed suit.

"Tango, Hammerhead, checkpoint four, over."

Lieutenant Colonel Barclay responded. "Tango, roger, out."

The countdown began.

***

0454 Hours

Colonel Krokos left the surging crowd of reporters and walked past a Cypriot police officer. He passed through a set of swinging doors and stepped into the relative calm of Larnaca airport's back offices. *How could the reporters still be there waiting like vultures at this hour?* he wondered.

He walked down the gloomy corridor with his most dignified stride, his hands locked behind his back, his head high. As the official assigned to represent the Cypriot government and coordinate its efforts on scene, Colonel Krokos had many responsibilities. Among those, the press conferences were the most distasteful, especially when he had nothing to tell them. In just a few short moments, though, he would be informing them of the untimely demise of four unfortunate Arab terrorists—and that *his* plan was successful. That would be more rewarding.

The spindly little colonel stepped into the airport police control center. It was less a command hub and more a drab room with two scarred and battered desks, a tired old captain of police, his sergeant, and several dozing officers. It wasn't much, but due to the crisis, Krokos was also in command here.

He had been en route to the tower to observe Delta's assault but decided to make one last, quick check on the airport's security. "Everything okay?" he asked the captain.

"Yes, sir," replied the captain with a tired smile. "Oh, only a minor, little problem, nothing important. Post number six, and a roving patrol, haven't checked in, but I'm sure it's just a radio issue. We have been having a lot of problems with radio batteries lately."

"Where is post six?"

"On the roof of the maintenance building."

"And did you send someone to check on it?"

"I was just about to," replied the captain, turning and snapping his fingers at one of the officers sitting behind him. The man stood, straightened his cap, and moved out the door.

"They're probably asleep," said Krokos.

"Perhaps. But it's more likely the radio."

"If they are asleep, I want a disciplinary report."

"Yes, sir," he answered respectfully, knowing he would tell the little man later that the radio was out, regardless.

Glancing at his watch, Krokos decided he didn't have time to reach the tower before the Americans assaulted the plane. "I will be here at the rear door of the building," said Krokos to the captain, pointing.

He spun and re-entered the hallway. *Such buffoons*, he thought. The next time something serious occurred here, he decided, they would bring in the national police to maintain airport security.

He stepped out the back door and stood in the dark staring at the dim white outline of Air France 622 in the distance. It had been a long thirty-six hours, and the past night had dragged by particularly slowly. *But it won't be much longer now*, he mused.

***

Akim and the two men carrying Striker had traveled about two hundred yards under the cover of the ditch-like ravine. They could no longer hear the shouts of the Shiites searching for them.

Striker tapped on the hand of the man gripping him under his arms until they stopped and lowered him to the ground. Akim knelt down beside him. The other men stood guard, weapons ready.

Striker gripped Akim's arm and pulled him closer. "What happened?" he asked. "Why didn't you show at the Alfonse?"

"There was a trap. I was attacked, but I eluded them. I took my brother's car and came here."

"How did they know *I* was coming here?"

"I don't know. I'm pretty sure they didn't follow me here, but I guess it's possible they did. I also sent my great uncle to Beirut to call you, and he has not returned. Maybe they grabbed him. I don't really know."

"Or, maybe they *let* you escape so you would lead them to me." Pulling the younger man even closer, Striker asked, "Was there really a message?"

"Yes, and I risked my life to get it, so maybe we're even. I need to get out of the country before they can get to me."

"We'll see. What is the message?"

"Mustafa, a.k.a. the Scimitar, is on Larnaca Airport right now."

"Shit," mouthed Striker. "Left pocket," he said, trying, but unable to reach his left leg pocket.

Akim found the pocket and extracted the portable satellite phone. He unfolded and extended the antenna. The glass face on the device was cracked, but it powered up and quickly acquired a satellite.

"Okay," said Akim, "it's on."

"Dial," said Striker, squinting his eyes and fighting the pain. Then he said, "Zero, zero, one, seven, two, niner, three, three, three," while Akim pressed the illuminated buttons on the phone.

A line picked up in the CIA's Langley operations center. A female voice said, "State your code and your emergency."

Akim handed the phone to Striker.

"Alpha, zulu, three, two, niner, seven, six, zulu."

"Go ahead," said the voice on the line.

Striker quickly passed the information on Mustafa.

***

Barely a moment later, Wilson called Sinclair and Barclay over the radio. He didn't wait for a reply.

"Flash message from Langley," said Wilson rapidly. "There is a fifth terrorist on the airport grounds. Repeat, fifth terrorist at Larnaca airport, over."

"Acknowledged," replied Barclay.

He jerked up a Motorola handset from a single charging console in the corner of the van and called Colonel Krokos.

"Krokos, Barclay here. Come in," said Barclay into the portable radio.

The Cypriot pulled his radio from his belt. "Colonel Krokos here, go ahead."

"Colonel, there is a fifth terrorist somewhere here on the airport grounds. How copy, over?"

Krokos needed only seconds to comprehend.

"I think I know where," replied Krokos into the radio. "We are going there now."

"Shit," muttered Sinclair in disbelief.

"Should we put Scott on hold?" asked Barclay.

"They're forty seconds out," said Sinclair, shaking his head. "If we don't hit them now, we'll never get another chance. We have to carry through."

Barclay nodded. "I'm gonna let Scott know what's going on."

***

It was two minutes to 5 a.m., noted Mustafa. He would allow himself two more minutes and not one moment longer. Then he would kill the two commandos lurking around the plane and disassemble his rifle. He had already repacked the scanner. He would then slip quietly out the back of the building, over the fence, and out across the rough, bushy terrain to his rendezvous. He would leave Abdul to his own devices. Foremost for Mustafa was his own survival.

Perhaps though, he mused, his plans could still succeed, and he might yet have a chance of getting this plane back to Beirut where his men could get control of it on the ground. Defeating and embarrassing the Americans in Cyprus, and getting the plane back to Beirut, would be the ultimate victory. The Muslim world would revere his exploits.

He scanned the immediate vicinity of the Airbus and saw no change in the situation. He leveled his rifle on the young commando on the tail section of the plane. Mustafa decided that this man had wired the plane with electronic devices or explosives. *Probably explosives*, he thought, *and he will initiate the assault.*

Mustafa knew he would have to be quick, but he would eliminate the man on top first, before he could detonate his charges. Then, he would cut down as many of the ground assault element as possible before retreating.

He was sure he could cut down quite a few, and they would have no idea from which direction they were being killed.

***

Krokos bounded back through the door into the police precinct. "Quickly," he shouted to the captain, "get your other man. Hurry now!" he screamed. "And bring weapons."

Colonel Krokos hurried across the tarmac toward the maintenance building with three Cypriot police officers in tow. He had picked up the officer sent to check on post six. He realized he should keep the Americans informed. Without slowing his pace, he raised his Motorola handset to his lips and called Barclay.

"Colonel Barclay," he whispered into the portable radio, already puffing to catch his breath, "Colonel Barclay."

"Yes, Colonel, this is Barclay."

"Colonel, I think the intruder is on the top of the flat-roofed maintenance building. My post there is overdue to call in. My men and I are going there to investigate."

Barclay asked Colonel Sinclair, "Should we go assist Krokos?"

"No," replied Sinclair. "The Cypriot police would just end up shooting at us, and our attention needs to be focused here. Let's just pray Krokos deals with it."

22

The three aircraft moved in loose formation. Captain Owen's light plane still displayed its anti-collision lights. The two army helicopters, flying side-by-side some three hundred yards to the rear, appeared only as dark, ghostly figures against the night sky.

"Hammerhead-six, Tango-one," said Barclay over the radio calling Barrington, "possible armed intruder on airport grounds. Cypriot police are trying to deal with situation. So far, no sign. For the moment, the terrorists are still quiet. How copy, over?"

"Roger, I copy," was Barrington's cool reply. "Coming in."

"Roger, out."

Barrington reached up and tapped Chief Smith on the shoulder. "Could be a hot landing zone, Chief," he said over the intercom.

"So what else is new?"

Barrington passed the word to each man.

Chief Smith's copilot adjusted an instrument on the console, part of a dim little screen with a grid of thin black lines. "Okay, Chief, I've got the NDB five-by," he said, referring to the navigation directional beacon that Jake Brady had planted on the vertical stabilizer of the Airbus. "We're on target."

"Roger," replied Smith without looking down at the instruments. He reported to Jake, "Jockey, Hammerhead, got your beacon five-by. It's calibrated, over."

"Roger, out," whispered Jake.

Behind Chief Smith, in the Blackhawk's troop compartment, the Delta men waited. Some stared at the dark floor in concentration. Others gazed calmly out the open doors of the helicopter. A cold wind rushed through the cabin, and specks of light glimmered off the dark sea below. Now that the cloud cover had moved out to sea, stars filled the predawn sky and flashed through the rotor blades, creating sparkling halos of light.

In the lead, Captain Owen crossed checkpoint three and came right twelve degrees. He was thirty-five seconds out. "Tango," he said into his lip mic, "Condor, checkpoint three, over."

"Roger, out."

The two helicopters continued straight ahead, on course. Five seconds passed and Owen pressed the new button on his instrument panel. The flares on his left wing strut sputtered into life and soon burned brightly. The smoke grenades popped with a flash and settled into a steady, hissing stream of grayish-white smoke. It was a ghostly sight. Owen shielded his eyes with his gloved left hand and concentrated on the runway.

Sergeant Major Scott Barrington glanced briefly out the right door of the Blackhawk at Owen's small plane some distance away. He could afford no more than a glimpse without risking his night vision, but he thought the effects were convincing. He wondered if Owen's plane might have actually caught fire from the flares.

***

Hamud informed Abdul of the approaching in-flight emergency—an aircraft with an engine on fire was coming in for a possible crash landing. The airport had no choice but to receive the plane immediately. No one would approach the Airbus, he assured Abdul. The terrorists were vaguely suspicious. Under the circumstances, they were paranoid of everything, but they were not yet alarmed. Three of them gathered starboard to watch the incoming plane. As Delta had expected from past observations, they did not show themselves in the doorway.

Abdul instructed Khalid Moussa to maintain surveillance on the opposite side of the plane, just in case. Through the tiny porthole in the portside door, Khalid stared at the tarmac and field beyond. He glanced back starboard frequently in an effort to see the plane crash that was about to happen.

In the predawn night, the flares and smokes mounted on Captain Owen's little plane created an impressive diversion as it loomed ever larger on the horizon. It was a bright ball of fire, trailing flame and smoke, as it bounced and coasted toward the Earth.

Gazing back out the porthole into the dim light across the tarmac, Khalid caught a fleeting glimpse of shadows moving near a cluster of airport buildings, but they disappeared as quickly as he had spotted them. He told himself that it was his imagination. He returned his attention to the ball of flame in the sky.

***

Mustafa peered through his scope at the Air France Airbus. It was time to leave. He had just enough time to make it to his boat before daylight arrived. He would leave his calling card by killing the two commandos, and then slip away into the night.

Braced against the low wall, he methodically steadied his rifle on his hand and arm. He carefully formed his sight picture in the scope. The one on top first, he thought, steadying his breathing and applying pressure to the trigger.

A sudden bright glow flitted across the periphery of his night-vision scope. He looked up into the distant night sky. He had already repacked his radio scanner to hasten his departure, or he would have heard Hamud explaining the incoming emergency. As it was, the apparition in the night sky stupefied him. The approaching object was a bright ball of flickering flame, unidentifiable as anything he had ever seen.

"What in the world is happening here?" Mustafa asked himself as he gaped at the looming ball of flame low in the night sky.

He tried to look at it with his night-vision scope, but it was too bright, so he watched with binoculars. He could make out only smoke and flame. It was obviously some type of aircraft, apparently on fire, and it was coming in for a landing. Several fire engines began pulling out of their bays farther down the row of buildings, moving toward the runways.

Very curious, he reasoned, *that such an emergency would develop just at this particular moment—the moment I most expected an assault by the Americans.*

He quickly rechecked the Airbus and the field around it with his scope. He detected no movement or change. *This must be a diversion*, he thought, *but if so, where are the attacking commandos?* He had expected them to crawl in from the field. *Perhaps they are on the fire trucks*, he mused, *or maybe they have a vehicle concealed in a hangar and plan to rush out at the last instant.*

I must kill them now. He took careful aim at the commando on top of the plane. Then a dull thump on the door behind made him spin around to face the threat. He assumed it was one or two police officers coming to check on the guard post.

Colonel Krokos had hit the locked door with his shoulder. Just behind him, lined up on the narrow, un-railed staircase, his three Cypriot officers waited.

Krokos flattened himself against the wall and signaled a man forward. The officer moved to the door. He thrust his twelve-gauge pump shotgun up to the doorknob, pulled the trigger, and burst through the door.

It all happened in the blink of an eye. There was a horrendous noise and a blinding flash. The shotgun blast caught Mustafa by surprise. The officer with the shotgun came running out onto the roof but lost precious seconds locating his target. Mustafa was dressed in a Cypriot police officer's uniform, further confusing the man.

On the stairway, Krokos signaled his remaining two men up past him and onto the roof. They were no match for Mustafa. He had more than enough time to cut all three down in rapid succession. The last two Cypriots had gotten off shots, but they were wild. It was still now. Three bodies were piled one on top of the other, mere steps beyond the doorway.

That was it, thought Mustafa. He turned back to the aircraft to finish the job he had begun three times.

The compact little Cypriot staff officer stood on the top step of the staircase, just behind the edge of the doorframe. He held his pearl-handled, nickel-plated .38 caliber revolver at high port. He had not fired it in eighteen months. He didn't know why he had raced off with the officers. Impulse, he supposed. He should have just sent them over here to check on the guard post. He was here now, however, and he had seen enough through the flashes of gunfire to know that he had just sent three men to their deaths.

He could feel his cold patrician blood coursing through his veins like ice water. It pounded in his ringing ears. He knew that his destiny was upon him. He would not shirk from it. He stood erect, as usual. He was calm. Krokos hesitated for only a handful of breaths. He stepped into the doorway, raised his arm, and aimed.

Mustafa heard the movement behind him and spun around, his reflexes like lightning.

***

Abdul and his men watched Owen's plane while carefully scanning the tarmac for commandos. Then the crack of distant gunfire shattered the still night air. They looked at each other in shock. They scurried from window to window, peering into the night in search of attackers. They found none. Someone had been shooting but apparently not at them. They looked back and forth between the incoming diversion and the surrounding field.

Finally, Abu Hassim yelled to Abdul. "There are too many things happening all of a sudden to be mere coincidence."

Abdul nodded. "We will take off."

***

Colonel Krokos felt as if he were moving in slow motion as he stepped into the doorway leading onto the roof. He was only vaguely aware of a rapid shuffling movement just in front of him. As he tried to aim at the blurry silhouette before him, he could feel, rather than see, his life flashing before his eyes. He knew with great clarity that his time on this Earth was about to end. Then, time stopped altogether.

Mustafa came around to face the new intruder, his pistol already drawn in a deadly blur. Krokos somehow willed his body to move, to step to one side. He heard a tinny clink as a round hit the metal wall next to his right ear. Fear gripped his throat like a vise. He could no longer breathe. The pistol in his hand felt too heavy to lift.

***

"Hurry," Hassim yelled at Abdul's back, as the smaller man scrambled toward the pilots. Abdul rushed into the cockpit, pistol in hand, screaming at the pilots to take off. The pilots, too, had heard the gunfire. They could see the fear in Abdul's eyes and the sweat on his brow. They quickly began to start the engines.

Abdul hopped nervously from one foot to the other as Hamud urged calm. "There's been a disturbance," he was saying. "It has nothing to do with you. Remain calm."

The instant Master Sergeant Palmer heard the engines begin to turn he tried to cut power coming from the APU, but it was too late. The APU had already provided the burst of electricity the aircraft needed—the Airbus could now complete starting its engines under its own power.

The unmistakable accelerating whine of jet engines filled the night air. Palmer reached up and disconnected the APU cable from the belly of the plane, otherwise it might drag the APU, possibly damaging the aircraft and endangering the hostages.

Abdul watched the frantically working pilots for a second, but he was too nervous to remain in the cockpit. He had to see what was happening in the back. He jammed his pistol hard into Captain Granger's neck and screamed, "Take off now! Or when I return you will die, I swear it!" He turned and raced back to the passenger cabin.

***

Mustafa adjusted his aim and began to squeeze off a second round to dispatch this new threat. Krokos fired. A .38 caliber slug entered Mustafa's forehead slightly above his black, bushy eyebrows. Somehow, the diminutive Cypriot staff officer had accomplished what a dozen Western intelligence agencies had tried to do for as many years. He had slain the notorious and deadly Scimitar.

23

Captain Owen and his diversion aircraft were close now. His little plane hovered on the horizon like a small sun about to drop into the sea. The choppers were mere seconds behind him.

Colonel Sinclair called Scott Barrington. "Hammerhead, Raven, we've got gunfire in the maintenance buildings approximately nine hundred yards from the target. Engines turning on the Airbus. They're onto us. How copy, over?"

"We'll be on them in ten seconds!" Barrington yelled into the mic. To the Blackhawk's pilot, he said, "Chief, get us the hell down there."

"Fast as I can," he replied, "but we can't put down in the wake of those jet engines. We'll crash."

"Wherever you can, Chief, just get us in close."

"Roger that."

Only seconds from the Airbus, Barrington called Brady. "Jockey, Hammerhead, blow the doors, now!" Then he radioed the snipers. "Eagle, engage."

Hunkered down on top of the huge tail section of the A300B Airbus, Jake Brady groped for a handhold. He fought to stay on the plane as the pilots worked to get the big jet over the wheel chocks that the Cypriot ground crew had put in place just after landing on the first day. Jake had heard his orders, and he was trying like hell to comply, but the Airbus swayed and bounced in protest. It was like trying to stay on a bucking mustang. The plane strained and rocked back and forth between the front and rear chocks. The twin jet engines roared in Jake's ears.

The terrorists were in utter panic, running from window to window, but they were unable to detect a real threat. They were still watching intently as fire engines pulled into place out on the runway, nowhere near the Airbus, their flashing red lights adding to the eerie scene. They watched in awe as Owen's plane approached the outer runway marker, lower and lower, its wings wobbling desperately as if struggling almost in vain to remain aloft. Captain Owen gave a virtuoso performance.

Even after hearing the distant gunfire, the terrorists couldn't determine what was happening and were still mesmerized by the approaching spectacle of Owen's little plane on the horizon. Delta's plan would have worked perfectly but for the intruder and the Cypriot's gunfire.

Despite the fact that one set of wheels was chocked, out of fear for his life, the captain was doing his utmost to carry out Abdul's instructions to take off.

Jake was finally able to grab the vertical stabilizer to keep from falling off. He quickly activated the detonator in his left hand. Delta's carefully crafted diversion came to an abrupt end for the terrorists. Abdul had returned from the cockpit and he, Abu Hassim, and Mohammed Halid were looking out the passenger windows near the right front door. They were hidden from Delta's snipers. Khalid Moussa was near the door on the opposite side that was wired with explosives.

The charges ripped the two closed doors from their hinges. The two massive passenger doors, one on the left front, the other on the right rear of the Airbus, fell inwards. The explosion of the door threw Khalid onto the floor before he was crushed to death as the massive door came crashing down on top of him. The other three terrorists were stunned by the force of the explosion.

Owen brought his plane down hard, bouncing several times and skidding to a stop on runway two-one, seven hundred yards directly north of the hijacked Airbus exactly as planned. Cypriot fire trucks, sirens blaring, red lights flashing, pulled out onto the runway, racing toward the little plane. Hammerhead's Blackhawk settled to a stop not twenty feet off the left wingtip of the huge airliner. Smith had adjusted his landing point to avoid the vortex of the jet's engines.

Commandos poured from the Blackhawk as the Little Bird moved into position above the Airbus, its two commandos ready to step the last few inches from the skid onto the top of the jet.

Captain Granger heard and felt the explosion, but it only heightened his fear. He applied near full power for the fraction of a second it took to force the big plane over the chocks. The jet bucked wildly as it bolted forward. He reduced power to avoid damaging the aircraft, but he continued to taxi.

Delta's men raced forward with their ladders chasing the fleeing plane. The Little Bird pilot crabbed his helicopter horizontally trying to maintain his position over the Airbus.

Inside, it took several seconds for the three remaining terrorists to begin recovering from the explosion. They could only vaguely hear the helicopter above the airplane. At first, they were too dazed to react. Chaos swirled about them.

Abu Hassim recovered first. He had been the farthest from the exploding door. He shook his head and finally managed to focus his eyes. He stumbled toward the rear of the plane. A death wail had erupted from the passengers. The children closed their eyes tightly in an effort to escape the clamor.

Barrington stared at the scene in disbelief. He realized that they were not going to succeed. A few of his men had actually made it to the plane, but they could not board it on the move. He shouted the order to abort over the radio.

The men all heard: *Abort—Abort—Abort*, surging through their headsets.

The two Delta operators standing on the skids of their helicopter above the jet remained strapped in as their pilot pulled up sharply to avoid the looming vertical stabilizer charging toward them. The small helicopter peeled away and disappeared as fast as it had arrived.

Barrington called for smoke to cover their withdrawal, and the men on the tarmac began popping smokes as they withdrew. The jet's engines quickly cleared away the ground smoke directly behind the plane, but the smoke grenades the commandos continued to drop as they ran toward the Blackhawk concealed the helicopter.

Twenty-two miles to the east, a U.S. C-17 medical aircraft on final approach to Larnaca Airport pulled up and veered left, aborting its landing.

Barrington was on one knee watching the murky silhouettes of his men as they reversed course back to the Blackhawk. The last men out of the chopper were already back aboard, but the first men out were still forty yards away and running to the waiting helo.

On the plane, Abu Hassim scurried aft. He dove onto the floor by the portside door, searching for the helicopters he thought he had heard. He could make out only thick clouds of muddy, gray smoke roiling up from the spewing canisters.

Abu Hassim lay in the open door, his Uzi dangling outside. He could not see the withdrawing commandos, but he fired into the smoke. In his confusion, he assumed the attackers were still coming toward him. When the terrorist had emptied one magazine, he loaded another and resumed firing.

Abu Hassim's aim was not accurate, but Barrington and his men could hear the whistle of bullets hitting all around them. Rounds sparked off the pavement as the commandos hastily reloaded the helicopter. Retreating under fire, the men were orderly, their discipline solid. Several bullets tore through the Blackhawk and rang through the cabin. Chief Smith glanced at his copilot.

"Shit's getting hot, Stan. Wish they'd come on." He increased power and prepared for takeoff.

"Two-ninety RPMs," remarked the copilot.

Out on the field, Delta's snipers searched through their scopes to acquire the terrorist firing from the airplane door, but he remained concealed by the doorframe and the waves of smoke drifting across the tarmac.

Over the firing and the mayhem, the turbofan jet engines of the Airbus whirred ever louder as Granger applied more power. The plane began to pull away.

Mohammed finally regained his senses. He and Abdul had been closer to the exploding door. Mohammed became aware of gunfire echoing through the plane. He turned and dove into the open forward portside doorway. The door itself covered Khalid. His blood was everywhere. Mohammed caught a brief glimpse of the Blackhawk to the rear of the plane. He began firing.

Directly below him he saw the dark silhouette of someone under the plane. Master Sergeant Palmer had been crouched behind the APU just under the cockpit. As the big plane began to lumber over him, he ran along just behind the front nose gear. Over the roar of the engines, he heard machine gun fire coming from the front passenger door overhead.

Palmer unholstered his .45 caliber Colt Commander and sprinted along beneath the belly of the Airbus for a distance. Then he jumped out to the side, aimed, and fired one round. The terrorist's prone figure offered only an eight-inch, moving target in the darkness, and Palmer just grazed him.

The terrorist returned fire. Palmer saw the fiery burst, then instantly two rounds thumped heavily against his body armor like karate kicks to the chest. A third bullet ripped through his arm. He spun, fell, and sensed the colossal rear double tires of the Airbus rapidly bearing down on him, only inches away. Palmer rolled to the side, but one of the massive tires caught part of his pants leg and briefly pinned him to the concrete. He would have one hell of a bruise, but he was alive. Mohammed resumed firing at the Blackhawk.

Perched atop the Airbus, Jake Brady knew that a terrorist was firing from the doorway below him. He took two bounding steps on top of the moving aircraft and lunged for the knotted rope he had installed over the passenger door, almost falling from the roof of the plane. Jake didn't hesitate. He grasped the rope and swung down into the open door. The plane veered crazily, and he landed hard and off balance, half on Abu Hassim, half off. He tumbled forward onto his face.

Abu Hassim quickly rolled over and sat upright. He flailed at Jake like a ferocious animal. He grabbed him by the back of the collar and pulled him into his clutches. Jake's back was to the big man. Hassim worked his huge right arm around his neck. Jake tried to draw his pistol with his right hand; he repeatedly slammed his left elbow into the terrorist's ribs.

He struggled to free himself from the hold, but Abu Hassim was twice his size and strength. The terrorist tightened his grip on Jake's neck, cinching his arm tighter under his chin. With his left arm, he pushed forward on the back of Jake's head, snapping his neck. Jake lay still. Abu Hassim pushed the lifeless body aside, rolled back over, and resumed firing.

Barrington's helicopter was under fire from two locations on the plane. Several rounds ricocheted upwards off the tarmac and zipped through the Blackhawk's spinning rotor. Chief Smith felt the ripple in the sensitive cyclic grip and casually mentioned it to his copilot. He leaned forward to flip a switch on the console. A bullet tore through the Plexiglas windshield and ricocheted off his Kevlar flight helmet and out a side window. Everyone ducked reflexively. Smith felt as if someone had just hit him with a brick.

Inside the Airbus, Abdul staggered about, confused and bleeding. He watched in horror, shaking his head, as first one, then the other of his comrades ran to the open doors to confront their attackers. Then, regaining some orientation, he headed toward the cockpit.

Sitting in the front row, the exploding door had knocked Marie to the floor. She was nearly in shock, and her nose bled profusely as she struggled to get up. She was between Abdul and the cockpit, and he was in panic. He struck her with the back of his hand. As she bounced off the cabin wall, he jerked his pistol from his belt and jabbed it into her abdomen. He rapidly pulled the trigger twice. She collapsed. Abdul stumbled over her body and fell into the cockpit. He jumped up, slammed and locked the door behind him, and fell back against it.

He waved his pistol at the pilots. "Take off!" he screamed in French.

"We're moving as fast as we can!" yelled Captain Granger. Out of the corner of his eye, he saw his copilot make a move. Didier lunged for Abdul's arm, but he never made it out of his seat. Abdul shot him point-blank in the face. Granger recoiled at the ear shattering noise only inches from his head. Didier's already dead body hung there in the air for an instant, twitching and spurting blood in bright red gushes. The bullet had exited his carotid artery and out through the windshield. Then Didier crumpled to the cockpit floor, spewing blood onto Abdul's shoes.

"Take off!" shouted Abdul, as he pressed the pistol against the side of Captain Granger's head. In shock, the captain returned his attention to his console. His movements were mechanical and jerky. He was in a robotic trance, eyes glazed as he stared at the gauges. The ritual of flying a plane, however, was habit. He increased power and the two huge jet engines responded.

A handful of seconds had passed since Colonel Krokos had confronted the intruder and Staff Sergeant Brady had detonated the passenger doors on the airliner. Most of the assault element was back in the Blackhawk. Two security men and Sergeant Major

Barrington remained on the ground. Barrington ordered his last two men aboard. He ran to the waiting chopper behind them.

Rounds showered the hardstand around the Blackhawk. The shooters seemed to be zeroing in on the helicopter. Barrington stepped up into the waiting chopper as bullets licked the concrete under his feet.

***

The blast that collapsed the rear passenger door had dazed Mike Elliot. As he came to, he was aware of an intense ringing in his ears. His head was splitting, his vision blurred. He looked around. A short distance away, Abu Hassim lay on his belly, his back to Mike.

The plastic zip ties still bound Mike's hands. He began scraping the plastic straps against the seat frame, as he had done for hours on end, but this time with all his might. It finally broke through, and his hands were free.

Mike released his seat belt, vaulted from his seat, and lunged at Abu Hassim. His hands were high over his head, clinched tightly together in a double fist. He forced the full weight of his body into those fists as they crashed down on the back of Abu Hassim's neck, knocking the man unconscious. The terrorist's body went limp.

Mike could hear more firing from the front of the plane. His breath came in awkward gulps, and his heart thundered in his chest. He jerked the terrorist over onto his back. He was standing straddled over Abu Hassim as he grabbed the pistol tucked into the man's belt. His hands and arms were nearly numb from being bound for so long, and it was awkward trying to hold the pistol. He struggled to cock the hammer.

Suddenly, Mike felt as if a steel vise had clamped down on his left calf. It felt like someone was spinning the lever on the vice tighter and tighter, crushing the muscle in his leg. He grimaced in pain. He looked down to see a wild-eyed Abu Hassim scowling up at him, his massive right hand clutching Mike's leg. Fingers like steel rods dug into tissue like jackhammers. It was excruciating.

The big man jerked Mike down to him. He landed hard on his knees. The Arab slapped the pistol from his hands and groped for his throat with his left hand. The 9mm pistol skidded unheard across the deck.

Mike blocked the first attempt to grab his throat, but Hassim quickly adjusted and found his target. Mike tucked his chin trying to protect himself, but Hassim was too strong. He could feel the grip tightening on his neck. He grimaced in pain, and his eyes rolled up.

He felt the life slipping from his body. He knew he had seconds to live. The only thing he could move was his left arm. Consciousness was about to slip away. He reached out and probed with his left hand and fingers. He got his palm on the man's face. He could feel Hassim's large nose, then he found an eye, then both.

Mike's vision was dimming. He began to feel at peace with just slipping away and being done with it all. No more pain. No more memories. His hand started to fall away from the big Arab's face. Mike was going limp.

As he faded into oblivion, he could see his wife, Lynn, in his mind's eye. The expression on her beautiful face turned to disappointment. He seemed to hear himself scream in rage, but the scream was in his mind.

Mike's eyes popped open wide. He could see the large, bearded face looking up at him through wide, dark, fierce eyes. Mike thrust his left arm out and drove the full length of his middle and index fingers into Abu Hassim's two eyes.

Hassim jerked his hand from Mike's throat and pulled it toward the sockets where his eyes had been, but never made it. The hand and arm seemed frozen in air. Hassim was already in shock, and his body twitched spasmodically.

Mike collapsed on Abu Hassim, gasping for breath, his face against Hassim's. Blood streamed down both sides of the Arab's head from empty eye sockets, now nothing more than large, deep pools of blood.

Mike's adrenaline was still pumping. His throat and lungs burned, but he finally managed to suck in a breath. He felt around with the bloody fingers of his left hand and found the pistol. He tried to get up but couldn't seem to move his left leg. Hassim had stopped twitching and was still, but he was taking no chances with this one.

He jabbed the pistol in against the terrorist's ribs but then stopped and didn't shoot. The man was already dead, and Mike knew he had more killing to do. *Don't waste ammo*, he thought. He managed to get to his knees, but he had to pry the dead fingers of Abu Hassim from his leg before he could stand.

He tucked the pistol into his belt. He stooped, grabbed the terrorist's legs, and with an enormous effort, flipped him out the door. Through the van's camera, Barclay saw Number Three hit the tarmac and tumble a dozen yards in the plane's direction of travel. Delta concluded, erroneously, that Jake Brady was succeeding in his attack.

Though it seemed to Mike as if time itself had stopped, and for him it momentarily had, his struggle with Abu Hassim had taken only thirty seconds. He saw a soldier lying next to the cabin wall. He checked for a pulse but couldn't find one. He didn't expect to—the young man's neck was twisted grotesquely at an odd angle. Mike turned and moved forward, limping badly. Then he forced himself to run, sprinting toward the sound of automatic fire coming from the front of the plane.

Running up the aisle, his vision clouded by tears, he was scarcely aware of the passengers screaming and swaying back and forth all around him. Some had unfastened their seatbelts and were moving around. He dodged them as he bolted forward.

He was moving fast by the time he reached the forward section of the cabin. He almost tripped on the bearded face of a dead terrorist sticking out from under the collapsed front passenger door. Mike hit the front bulkhead with his shoulder.

Another terrorist was lying on top of the collapsed door, firing his weapon outside toward the rear of the plane. The terrorist sensed movement behind him. He rolled over onto his back, swinging his small machine gun around as he did. He fired wildly, and a string of four or five rounds whizzed past Mike's left ear, poking a neat row of holes in the roof above his head.

Mike recovered, his pistol ready and gripped tightly in both hands, arms extended. He fired once and the round entered just under the terrorist's chin, bursting into a soggy, pink spray of blood as the bullet exploded from the top of the man's skull.

Mike sank to the floor, the life-giving adrenaline deserting him and draining his body of strength. He was vaguely aware of the flight attendant next to him on the floor. She lay slumped over just outside the cockpit door. Then he realized that the plane was moving.

He struggled to reconstruct the string of events that had just occurred. He knew that three terrorists were dead. He had killed two, and he could now make out the head and shoulder of the third terrorist, sticking out from under the collapsed aircraft door on the floor just in front of him. *Was there another one?* Mike slowly raised his eyes to the cockpit door.

He looked back at the flight attendant, and with difficulty, pulled himself the remaining three feet to her. It was Marie, and there was no pulse. He reached up, aimed his pistol, and tried to open the cockpit door. It was locked. He laid his head back against the wall.

An intense pain surged through his shoulder and neck. He even wondered if he might have broken something but dismissed the thought. His throat was badly bruised, and the fire-like pain in his left calf pulled at his attention as well.

He looked up and spotted his wife, Lynn. She was in the third row, aisle seat, only a dozen feet away. She unbuckled her belt and bolted from her seat toward her husband. Mike managed to stand, and he pulled her tight against his chest. She cried as he kissed her.

She was stunned by the exploding door and had not seen or heard Abdul shoot Marie. Now, she looked down, saw her, and screamed. She looked back up at Mike expectantly, and he shook his head. Lynn dropped to the floor, her hands still bound. She pressed her body against Marie and wailed in agony. Mike bent down, put his hand on her shoulder, and yelled to her, "I love you."

He stood and turned to face the cockpit door. Through gritted teeth, he growled, "No, dammit! It ends here!" He felt the plane swerve in a wide arc. The centrifugal force pressed him against the wall. The plane was turning onto the runway.

Mike knew he had to get in there. He held the pistol tightly in both hands, cocked it, and pressed the muzzle against the lock. Pushing against the door with his forehead, he hesitated. He might kill a pilot—or, more likely, he would walk into a slug. He almost stopped but didn't.

He felt the aircraft's acceleration begin to build. They were taking off. He pulled the trigger and the pistol jumped in his hand. He fired again and felt the door give way under his weight. He fell into the cramped cockpit, crashing into Abdul who struggled to get his pistol into firing position. The terrorist clutched at Mike with his free hand. Mike's momentum carried him forward, and Abdul tumbled backward onto the console between the two pilots' seats, Mike coming down on top of him.

He pressed his pistol into Abdul's abdomen and fired twice. Abdul quickly lay still. Sprawled on top of Abdul's body, Mike turned his head to Captain Granger and screamed, "Cut it, dammit!"

"Get him off!" yelled Granger, slapping at the dead terrorist.

Mike rolled back with all his might, pulling the body with him so Granger could get at the throttle levers. He landed on his back on the cockpit floor, Abdul's body tumbling on top of him with a heavy thud. Granger reduced power. An instant later, he brought the Airbus to a halt some three-quarters of the way down the long runway. He killed the engines, leaving the plane's internal APU to power the lights and radios. The Airbus sat quietly on the centerline of the runway, its turbofan engines gradually winding down.

Granger sighed. "*Mercy Dieu.*" He turned to Mike. "What about the rest of them?"

"Dead." Mike shoved Abdul off to one side. The dead man's blood and tissue covered his entire midsection.

"Are you all right?"

"I'm okay." Looking down at his torn and blood-soaked shirt, Mike waved him off. "It's mostly his, I think."

"Are we safe now?" asked Granger.

"Yeah, I think so."

Granger sighed and picked up the radio headset.

Hamud passed the word to Delta. Barclay's van raced toward the plane. Sinclair called Barrington and instructed him to bring the choppers to the plane. He then dispatched a Delta security team to the maintenance building to investigate.

"Take her right up to the door, Jimmy," Barclay told his driver. The Delta soldier drove the van up to the open front passenger door. Barclay, Sinclair, and the driver swung out the doors and hastened up a small ladder onto the roof of the van.

Pistols drawn, crouched down, they ran the length of the van to the aircraft's door, where Barclay took up a covering position.

Between the van's roof and the lower edge of the door was at least a ten-foot gap. Sinclair and the driver popped four quick-release latches securing a lightweight fiberglass ladder. They hoisted the ladder into place against the side of the Airbus. Sinclair climbed up first, pistol drawn, followed by Barclay and the driver.

They had heard Hamud's *all clear*, but they were still cautious. Inside, pistols drawn, they scanned the scene. Sinclair went forward; the other two men headed aft.

As he moved toward the cockpit, Sinclair could hear the Blackhawk's rotor as the chopper landed next to the plane. *So far, so good*, he thought. *Haven't been fired on yet*. Within seconds, Barrington's men would have the plane secure. They would now have the force to deal with any remaining threat.

Sinclair eased down the small corridor leading into the cockpit then rushed in, pistol at combat ready. The cockpit was a grisly scene, but calm. The floor was slippery with blood. Mike Elliot sat on the floor in a pool of crimson, slumped against the wall, a bloody pistol on his lap. He stared up at the army colonel. Captain Granger sat in the command chair, head hung low, breathing deeply. Splattered blood was everywhere in the cockpit, and two dead, bloody bodies littered the cramped space.

Sinclair leaned down, grasped Mike's pistol, and carefully took it from his hand. He stood up straight, replaced his own pistol in its holster, and then eased the hammer down on Mike's weapon.

"What happened here?"

Granger said, "This young man just saved us all."

"Are you wounded?" asked Sinclair, kneeling down in front of Mike.

"I don't think I'm shot, just banged up."

The roar of jet engines and the screech of tires could be heard in the distance as the U.S. C-17 medivac plane landed on an adjacent runway.

Lieutenant Colonel Barclay came to the door, and Sinclair stood to confer with him. "Sir," said Barclay in a low voice, "Scott's boys are aboard. They're checking things out. I found three dead terrorists back there. This one makes four," he said, pointing to Abdul.

"Do we need a medic up here?" asked Barclay.

"Yeah, go ahead and bring one in," said Sinclair, looking at Mike in wonder.

Lynn pushed past Barclay and Sinclair. When she saw Mike on the floor, a wide circle of dark blood covering the entire front of his shirt, she screamed in horror. Sinclair grabbed her by her shoulders. "He's all right," he repeated several times.

She collapsed next to her husband. She put her face next to his and kissed him repeatedly. Her tears ran across Mike's face in streams.

Sinclair turned back to Barclay.

Barclay continued, "Security team reports the maintenance building is secure. Quite a mess. Five Cypriot police officers are dead on the rooftop, another reported dead on the perimeter. Apparently Krokos himself killed the intruder after all his men were gunned down."

"I'll be damned," said Sinclair shaking his head in disbelief.

"We don't know who the intruder is, but he managed to kill six Cypriot police officers undetected, and he had a professional grade, silenced sniper rifle, a silenced .22 caliber pistol, and a radio scanner."

"Shit," responded Sinclair. "I guess we were lucky after all."

"Yeah, if he hadn't been discovered we could have lost half the team."

"Make sure we have plenty of photos of him and his equipment. Take his prints and DNA. We'll want to figure out who this guy is."

"Will do," replied Barclay. "Sir, there's one more thing."

"Yeah?"

"Jake's dead."

Sinclair turned back to Mike and Lynn. He pulled a knife from his boot and knelt down. He gently held Lynn's arms and cut her bindings.

Mike suddenly felt dizzy and shook his head to clear his vision.

Sinclair asked him, "You sure you're okay, son?"

"I'm okay. Are we really safe?"

"Yeah, it's over. Did you kill all these men?" asked Sinclair with astonishment.

"I killed three of the terrorists; another one was already dead, under the door. I saw a dead soldier and a dead flight attendant back there. The dead woman's name was Marie, and she was a true hero," replied Mike. "I guess the hijackers killed them both, I don't know."

Shaking his head, Captain Granger stammered, "My god, Marie is dead." Then he added, "This one here, Abdul, killed my copilot."

Looking at Mike in astonishment, Sinclair said, "You took out three of them, alone and unarmed, including Number Three."

"Who's Number Three?" asked Mike weakly.

"The big one."

"Oh, yeah, that was my second encounter with him. He won the first one; I won the second. But Colonel, I *had* to kill them," said Mike shaking his head. "I had no choice."

"Hold on, son, you don't have to explain any of that to me," said Sinclair, putting his hand on Mike's knee. "What's your name, young man?"

"Major Mike Elliot, sir."

"I figured as much. We were told you were aboard. Turns out it was a damn lucky thing, too. You did a good job, son. I only wish we could have served you all better. But, no, you did a real fine job."

Stepping back to let a medic past, Sinclair said, "Major, we could use a guy like you on Delta."

"I'm trying to settle down," replied Mike, looking at his wife. "I'm just going to take care of her."

Moving toward the door, Sinclair said. "You took real good care of her, son. You sure as hell did."

Epilogue

Arlington National Cemetery

The June day was warm and sunny. Rows of white granite headstones stretched across the smooth, bright-green grass. A solitary Army bugler in dress blues stood among the markers playing taps.

Across a small stone pathway, under a stand of elegant oaks, an honor guard stood at attention, saluting.

Eight Delta Force operators, neatly trimmed, in crisp, dress blue uniforms, approached the open grave carrying Staff Sergeant Jake Brady's casket. Jake's parents stood near the grave, their hands over their hearts. Mike and Lynn stood beside the parents. Lieutenant Colonel Steven Barclay, his wife by his side, stood on the other side of Jake's parents.

Jake's father was a retired U.S. Army soldier. The Army had not informed him of exactly how his son had died, and the parents had not asked. The official death certificate listed the cause of death as *combat action*. Jake's parents knew what he did for a living—and what he had lived and died for. There was no need to ask.

Surrounding the gravesite, dozens of Delta operators in civilian clothes also held their hands over their hearts. Delta's officers and staff also wore dress blues and stood saluting. Sixty plus Army Green Berets, men from Jake's days before Delta, were also in attendance.

The chaplain made his remarks, and then the pall bearers carefully folded the U.S. flag covering Jake's coffin. Colonel Sinclair took the flag and knelt on one knee in front of Jake's parents. He gave his condolences and presented the flag to the father.

Jake's dad caressed the flag several times and then handed it to his wife. She clutched it to her heart with both arms. A staff officer stepped up and handed Sinclair a small, glass-covered display case. It contained a Purple Heart and a Silver Star. He presented it to the father. Jake's dad clutched the little box and then broke into tears.

The ceremony ended quietly. The soldiers present each passed by the casket, touching it, wishing a silent prayer for Jake, his family, and the Unit.

Many of the Delta men present, as well as Mike and Lynn, would now be moving to the State Department for a memorial service for young Dean Bradford.

As the crowd began to disperse, four men approached Mike and Lynn. The CIA's Max Hardwick and Jonas Ward stopped in front of them. Jonas used a cane and practically had to drag his right leg. His left arm hung uselessly by his side; he could no longer move it.

Along with Max and Jonas, there was a man in a wheelchair that Mike didn't know. He was missing his right foot halfway up his lower leg. His left arm was in a cast, and he had numerous stitches in various cuts on his face. He was being pushed along by a handsome, young Arab male wearing expensive-looking Ray-Ban sunglasses.

Jonas had saved Mike's life in the Brazilian jungle, and Mike had never had the opportunity to thank him. Jonas was nearly crippled in the explosion that killed Mike's first wife and daughter. Mike would have died too, if not for Jonas.

Mike slowly stood. He was healing well, but he, too, needed a cane to steady himself. He stepped toward Jonas, put his arm around him, and squeezed him for a long while. Then Mike took a step back.

Max gestured toward the man in the wheelchair and said, "This is John Striker, our new director of operations. He wanted to meet you."

Mike leaned over and shook Striker's hand. "My pleasure."

Striker nodded and grinned. "Good job. You managed to do something Delta was unable to. That's impressive."

Max said, "We knew you were on the plane. We pretty much predicted what you did."

"I was just lucky," said Mike.

"Whatever you say," replied Jonas.

Max shook Mike's hand. He nodded to Lynn. "Mrs. Elliot," he said.

The men turned and headed slowly back up the hill toward the road. Max looked over his shoulder at Mike and said, "We'll be in touch."

"What was that about?" asked Lynn, looking up at her husband.

"Nothing. I'm not going back to work for them. I'm done with that. I'm going back to the DIA to be an analyst and push paper."

Mike put his arm around Lynn, and they made their way slowly toward their waiting car.

Author's Note

Dear Valued Reader,

Thank you for reading The Dawn's Early Light. Writing a novel is quite a journey. You get an idea for a story and you set out writing it. The story develops, though nothing like you imagined it would. Characters come and go, they thrive or perish, and the plot thickens. It is truly a great journey of discovery and growth for an author, and with any luck, for the reader as well. I hope you enjoyed reading it. If you did, please be so kind as to visit Amazon.com, or Goodreads, and leave a review—reviews are an author's lifeblood. I am eager to hear your feedback. It will guide and shape my future writing.

Thank you,

Lee Duffy